val harris
SEA CREATURES

Val Harris

CAVA BOOKS

A CAVA BOOKS
publication

First published in Great Britain
October 2009 by CAVA BOOKS

Cava Books is an imprint of GINGERCAT BOOKS Independent Publishers
The Barn, Dippenhall, Farnham, Surrey, GU10 5ED, UK
www.cavabooks.co.uk and www.gingercatbooks.co.uk

Design and typeset for this edition: www.no-mo.co.uk
Typeset in Garamond

"Printed and bound in Great Britain by CPI Antony Rowe,
Chippenham and Eastbourne"

ISBN (13) 978-0-9555997-4-3

A CIP record of this book is available from The British Library

Also by Val Harris

Whisky 'n' Ginger
The Siren

Wherever I go, mysterious figures, I see you, turning the corner…you, you, you…Grey is the landscape; dim as ashes; the water murmurs and moves. If I fall on my knees, if I go through the ritual…it's you, unknown figures, you I adore; if I open my arms, it's you I embrace, you I draw to me…!

Edited extract from:
An Unwritten Novel by Virginia Woolf

(By kind permission from The Society of Authors as the Literary Representative of the Estate of Virginia Woolf)

CORNWALL

1

JENNA

Our house was full of the sea. Dad was an artist and the seashore's kleptomaniac. He filled every space in the house with shells and stones, feathers, driftwood, smooth pieces of glass, and tiny pink and grey shells, which he threaded up and turned into necklaces and bracelets for me. Pieces of eggshell that had fallen from the sea-gulls nests on the cliffs would find their way onto the mantelpiece, along with clumps of dried kelp and sea grasses. Then he would disappear into his studio – the glasshouse in the garden – and paint. Sometimes I would sneak a peak through the glass and watch him work. I was so proud of my dad.

I inherited his squirreling instinct. Not my sister, Olivia, though. Her grown-up house is entirely minimalist and uncluttered. Not a thing out of place. Nothing found and rescued. All new. Modern. 'She's got a good eye for a piece,' dad said. Olivia lives in London and 'does' Sotheby's and the Royal Academy, and buys from smart Mayfair galleries. She takes tea in Fortnum and Mason and dinner at La Gavroche. She has a Harvey Nichols credit card. She never comes back to Cornwall. She is married to Michael, an investment banker in the City.

Lobster pots, nets and lamps cluttered our house by the sea in the old days and, for a while, half a broken sun-bleached wooden dinghy lay in the living room. Olivia and I, and Charlie, our brother, perched on top of it while dad took photos and sketched us for a painting. Then mum put her foot down and made him move it back down to the beach.

That was before everything changed

I found a sketchbook in a box a few weeks ago for a painting dad did, called Sea Creatures. I remember he told me it was an, 'analogy'. I wasn't sure what he meant by that, but the painting was of us children on the beach, along with a starfish representing me, a seahorse representing Olivia, and a crab that was Charlie. There were also some old photographs of us children with mum and dad. I took them out and hid them in my satchel, the old brown leather school satchel I still use, even now. It smells of the past and things faintly familiar. Every time I open it I hear the school bell, the scrape of chairs. Good things and bad things.

Dad did quite well as an artist. He sold his paintings to local galleries and to others as far away as Truro and Exeter, and even London. Once, one of his paintings was hung in an exhibition at a gallery in St Ives, and we piled into his battered old Ford estate to go and see it. But mostly he earned a living from commissions. His work was popular and he did well enough for us to be able to live in a cosy whitewashed cottage with black window frames and a pretty garden, down at the bottom of a narrow lane between the high hedges. It was called Beach Lane Cottage, and it was just outside Looe in Cornwall.

I was literally a sea baby. Mum and dad were out on the shore one evening and mum said: 'Oh my God, Brendan, I think she's coming.' There was no time for her to get back up to the cottage.

Ten minutes later I was born on dad's coat on the sand, with the tide charging in. He wrapped me up in his coat and rushed back to the cottage to call the hospital. We left mum on the beach with the kelp and the crabs and the Atlantic thrashing towards her. Not long after, with mum safe, we were all on our way to Liskeard.

That was it, my entrance into the world, my beautiful world where the sea creatures live and the sky breathes out its fresh, wild air as warm as tropics or as cold as the Arctic. Mum didn't know she was having a girl, but her guess was right.

Later that night there was a beautiful moon – a sliver of a curve glowing on a blue-black sky. Dad painted me with that moon, curled up in a seashell.

Whilst dad painted and combed the shore for ideas, mum ran the Blue Moon Café along by the river in West Looe. It had a curved bay window with blue frames, wooden floors and an old fireplace. Mum found eight different tables, and chairs to go with them, from the second-hand market and she tie-dyed a couple of old sheets to make eight patterned blue-and-white tablecloths. In one corner she set up a small stall selling trinkets and other bits and pieces: shell earrings, little boxes embedded with shells, and pieces of sea-smoothed glass which dad found on the beach, silver bracelets made from bent forks and spoons, wind chimes, and tin fish, flattened and beaten so you could see scales and dimples on them.

She baked and prepared everything herself – bread,

cakes, biscuits and scones, and hot dishes like Welsh rarebit, egg and chips, toasted sandwiches, and Cornish pasties of course. It was open all year round, and in the winter she did a special for lunch, like steak and kidney pie or a hotpot. The café was always busy, mostly with local people because the visitors tended to stay over in East Looe, where all the shops and the beach were.

Mum had a smile like the sun breaking over waves, and a good word on her lips for everyone.

They were creative people, Rowena and Brendan Moon. Dad was a dreamy absent-minded Piscean while mum, on the cusp of Aquarius, had a practical side to her own artistic nature. No time for dreaming. Up early to make sandwiches for the shop. Baking at night. Scrubbing floors and tables. Feeding children; baths, colds and chickenpox, whilst dad painted on, and the smell of oil and linseed permeated our world.

Everyone loved dad. And he loved them back. He'd spend time at the local pubs, listening to the fishermen's stories, joining in the sea shanties, then stumbling home in the early hours.

Mum had a friend, Mary-Ellen, a potter, who helped out when mum was really busy. She made pots and dishes to sell in the café.

Then Olivia arrived.

I was just about to turn seven and my brother, Charlie, was a bright happy little four-year old, adored by us all. It was a happy house, full of sunshine and smiles. At least that's how I remember it.

Olivia was a handful, even at a month old. A screamer. A

demander. Suffering from colic. Awake night and day. Mum was exhausted. Dad was exasperated. He was just gaining ground as a respected artist; his work was in high demand and it was more than his temperamental personality could cope with.

It was chaos. I remember the screaming. I remember stroking Charlie's hair through the cot sides, late at night, when he was crying; no, make that sobbing. Mum had no time for him. He was abandoned because of Olivia, not because mum wanted to but because she had no choice.

Charlie fell quiet. He'd play in the corner of the nursery, muttering in his baby language, watching videos and clutching his old rabbit.

Days, weeks, months passed, and although we muddled through, everything was on the verge of falling apart. Dad had begun spending more time at the pub than he did in his studio. He and mum argued a lot and she was exhausted. Once I heard him say that Olivia was a changeling, put there by the Piskies as a punishment. I didn't understand what that punishment could be for, and mum was really upset and irritated. She had no time for folklore. She had to carry on the practical tasks of running the café. Dad hadn't sold a painting for a while, and so the money from the café was all we had.

Eliza, a girl from the village, started to look after us; dad should have taken over in the afternoons but, mostly, he wasn't there. His studio was empty.

I was at school, way up on the top of Lark Hill. I used to dawdle home across the fields and along by the cliff instead of taking the road. Mum would scold me when Eliza told her I wasn't back until gone four-thirty. I just wanted time to myself, before I had to help Eliza with Olivia and Charlie, or get the vegetables ready for supper. Sometimes dad wouldn't come home for supper, and it was way after I'd gone to bed that I'd hear him coming up the garden path, shuffling, banging the gate behind him. Even then he might not go into the house, but stumble into his studio in search of more whisky from the stash he thought was secret. But we all knew about it. One morning I found him asleep on the studio couch. Mum had locked all the doors.

I didn't understand what had happened to my father, why he preferred to be out at the pub than home with all of us. Every night I prayed for him to change and go back to being the old dad, and I prayed to the Piskies to help us.

We stopped going to the beach together, dad and I. So I went on my own. By then I knew the seashore better than anyone – its tides and dangerous areas, its secret caves and rock pools.

I couldn't bear to see my parents falling apart, too tired or angry to talk to each other about what was happening. It was taking its toll on me too. My teacher complained about me falling asleep at my desk in the afternoon. It was a small community and everyone knew what was going on. She asked my parents to find another way of dealing with their problems, one that would allow me the freedom to do my homework and get a good night's sleep. I think that teacher must have known that I was the one who got up in the small hours to take Charlie to the toilet, or to soothe Olivia, because mum was too tired to hear and dad was blotto in the studio.

How long can something like that go on without cracks starting to show and something breaking? It was routine for such a long time that no one really noticed what was happening to mum. She was exhausted, of course, angry with dad and tetchy with us if we didn't do what she asked right away. Olivia was the worst but she was the youngest and mum had a soft spot for her, so her misbehaviour often went uncorrected. I took the brunt of it but it didn't bother me really. I did my chores, and made myself scarce when I needed time to myself, or when mum was having a rant. I watched her beautiful face begin to crumple at the edges and ripples, like the grooves the sea made across the sand, appeared on her forehead.

One afternoon I was up on Lark Hill after school, enjoying a spell of hot sun in April and staring out at the sea's dark blue horizon. I imagined myself out there in a little boat, lying back in my red swimsuit, with my hand drifting through the waves.

I saw dad's old car on the cliff road; it was heading east. I watched it winding in and out of sight behind the high hedges and around the bends until it disappeared from view. It didn't emerge again; if it had done I would have seen it just before the five-bar gate that led up to the main road; I kept my eyes fixed there for ten minutes but it didn't appear. I thought the car must have broken down; it was old and hardly ever serviced because he couldn't be bothered to take it to the garage.

I thought dad might need my help so I hurried back down to the house and got out my bike. I hadn't used it for a year. It was covered in cobwebs but it worked fine once I'd brushed those away; the chain was okay and so were the brakes. So I set off along the road in the direction I'd seen dad's car going to find out what had happened to him.

There was only one cottage before you got to the main road: Mary-Ellen's. Since mum was too tired in the evenings to make things for the stall, Mary-Ellen had been helping her. She made pots and plates and photograph frames in the little pottery where she had one wheel, an oven and a stack of clay. Sometimes she let me watch her making the pots on the wheel, pulling up the wet clay and moulding it into a shape. I had a go once, but the clay collapsed under my hands and went flapping around like a rock eel just caught in bucket; we laughed and laughed. I really liked her. She was the only one who let me be the child I still was.

She would give me some of her homemade lemonade; it was quite sour but I drank it anyway. She had a funny little laugh, like bells tinkling, masses of long red curly hair and a smile as wide as the bay. Her house smelled of coffee and incense, and she liked the seashore as much as dad and I did.

I thought she was one of the Cornish Piskies that dad was always telling me about.

'They live all over the place, up on the cliff paths, on the moors, under rocks and roots. Mostly they're cheerful little people but make sure you're good. They don't like bad children,' he warned me with a twinkle in his eye. And he told me stories of people being lured into bogs by Piskies pretending to be a light in a cottage. Even though he laughed about it, I began to wonder just how much power the Piskies had.

When we were out after dark dad would sing this song:

'Jack o'lantern, Joan the wad,
who tickled the maid and made her mad;
light me home, the weather's bad!'

Then he would tickle me until I begged for mercy. Whenever something good happened I would thank the Piskies, but if I did something bad, I was afraid they would lure me away with their songs and never let me go back home again.

Mary-Ellen kept goats and chickens in her back yard and sometimes she gave me some eggs to take home: three usually, one for each of us. At Easter time she would hard-boil the eggs and paint them with funny faces, and she would bring them down to us on her way to church. We Moons would all traipse up to that ancient little church near enough on one Sunday every month. We were all christened there. Mum had been raised Catholic, but she didn't mind going to the local church. Not dad though; he said he was an agnostic, and he wouldn't even come in for our christenings.

The hedges either side of the lane were too high for me to see right over, even up on my bike, but I caught glimpses of the sea through the gaps and I heard the sea gulls screaming over the cliff tops as I pedalled past. Sometimes I heard the cry of the peregrines that nested on the cliff face. I loved to be on the beach and see them flying as fast as fighter jets above me.

It was great weather for the end of April and I'd taken off my sweater before I left home. The sun warmed my skin and even the breeze didn't set goose bumps along my arms. Some peacock butterflies were enjoying the warm spell, fluttering along the verges, and swallows were already screaming and chattering as they zipped through the sky above. I turned out of the long bend just before Mary-Ellen's house, but there was no sign of dad's car. I came to a halt outside the cottage, walked my bike through the gate and parked it up against the wall, next to Mary-Ellen's car. Then I wandered around the back, as I generally did, and knocked on the kitchen door. It was usually open when she was in but not today. There was no answer and no sign of Mary-Ellen, so I thought she was probably out in her pottery shed. I looked but she wasn't. I called her name but there was no reply; I guessed she was out walking. I turned to leave but then I heard her voice.

'Jenna, sorry my lovely, I'm upstairs and I didn't hear you at first.' She was hanging out of the bedroom window and looked a bit flustered. Her thick red hair was mussed up a bit and I did stare. Her hands went up to it.

'I was having a doze,' she explained. 'I had visitors last night and I think we drank too much of my elderberry wine,' she said and laughed loudly, like fairy bells.

'I was wondering if you'd seen dad, if he'd called in here?' I said. 'I was up on the cliff and saw his car coming along the lane and then it vanished. I thought perhaps he'd broken down and so I came to look for him.' It was my turn to explain.

She shook her head. 'No love, I haven't.'

'Sorry to wake you up,' I said.

'That's alright love,' she replied, but she didn't ask me in or offer me lemonade like she so often did, so I said goodbye and went back to my bike. It wasn't until I was leaving that I noticed the tyre marks that went across the verge and into the field around the far side of Mary-Ellen's house, behind the high wall. The visitors must have made them the night before.

Later I told dad about how I'd cycled along the cliff road because I'd seen his car go by and then it seemed to disappear and I thought he'd broken down. He laughed and said he'd only stalled it and got it going again after a few tries. Then he kissed my head and told me I was very sweet to worry about him.

I was nine when an au pair came to live with us. There was talk of an inheritance mum had received out of the blue from some distant relative in Australia. She decided to spend it on employing permanent help and renovating the café. Eliza had already left us to work in Truro, and mum was desperate.

Anya was a tall, confident girl from Norway, with nut-brown hair and piercing blue eyes. I was mesmerised by those eyes the first time I saw her. She was also extremely capable and had our disorderly house shipshape within days.

Mum unfolded from her exhausted and crumpled state. Olivia was taught, through Anya's uncompromising determination, a routine. Charlie got plenty of attention, and I was allowed some freedom to be a child.

Dad even cleaned up his brushes, and his act, and soon there were paintings for sale again. He whistled and he smiled, and he and mum began to talk to each other and even to laugh together again. It was a miracle.

Dad took me for walks again on the seashore and we began to collect bits and pieces, just like in the old days. The laundry sink was crusty with sand and shingle, where I'd rinsed out shells and washed pebbles. But I noticed that

Charlie was withdrawn and sullen. Although he sometimes came for walks with us he didn't like the seashore in the way that dad and I did. For Charlie it was a place to run around and kick a football, to play cricket, to fly a kite and sail a boat; dad did none of those things. He and I dug and scuffled in the sand while Charlie sulked and went off on his own to kick a ball around. I suppose no one really noticed what was happening.

Anya did though. She noticed what was happening to all of us and she set about repairing it. Her presence alone had brought about a monumental change, and Beach Lane Cottage was filled with the sound of people enjoying themselves.

I thanked the Piskies, of course, for sending her to us.

I was relegated to the routine of school, homework and play. She made a point of collecting me from school so that I couldn't linger on the cliffs anymore. In the summer, after the children had had their tea, which was always at five o'clock, she let me go off on my own for an hour.

Of course I went straight to the seashore.

At the weekends we all went. Charlie and Olivia and Anya would play all the games that Charlie wanted to play, and even mum found time to join us. Olivia paddled and splashed in the shallows when the tide was out. I even relented and took her to hunt for the tiny fish that hid in the rock pools, and the little crabs that slept under the stones and rocks. She squealed whenever we found a crab; she would run away and sometimes I chased her until mum and Anya told me to stop.

Despite the initial mending of their relationship, things were still not perfect between mum and dad; it gradually began to deteriorate again, despite having Anya around. Mum hated to see dad drinking but the more she nagged him about it the more distant he became, disappearing during the day and coming back late in the evenings.

I missed the old days so much, when we all had supper together and I would go and fetch dad from his studio to join us. Everyone laughed a lot then, and mum and dad used to hug each other.

Now I was afraid to go to his studio, afraid of what I would find, or the mood he might be in. Once he even threw a paintbrush at me. And there were days when the blinds were pulled down and he didn't come out at all.

Once I heard Mary-Ellen laughing with someone in the café about artists and their moods, and too much beer and whisky.

I thought I knew when everything had changed. I thought it was when Olivia arrived. But I never said anything. If only she'd been an easy baby and mum hadn't been so tired and irritable, and dad had been more sympathetic and had helped more with the little ones. Instead he had withdrawn and spent more and more time in his studio or the pub to escape the chaos, and he and mum had grown further and further apart.

Sometimes I heard them arguing late at night, on the occasions when he did come home and she let him into their bedroom. They argued in harsh whispers and I had to hold my breath to hear them through the wall, but I could never make out what they were saying. I lay listening until it went quiet and then thoughts tumbled around my in brain like clothes in a dryer.

I would wake heavy-eyed in the morning and drag myself out of bed. Mum scolded me for it and I didn't argue, but Anya always had a kind word for me. I think she knew how anxious I was.

Mum left for the café one morning, and that was the last we ever saw of her. It was midsummer's day, nineteen eighty-six. I was eleven years old. The first we knew was when Mary-Ellen phoned to ask where she was. I heard dad talking to her on the phone.

'Hasn't arrived?' I saw him look at his watch and I looked at mine. It was almost nine-thirty. Mum had left the house nearly two hours before. I waited behind the half-closed door, listening. 'Where on earth can she have got to?' I could hear the irritation in his voice. 'Perhaps the car broke down.' He sighed. 'I'll go and see if I can find her and call you back.' As he put the receiver back on the cradle I scuttled into the living room.

I heard him pick up his car keys and then he called out to nobody particular: 'Just going out for a bit, back soon.'

Dad didn't find mum. He scoured all the lanes, the village, the cliff tops, and the road into Looe and out again. I was old enough to realise that something was badly wrong. When Olivia and Charlie asked where mum was that evening, dad told them she'd had to go up to London for the night. They accepted it. But I didn't.

I'll never forget that long day and night. I couldn't sleep. I kept wondering what I'd done that was so bad that had made the Piskies take her away from us. I lay awake listening to every sound, praying for them to set her free and send her home. My window was open and I kept thinking

I could hear footsteps; once I thought I heard her voice, calling my name. I rushed to the window and whispered 'mum, are you there?' But there was no reply.

Three more nights passed by and then a week but there was no news. The police listed her as a missing person and the story of her disappearance went out on the local news. The local paper also printed a story and her picture. Everyone was talking about it and people who knew mum from the café called by to see if they could do anything to help. Her car was found eventually, abandoned in a car park in Polperro. The police took it away, for investigation.

Despite what they'd been through over the past few years, and the distance that had grown between them, I had never seen dad so desperate. There was nothing to give us an inkling of why she might have vanished from our lives. As far as we knew, she'd left everything behind: her clothes, her belongings, her personal things, even her passport. The police said it didn't seem to be the action of someone who was planning to disappear, but they insisted there wasn't any reason to suspect anything sinister. They did question dad and Mary-Ellen and dad told me not to worry, that it was just routine. But people talked. I overheard snatches of conversation – locals saying that maybe they'd both had something to with it: 'Because, well, you know what's been going on!'

What had been going on I wondered? It scared me, that kind of talk, and I was afraid to go onto the beach in case I found mum washed up.

Dad took copies of mum's photo, with her name on it, to train stations in Looe, Liskeard, Plymouth and Truro; he even went as far as Exeter. He went to all the local villages and stuck her photo up wherever he could; he handed it to shopkeepers, pub landlords and people in the street. I begged dad to let me help him and he agreed. Every time I handed one over, I was certain that someone would say: 'Oh yes, I've seen her, she's staying in such and such a place'; and then dad and I would rush over and find mum, who had just forgotten who she was for a little while. We'd bring her back home and everything would be fine.

But weeks went by and still mum was missing. I'd stopped eating and sleeping properly. If I did doze off, I'd wake up in a complete panic, shouting out for her. It was horrible. The house was full of her perfume, the ghost of her voice, the songs she hummed, but she was nowhere to be seen!

All the time I kept thinking that if the police couldn't find her, what chance did we have? Dad and I had done our best, but dad had turned to drink again. Black moods and depression followed, and even though we really needed him he didn't seem to understand or care. The studio was dark: the blinds were down and the door was locked. I went to knock for him, pleading with him to come out, but he didn't answer.

Thank goodness Anya was still with us and Mary-Ellen was around, although she spent most of her time looking after the café. I really think we would have been taken away and put into care if it hadn't been for the both of them; dad was incapable of looking after us.

Olivia had just turned four and so she was too young to really understand what had happened. Without mum she had to have someone to cling on to and Anya became her life support; I was a close second, and Mary-Ellen helped too. Olivia asked for mum over and over. She made me feel so exasperated because we all wanted mum, but when she wailed and wailed for her my young heart went out to my sister.

Charlie and I were both at the local primary school when mum disappeared. Olivia was due to start in the autumn. It was my last month there, before we broke up for the summer. I would go to senior school in September. I suppose dad was right to carry on sending us to school, but it was so hard for Charlie and me. Looking back I think he suffered the most. Some of the kids at school were being really mean about what had happened to us. They teased Charlie all the time – telling him that his mum ran off because he was stupid. Charlie was so sensitive that he would often burst into tears and then they would laugh at him. Eventually he began to lash out and got into trouble.

Finally, in a sober moment, and because both Anya and Mary-Ellen insisted, dad went to the school and asked the teachers to talk to the pupils and make it clear that it was not appropriate to be so cruel. He asked them to take action if it happened again. He really could come up trumps sometimes.

But despite dad's intervention, Charlie continued to get into fights and he rebelled against just about everything. Dad was exasperated, frustrated and angry, and he couldn't concentrate on his work. Charlie spent more time on his own, responding moodily if anyone tried to talk to him.

A year after mum disappeared, dad decided it would be better to send Charlie to Cunningham Manor, a boarding school in Devon and thus far away from the centre of the problem. Dad and I went with him on his first day. He put on a brave face, but I knew Charlie was upset about it, and I was too. I would miss my brother. It just wouldn't be the same.

I think that decision was the last straw for Charlie and his relationship, or the lack of it, with dad. I suppose dad just wanted to get on with his life, and Charlie was a drain on his resources. Or maybe dad really thought he was protecting Charlie.

Whatever the reasons, I suppose the consequences were inevitable.

LONDON
TWENTY-TWO YEARS LATER

2

JENNA

The smart shiny lift sped up to the tenth floor and I glanced at myself in the mirror. Still the same old Jenna Moon: long dark wavy hair, brown eyes, over-curvy figure in jeans and a white cotton blouse, and some hastily applied make-up. The freckles sprinkled across my nose and cheeks from years of sun and wind by the sea almost made me laugh. I looked completely out of place in this smart apartment block. I sighed. I didn't want to be here but Olivia had been unnaturally insistent. So I'd packed my rucksack, driven to Exeter and got myself onto a train; my sister had reserved and paid for a first-class seat.

'Get in a taxi at Paddington and I'll pay for it when you arrive,' Olivia had said briskly on the phone.

'That's not necessary,' I'd replied with a hint of irritation. 'And what's this all about? What's the urgency?'

There was a brief pause. 'I can't tell you over the phone Jenna, but it's very important. Please come. I'll explain everything when you arrive.' Something in her voice had made me agree; she wouldn't have suggested it if it hadn't been really important.

She knew how much I hated London. It was as much as she hated Cornwall. It was the difference between us. I was at home by the sea, with the gulls and the wind and the tide. She was at home in the heart of the city, with the traffic, the buildings, the noise.

The lift came to a perfect halt and I sucked in my

breath as the doors opened and I stepped out onto a plush carpeted corridor. I looked to right and left for a guide to the apartment numbers. Sorry, make that corner penthouse suites. Penthouse Apartment 4, 10th Floor, West India Quay, with its open plan layout and private terrace, was the benchmark of city wealth and social standing. Even I was taken aback by it, especially the views over the river and the arcing skyline of London.

Earlier that morning I'd been walking along the cliff tops behind Beach Lane Cottage, where I'd lived all my life, breathing in the cool fresh air from the sea, listening to the waves and the cries of the gulls and the peregrines. Just half a day later, I was up among the rooftops of a choking metropolis, with the chilly breeze of the air conditioning system around me, and the cacophonic roar of the big city, muted by double-glazing, not daring to penetrate the sterile environment of Olivia's penthouse apartment.

We kissed awkwardly and she shooed me towards the bedroom I would inhabit for a night or two. It was immaculately furnished and unfussy: a spacious white room with a black lacquered wardrobe, a black wood bed 'dressed' with a thick scarlet silk cover and black silk cushions embroidered with a simple red Chinese bamboo pattern. The floor was pale maple wood and there was a beautiful Chinese rug lying between the bed and the sliding glass doors that led to the balcony. On the balcony was a small wooden bench and table, and pots of bamboo. The en-suite bathroom was also all white, with a marble shower and sink and smart, gleaming chrome taps. A Chinese wrap lay on the bed for my use, and red embroidered slippers sat on the floor. I thought of my old soft cotton pyjamas in my rucksack, and I wanted to take them out there and then and hug them.

'Will this be okay for you, Jenna?' Olivia asked, the tone of her voice implying that it couldn't possibly be anything else.

'Oh it's wonderful,' I breathed, still holding onto my rucksack and my old leather satchel, afraid to put them down anywhere. I was thinking of my own comfy old room at the cottage, with its threadbare rug on painted bare boards. I wasn't bothered about scratching, spilling or dumping things there.

'I'll let you freshen up and then we can have a drink and a chat,' Olivia said brightly and left me to it. I sensed she was anxious to get away. Perhaps she needed to have a drink before I started asking questions. The weirdest thing was that even though Olivia was my junior by nearly seven years, I felt like an incompetent child in the company of this self-assured mature sister of mine.

I took out my pyjamas and hung them on the hook in the bathroom. I washed my face and hands, and revelled in the softness of the pure white towels in the bathroom. I even found myself looking forward to a shower later, before I went to bed. But I bet my money on the sheets being a bit stiff and crackly, not soft like the old flannelette ones I had at home.

With the old rucksack and satchel stuffed into the wardrobe, my jeans and cotton blouse folded up, and me newly changed into a pair of black linen trousers and a thin jumper for protection against the air-conditioning, I ventured out of the bedroom to find my sister.

Olivia already had a gin and tonic in her hand

when I emerged from the bedroom, and she poured one out for me.

'Cin, cin,' she said, and took a large slug from her own glass.

I raised mine and then sipped at the strong alcoholic drink. I wasn't used to drinking more than a glassful of cider down in Cornwall.

'Sit down,' said Olivia; it sounded more like an order than a gesture of hospitality.

I looked at her in surprise but dutifully took a seat on the huge plush sofa behind her, and took another mouthful of my drink.

'I've heard from our mother,' my sister calmly announced, without even waiting for me to settle.

I literally spat out the gin and tonic I was about to swallow and coughed. 'Sorry,' I said, 'I thought you said you'd heard from our mother.'

With a level stare she said: 'I did. Not directly, but through a lawyer.'

I took a deep breath and, as carefully as I could, I leaned over and put my drink down on the side table. But my heart was thumping with a force like the waves that pound the rocks at home and I began to tremble violently. I had to fight to take a breath again. What had made Olivia say such a thing? I stared at her in bewilderment.

My sister was watching my reaction. 'Are you okay?'

I shook my head. 'It's impossible,' I squeaked, still fighting for breath.

Olivia smiled wryly. 'I know. Big shock. But I'm afraid it's true.'

'She is still alive then?' I said, more to myself than

to my sister. A crazy slideshow had started running through my mind. Pictures emerged from the past: a flicker-book of images.

'Apparently so.'

The missile that had been winging its way towards me reached my heart and hit it with an almighty thump. I almost cried out with the pain of the impact. My head was spinning from the news and from the effect of the gin and tonic on my empty stomach.

'When did you hear from the lawyer?' I managed to ask in a faint voice.

'A few days ago.'

'I don't understand. How can it be her? What does she want? Why did they contact you?' I babbled incoherently.

'I'm sorry to be so blunt,' Olivia said in response to my confusion. 'I'm still trying to get over the shock of it myself.'

Then I burst into tears. Great huge heavy tears full of the burden of loss and now mixed with utter confusion.

Olivia came to sit on the arm of the sofa, awkwardly patting my shoulder.

'I know. It's crazy, isn't it? Twenty-odd years of nothing, of thinking she was dead, and then suddenly, out of the blue, she's here and she wants to see us.'

I sniffed and Olivia fetched me a box of tissues from the kitchen.

'Sorry,' I said, dabbing at my eyes and trying to get a grip of myself. I don't think I had ever cried in front of her before. 'Why?' I asked again, once I'd pulled myself together.

Olivia shook her head. 'I don't know. But she wants to

meet us. That's why I got you up to London. I'm so sorry I didn't explain over the phone, but I wanted to make sure you came and I was afraid you wouldn't if I told you beforehand. You understand?'

I nodded vaguely and stared at Olivia, mystified. Mum, here in London, wanting to meet us? It just didn't make sense. Why, after all these years of silence, of us wondering whether she was dead or alive, why on earth did she want to throw herself back into our world?

'What made you agree to it?' I asked my sister. 'Why didn't you just tell the lawyer to tell her to go away and leave us alone? Didn't you say we thought she was dead?' It wasn't true though. I had never believed she was dead. Something had always told me otherwise.

'I don't know, Jenna. It was such a shock but also it was…well, it was if I'd been waiting for that call all my life.' She shrugged apologetically, but I knew exactly what she meant.

'How will we know it's really her? I mean would we know who she was if she passed us in the street?' I persisted, still unable to accept this impossible piece of news.

'Why would someone want to impersonate her? I have no idea why her lawyer has contacted us, but I think we'll know when we see her.' Then she added, with a sense of bitter irony: 'To be frank, I'm rather intrigued to meet this person who so readily abandoned her family. I want to know what a selfish, callous woman looks like.'

How like Olivia, I thought. Already taking the cold and calculating route, whereas I was ready to collapse in emotional turmoil. A chill, like a cold fog on the moor, was settling around me. I wanted to curl up somewhere and forget. My hand went to the Pisky hanging around my neck, but hidden beneath my blouse. Olivia had always scoffed at my belief in the fairy folk.

'Look, there was a time when I would have given anything to see her, but that passed by long ago. I've allowed myself to forget she ever existed,' she admitted.

'I don't know if I can do it,' I said thinly. 'I can't let her hurt me again.' I almost choked again with the feeling of grief. A moment of silence passed and then I asked: 'Do you ever think about her, I mean from the past, when we were a family, before…?'

'No,' Olivia said abruptly, 'I don't.'

I stared at the hard look on her face, almost envying the line she had been able to draw, but I didn't believe her.

Then her face crumpled. 'I can't afford that sort of sentimentality in my life,' she said. 'It would destroy me.' She took a slug of her drink and closed her eyes.

'Poor you, it must have been so hard when mum left. You were so young and bewildered, and she adored you. I just couldn't understand why she'd leave you. Leave any of us. I thought it was my fault for a long time, and I blamed you too. Well, you were such a pain back then, such a demanding, selfish kid.'

'Thanks,' said Olivia quietly. 'I don't really remember myself.'

We sat in another gap of silence, trying to get to grips with this bombshell. It was the first time we'd ever discussed our feelings about mum leaving. Dad had never encouraged it and time had slipped by without us ever making the effort.

'How did she find you?' I wondered aloud.

'I've no idea. How would she know I was Olivia Hobbs, not Moon? I wonder if she knows that you and dad still live in Beach Lane Cottage?'

Of course, a lawyer could have traced these things, I was sure.

I reached for my drink, drained it and held out the empty glass to Olivia. 'Another one, please.'

A faint smile appeared on her face and she got up to fetch it. Olivia was well aware that drinking alcohol was not a habit of mine.

'She's asked for Charlie too, I presume?' I said as she went into the kitchen.

'Yes. He actually replied to the message I left on his phone, but he couldn't come here this evening for one reason or another. I heard he was up on some drugs charge recently and will be going to trial. Did you know?'

I nodded. Charlie got in touch only when he wanted to and he always called when he was in trouble. This time it was serious. Charlie was facing trial at the Crown Court and it was more than likely he'd be given a prison sentence.

Charlie had been expelled from school in the sixth form, his final year, after being caught with cannabis. He'd run off to Newquay before dad could get to the school to collect him. Dad didn't chase after him, though; Charlie was almost eighteen and dad said he was old enough to make his own decisions. That might have been true, but Charlie was a wild child, always searching for the next thrill and I worried about him being on his own. Dad had wiped his hands of his son. I tried to talk to him about Charlie but he wasn't interested. Once I even ventured to tell dad that he should take some responsibility for what had happened to his son, but he didn't want to know, and we ended up not talking for a week.

I never stopped loving my wayward brother and I prayed that he would be safe.

Olivia and Charlie had no time for each other. 'Why can't he get over himself and get a life?' she had said to me on more than one occasion. 'We all came from the same place and we all had the same crosses to bear! Why should he resent my success?'

This was true, but some of the circumstances had been different. I never passed judgement on either of them and I kept in touch with both of them. But it was almost laughable and pretty ironic that when Charlie finally did get himself a life, he had ended up in Olivia's world, or at least in her husband's world. I thought about how embarrassing it must be for Michael now that Charlie was up on a charge for supplying drugs to the very people he worked with. He must have been beside himself!

'What does Michael make of the phone call about mum?' I asked Olivia, when she returned with the drink.

'He thinks it's a tall order, calling your daughter out of the blue after disappearing off the face of the earth twenty years ago, and expecting her to jump to attention.'

'Did you? Jump to attention?' I asked.

Olivia shrugged. 'I was so taken aback I didn't know what to do really. The lawyer said that Mrs Moon was sorry to spring this on me and completely understood if I refused, but that it was a matter of great importance.'

'For her, or for us?' I wondered bitterly.

'When I put the phone down I expected to feel cold and angry, but I didn't. I suddenly wanted to go back. To the night before she left, when she lay down on the bed with me and read my favourite story,' Olivia said with a distinctive quiver in her voice.

I saw at last the core of my sister, the vulnerable, unhappy core of her. It was a cold feeling and I shivered. It was my turn to comfort my sister. I put an arm round her and we hugged for the first time in years.

'We're to meet at The Savoy,' Olivia said.

'What?' I exclaimed. 'The Savoy! That's not like her. Well not the "her" we used to know, I suppose.'

Olivia didn't comment. Her demeanour seemed to change, the show of vulnerability hardening over again. I saw her face tighten. 'I wish she was dead.'

I shivered. 'No you don't'.

Olivia looked at me intently. 'Yes I do, Jenna. I wish she was dead and buried, and the past with her. It would all be so much easier for us to live with. That woman has haunted me since the day she left and she will continue to do so into the future. And now the nightmare has turned into a reality!'

I watched her lift her chin, breathe and settle in her chair. An air of complete confidence descended around her. It was masterfully managed. I imagined her doing this in her working life. Getting the better of her competitors with that mask of steely determination, devoid of pity.

'Look,' she said, her composure swaddling her tightly again, 'we can't sit here all evening, letting the past tie us up in knots. We'll go out for a meal and let the company of strangers take our minds off it.'

The last thing my sister was prepared to do was let a mother who had abandoned her more than twenty years ago now force her to sink into misery and pain.

I supposed a distraction would be best, but I would rather have gone into a darkened room and curled up on the bed or, better still, run back to Cornwall and pretend this had never happened.

'Right,' said Olivia, 'we're going to Leo's. It's a place I know in Blackfriars. It has great food and great wine.'

'Sounds fine to me,' I said. I didn't really care where we went but it was a surprise to suddenly find myself actually finding some enjoyment in my sister's company. Perhaps it was because we were at last talking about the disappearance of our mother, sharing the loss we had each felt.

'Will Michael be coming for dinner with us?' I asked as she went to change. Guiltily, I found myself hoping she would say no. I found him a bit pompous and quite difficult to talk to.

'I don't think so, he's working late, but I'll tell him where we are and then he can join us later,' she replied, a little too casually I thought.

Whilst Olivia was changing, I moved slowly around the large open-plan living room, dining room and kitchen area of the penthouse apartment. There were huge glass windows on two sides, with great views of London. A large terrace overlooked the river on another. The terrace was more like a rooftop garden jungle, with lots of tropical plants creating a shady area. A round bubbling pebble fountain was set in the centre of the terrace. In one corner the floor was decked with narrow weathered oak boards, where there were chairs, a table and a large parasol. Typical Olivia, I thought, everything was perfect. The plant leaves were shiny; the furniture was immaculate; the large modern urns were beautifully aged; the water in the pebble fountain was crystal clear, with not a speck of algae. I pulled one of the sliding doors open very slightly. The sound of London made me jump back; it came rushing in towards me, like a wailing banshee! I quickly pushed the door shut again. The peace that the closed doors maintained inside the apartment was definitely more preferable. How could anyone sit out there and have a conversation? Or did you just get used to it and no longer notice it? I watched a plane, a large loud creator of pollution, on its ascent from Heathrow, and imagined the noise of it as it passed almost directly overhead. How could Olivia prefer all this to the peace of the Cornish coast? But of course we were very different people. Olivia had never really enjoyed what the coast had to offer; she had never explored like I had, the sea and the beach, the cliffs and the fields. She played on the surface, but it seemed as though she was never wholly aware of what was around her: the insects and plants, the birds and the butterflies, the moon and the tides. She had never been interested in any of it, let alone collecting things from the beach, like dad and I had done.

A painting in the corner of the room caught my eye. I recognized it instantly and felt a rush of déjà vu. It was one of dad's: an oil painting of a starfish, a seahorse and a crab on a wild beach, along with us kids. It was the one he'd called Sea Creatures. It used to hang in the cottage but then it disappeared. I'd asked dad where it was but he was vague about it. He had said it must be around somewhere.

'I bid for it on eBay,' Olivia said behind me and made me jump. I had not heard her come back into the living room.

'Oh,' I replied, and wished it were mine. Surely it would

have meant more to me than to my sister.

'Yes. Found it purely by chance when I was looking for something else.'

'Who was the seller, do you know?' I asked, curious to know who had not wanted to keep such a beautiful painting. Sad that dad had sold it.

Olivia shrugged. 'Someone in Truro, I think.'

I almost asked her what had made her buy it but of course I knew the answer. Olivia was a collector of art, and her father was an artist whose work was well regarded and collectable. I doubted it was for sentimental reasons.

'It's a collectors' piece,' Olivia said as if by explanation and reading my thoughts. 'It wasn't cheap.'

'Well you'd know,' I replied.

Yet even dad's notoriety had not brought them closer together. Normally Olivia would be fawning over someone famous with whom she had connections, but she was still too angry with dad. I was sure she blamed him for the disappearance of our mother, and she was angry about how he had neglected his children and the fact that he seemed to love alcohol more than he loved us.

But also I think she was annoyed with him for not pushing himself or his art as far as he could have done, especially as he was such a reputable artist with his earlier works quite sought after. He only sold his paintings through local galleries now. I think she despised him for not seeking the upper echelons of the art world. But of course she didn't understand him at all. Dad just wasn't like that. Painting was his life, not patrons and critics and those he viewed as the 'pimps' of the art world. Neither did she understand that he was afraid – of the black moments, the depressions, the vicious circle of it all. There were so many times when he wanted to work but couldn't. It was his crock of demons, the freezing of his artistic capabilities, the death of his personal creativity. Drink was his only companion then. Even I had given up trying to find cracks to slip through and save him. Somehow I just couldn't find the words to explain it all to her.

'Ready?' she asked, changing the subject.

I glanced at her dinner outfit: casual city-girl chic. Black designer crepe de chine trousers that hung perfectly on her long slim legs, a soft black cashmere jumper, designer shoes, and a handbag shrugged over her shoulder. Her short blonde hair was perfectly cut and shaped, her lips just lightly coloured, her cheeks touched with blusher, her startling blue eyes enhanced with a smudge of brown, some eyeliner and a touch of mascara. There were diamonds at her ears and around her wrist. Simple. Perfect.

It reminded me again of just how much she resembled mum, and a feeling of envy touched my heart. Dad had pointed it out on her wedding day.

'Yes,' I said. 'I'll just grab my bag and jacket.'

Next to Olivia I was, of course, the country bumpkin. I wasn't particularly in touch with fashion and design. I wore what I felt comfortable in: generally jeans and tops and sometimes a sundress or a skirt in the summer. The sum total of my jewellery was an old silver fork bracelet mum had made a long time ago, my Pisky necklace and some African beads and earrings that came from a place that had changed my life. The black linen trousers and long cream jumper I had on were from my teaching days; they were probably the only really smart clothes I possessed.

We jumped into a taxi, hailed as we stepped outside of the apartment block. The journey wove us through the City of London. I have to admit it looked almost enticing at night. A slight fall of rain had buffed and varnished the streets and they gleamed under the lights.

I liked the look of the river. It would be good to take a walk, or jump on a riverboat and see where it took me. But my visit held something other than a day of exploration. Or perhaps that was exactly what it would be: an exploration. I shook my head. It was just all too much to think about. My thoughts were jiggling around. One of those was about whether tomorrow would reveal the answer to the huge dark question that had hung over us since we were children.

'Hey, are you still with me?' I realised that Olivia had been talking to me.

'Sorry, I was miles away.'

'I said, 'What do you think of London by night?''

'Oh,' I responded, looking out at the glittering skyline of the city along the edge, and beyond the river, 'I rather like it.'

'Yes, it looks pretty good doesn't it? I bet you like the river best.'

I smiled. 'Yes, as a matter of fact I do.'

'Maybe you could come up another time and we could do a river trip,' my sister suggested out of the blue.

I turned towards her in surprise. It was the first time she had ever suggested that we do something together.

I shrugged. 'If you like,' I replied and smiled. We were acting now as though the world was still turning the way we knew it.

Then we both said, almost together, 'Let's see what happens tomorrow', and we laughed a bit awkwardly.

I looked out of the taxi window again. We were in the City now, the lights still on in the office blocks. The taxi drove under Blackfriars Bridge, turned down a side street and came to a halt outside a restaurant between the arches.

It was certainly not what I'd expected. We were in a dingy street, and from outside the restaurant didn't look anything very special. Not Olivia's usual style. We climbed out and Olivia paid the driver.

I could hear noise and laughter as we approached the door. It opened just as we reached it, letting out a group of chattering men and woman who squeezed passed us. Olivia and I entered a surprisingly sophisticated reception area. The bar beyond was buzzing with customers.

'Welcome ladies...oh my God, Livvy, it's you dahling!' gushed a rather handsome man who hurried from behind the desk to engulf my sister in a hug and a kiss on each cheek.

'Hello Gino, how are you?' she said, removing her jacket and handing it to him. Awkwardly, I took my off own jacket, which was whisked from my hand to be checked into the cloakroom. Two cloakroom tickets were deposited into Olivia's handbag.

'It's so lovely to see you,' said Gino, in a rather tight sweet voice. 'And who is this adorable creature?' he said, glancing at me. I almost laughed aloud at the preposterousness of his remark.

'This is my sister, my older sister,' she explained. I held out my hand and the silly man bent down and kissed it.

'It is an honour to meet you. Do you have a name?' he

asked, winking at me.

I laughed. 'Yes, it's Jenna.'

'Jenna Moon,' said Olivia.

He put his hand to his heart. 'Oh what a fabulous name. How magical,' he gushed.

'I thought you'd like it,' said Olivia, as if she had revealed an important secret.

Gino nodded and then gestured for us to follow him into the restaurant area. It was a lot bigger than I imagined, dimly lit and full of diners. The food smelled good and I realised I was starving. I hadn't eaten since I left Cornwall earlier that morning.

'I hope we've got a good table,' said my sister importantly.

'For you dahling, of course!' gushed Gino and ushered us to a table in the corner. It looked like all the rest to me but I suppose its position meant that there would be less waiter traffic around it.

We took our seats and Gino left. A waiter appeared to take an order for drinks.

'Gin and tonic?' Olivia asked.

I shook my head. I'd had enough of those. 'Just some sparkling water please,' I said.

'The same for me too,' she said, 'but we'll have some wine with the meal. The usual bottle please. Red okay for you?' she asked me.

'Fine thank you.' I was glad that she was taking charge. I picked up the menu and started to look through it. Olivia was looking around the restaurant and she waved at various people at other tables.

'City friends of Michael's,' she explained. 'It's a popular

venue after work.'

'Does Michael work late very often?' I asked from behind the menu. For some odd reason, I didn't want to see the expression on her face.

'Nearly every day,' she replied breezily. 'We both do. Par for the course in our industries.'

Olivia was an editor for one of the big publishing houses. I knew it was a busy job and I assumed she meant that she was always out late, wining and dining clients, agents and authors. She certainly had some famous writers on her list.

'Busy entertaining or attending glittering industry awards?' I commented lightly and dropped the menu onto the table.

She looked at me aghast. 'You've got to be kidding. I won't deny that happens once in a while, but mostly I'm stuck in my office or a boardroom, meeting an author, discussing an author, listening to an author whinging, battling with an author over something they clearly don't want to change or give up in their precious book, even though I know we are never going to sell it to its fullest potential unless we do. That's my life!'

'I hadn't realised it was so intense,' I said meekly.

'Hmm, you have no idea. But don't get me wrong. I love what I do, but it's not always the life of riley and glamour.'

Olivia was currently working with Imogen Bell, an ex-model and a best-selling author. She wrote tales of the modelling world, providing an insight into catwalks, catty girls and the beds they slept in, designers, and the whole excessive lifestyle. It was a formula that made the author rich and famous and the publishing house even more rich and famous.

'How's it going with Imogen's latest?' I asked. I hadn't read any of her books; they weren't really my type.

Olivia smiled. 'Now there's an author I will always have time for. She listens to what I say and she's such a natural.'

'Do you still deal with Joanna Mills?'

She nodded and grimaced at the same time. 'Oh yes, Joanna's still on my books. She can be a bit of a tricky customer. Rather full of herself and loathes a critical editor. I have to tread very carefully indeed. Honestly, some of these authors are like petulant children. But Joanna has her work ready for deadlines, and she generally behaves in a professional manner once the book is ready for printing. She knows how important it is for her own reputation.'

I confess that I quite enjoyed hearing tales of Olivia's business. It didn't happen very often because we hardly ever found time to see or speak to each other. Every once in a while we had a phone conversation, usually when Olivia was feeling low; she never explained why and I never asked, but I suspected it was something to do with Michael. It was then that I heard all about what was going on in the literary world. I'd let her ramble on until she began to sound like herself again. Then she would suddenly break off with some excuse about having to go out, or off to a meeting. It might be another six months before I heard from her again.

Olivia turned her head towards a man who was approaching our table. He was walking very fast, this little man in a very smart suit and with the smallest feet I had ever seen on a man.

'Leo,' she said and he leaned down so they could kiss each other on the cheek. 'Lovely to see you.'

'Lovely to see you too,' he gushed, with a hint of an Italian accent. He turned towards me and Olivia introduced me.

'Hi,' I said, stretching out a hand. 'Pleased to meet you, Leo.'

Solemnly, he kissed the back of my hand. 'Friends or family of Olivia's are always welcome at Leo's.'

I smiled. 'It's certainly a busy place.'

'Of course, my dear, it's the best in the City, that's why. Anyone who is anyone comes to Leo's.'

'Oh Jenna's not into that sort of thing, Leo. She comes from Cornwall,' said my sister.

I was suddenly annoyed. 'You make it sound as though Cornwall is a dirty word? Don't you think we have any sort of sophistication down there?' I glared at Olivia.

Leo laughed. 'Well you don't, do you?'

'Some very successful chefs have come from Cornwall,' I heatedly reminded him. 'Personally, though, I don't think I could keep this sort of thing up every night.'

'Touché!' Leo replied. 'My apologies and please enjoy it while you're here.' He looked at me and said, 'By the way, we have Cornish Turbot as a special this evening,' emphasising the word 'Cornish'. 'It's quite fantastic, and so is the crab soufflé.' And then, with a flourish like a cavalier, he swept towards another table.

'That was unnecessary,' I said to Olivia.

'What was?'

'Making some point about Cornwall. The world is filled with all sorts, Olivia, not just your sort. You shouldn't forget that's where you started your life. And the best fish on the menu comes from Cornwall,' I added for emphasis.

She took a sip of her drink. 'Thank God it's not where I'm going to finish it!' The she saw the look on my face. 'Okay, okay I'm sorry. But you know how I feel about it. I was like a fish out of water there, excuse the pun. Couldn't wait to get away. I'm sorry if I embarrassed you.'

I shook my head, still irritated.

The waiter arrived and I ordered what Leo had recommended. Cornish was good enough for me!

Olivia's mobile rang and she fumbled in her bag to find it; she looked at the screen and pressed the receive button quickly. 'Hi, Michael, where are you?'

I watched her face as she spoke to her husband. It was eager. And then it fell.

'Oh, Jenna and I were so hoping you could join us at Leo's, but I quite understand, darling. Yes, see you later at home. Ciao.' She snapped the phone shut and laid it on the table.

'Working late?' I asked.

'Yes, they've got some deadline to work to so it could be hours.'

Despite the cheery façade, I could sense the disappointment in her voice. Something made me think that all was not as it should be.

A bottle of red wine, from Leo, appeared and then our starter arrived. We ate and eulogised about the greatness of the food and the quality of the wine that, I had to agree, was exceptionally good. By the time our main course arrived we had nearly finished the bottle, my share interspersed with glasses of water. My head was beginning to take on a fuzziness that could have been unpleasant but in fact was rather useful. It helped to take my mind off my reason for being there. The wine also helped us to open up a little bit with each other.

'So, Jenna Moon,' said my sister, leaning back in her chair and eyeing me mischievously, 'is there a boyfriend?'

'No,' I said immediately, but colouring slightly at her intrusion into my private life. It was true. There wasn't anyone now but there had been someone a while ago. Chris, or Christopher Wilson to be exact. We'd met at Teacher Training College in Plymouth. He was tall with sandy-coloured hair, a wide, open smile and a winning way with people and the pupils they'd allowed us to practise teaching on. I knew from the first moment I met him that Chris would be a great and inspiring teacher. He certainly inspired me.

I admired Chris from afar, or rather from behind the wall of hair I used to let fall across my face. It had always been at trick of mine when I was wary or shy of something. We were in the same group working on a joint project for our degree course. Behind my shield I watched how he so easily lapsed into laughter and how infectious that was to other people. I liked his hands too. They were large and strong looking but I imagined the gentle way they would handle something precious or delicate. I used to daydream about what it would feel like to have my own hand wrapped in one of his or, even more delicious, to feel it stroking my skin. Sometimes we would be in a group discussion and Chris would wake me from one of those daydreams. Then I would blush.

'Earth to Jenna,' he would tease after questions had landed on deaf ears.

But I liked the way he always sought my opinion.

Maybe it was because I was as passionate as he was about teaching.

One day he asked me to join him for coffee in the refectory. 'Got an issue I'd like to thrash out with you,' he said vaguely, and I'd agreed.

'Will you go out with me?' he said before we'd even sat down.

I'd nearly collapsed into my chair with surprise. Then I feared I'd misheard him and I was afraid to reply in case I gave the wrong answer.

'Well give a bloke some hope,' he'd said with a laugh, but I'd still been unable to find my voice.

'Earth to Jenna?' he'd tried. 'I asked if you'd go out with me, not if you'd have my babies.'

I'd pulled at my lip with my teeth, something I always did in tricky situations. He'd said, 'See, that's what I like,' and pointed at what I was doing.

It had made me laugh and I'd said, 'Yes!'

'Yes what?' he'd asked, and when I replied, 'yes please' we'd both fallen about laughing.

'Marvellous,' he'd said. 'There's a great movie on tonight.'

And that was it; we were an item. I had been a bit scared at first, scared of his expectations sexually. I'd only ever kissed a boy at school and had no idea of what to expect of anything else. I was still a virgin, for heaven's sake. There hadn't been any serious boyfriends before Chris. I was too afraid of being rejected.

Chris did kiss me that night. We were sitting on a park bench, and it was a magical moment: a clear star-studded sky, a full moon, a ship's horn out to sea, and seagulls and traffic in the background. Then the earth spun, but not quite in the way I'd expected. I threw up all over his shoes! It was a result of too much cider. I just wasn't used to drinking.

Chris didn't seem to mind. He'd laughed his head off, washed his shoes in the pond, picked me up, put me over his shoulder and carried me to my room in the university. He'd undressed me to my underwear – I'd felt too ill to protest about that – and put me to bed; he left some water and a bucket beside the bed.

'Sleep tight, Jenna Moon,' he'd said and planted a soft kiss on my forehead. The room spun again but it wasn't the cider this time. It was love.

That was the beginning of a relationship in which I learned all about how men and women work, physically and mentally. Everything was perfect and we both qualified with flying colours. Although we ended up teaching in schools about twenty miles away from each other, our relationship had continued to flourish. Then I went to Rwanda.

Olivia interrupted my flashback. 'You need someone, darling,' she said. 'Someone to take care of you instead of you taking care of everyone else; well, dad anyway.'

'No I don't, thanks very much,' I disagreed, returning to the present. 'I can take care of myself, and I like having dad around, particularly since Mary-Ellen spends less time with us now.'

'Oh,' she said, 'what happened there?'

I shrugged. 'I don't know. Dad's very difficult when he's working, as you well know.'

'That can't be anything new to her. She's been a part of his life for years. You knew they were having an affair before mum left, didn't you?' she said, somewhat harshly.

45

A second sense of déjà vu washed over me and I remembered that day on the cliffs, when dad's car had gone out of sight and a tousled-haired Mary-Ellen had greeted me from the bedroom window.

'You were little more than four years old, how did you know what was going on?' I retorted.

'Oh I didn't, not then, not when it was happening. I found out later,' she replied.

'Well it's water under the bridge now,' I said, not wanting to discuss it. I knew well enough that she was right but I had always shied away from the truth.

'You're on dad's side, I suppose, but what if it was the affair that drove our mother to leave? God knows they were unhappy enough.'

I stared at her in surprise. 'For someone so young at the time, you seem to know an awful lot about it.'

She returned a look as though she had a secret.

'What?' I said.

'I've not told anyone this before, but I kept in touch with Anya. You remember our au pair? She's the one who put me in the picture. She knew everything that was going on.'

I stared at her open mouthed. 'Anya?'

'Yep. She left her address in the book in the study when she went back to Norway. I came across it and later on, when I was about fifteen, I wrote to her. She replied and we've kept in touch more or less ever since. I even met her in Norway when I was over there on business.'

'Well you kept that quiet,' I said, rather envious that she'd been in touch with Anya all these years. She was the girl who had kept me sane and grounded when I could have lost my mind. In fact, she had kept our whole family together before and, for longer than she needed to, after mum left.

'It wasn't deliberate. I didn't think anyone else was interested.' Olivia defended herself. 'Any one of you could have written to her if you'd wanted to.'

'We kept in contact, cards and news at Christmas and birthdays, but not the in-depth communication that you've obviously had.' I suddenly felt guilty for not doing more to keep the relationship alive.

She shrugged. 'Well you could have done. Anyway, Anya confirmed my suspicions about dad and Mary-Ellen, our mother's so-called best friend.'

Olivia could never bring herself to refer to our mother as 'mum'.

For a second time in less than twelve hours I had to ingest some rather unsettling news. Of course, I'd wondered about dad and Mary-Ellen but I'd never really believed that Mary-Ellen was instrumental in the breakdown of their marriage. Now that belief was carefully unpicking itself.

But also I remembered the whispered arguments between my parents, the hushed but heated discussions late at night. Was that what it was about?

'Did you ever confront dad with your suspicions?' I asked.

'Once, when we were arguing about something.'

'So what did he say?'

'He denied it. Told me not to be so ridiculous.'

'But you didn't believe him?'

She shook her head. 'The evidence was overwhelming.'

'What evidence?'

'What Anya told me. The way they were when they

were together in public. Hardly speaking to each other, even though she'd known us all for years. It didn't make sense. Later on I realised that that was how people behaved when they had a secret.' My sister grimaced when she said that. I wondered what she was thinking about.

'But this is all hearsay from an au pair,' I continued. 'You couldn't possibly have worked that out for yourself.'

'Not then, but later, when we were at school,' she insisted.

'The whole village knew they'd hooked up by then, and that was after mum had left.'

'Oh Jenna,' she sighed, 'there's no point in this discussion. You'll always defend him to the hilt, and I'll always find something to put him down.'

Of course I was defending him. Dad had always been there for me. Yes, I found him frustrating but I loved him dearly, all the same. And we had so much in common. Olivia had always been mummy's girl, the apple of her eye, the youngest born, the one who got all the attention.

Where had that left Charlie? Stuck with 'middle child' syndrome? The misfit, neglected and overlooked by both parents. What a dysfunctional family we had turned out to be!

The silence then was awkward and volatile. I tried to think of something to diffuse it. Olivia, I sensed, was brooding on more than just the news we were sharing this evening.

'Did you ever buy that place in Majorca?' I asked, remembering a conversation from the past.

Olivia glanced at me in surprise. 'Did I tell you about that?'

'Yes, during one of your rare phone calls to Cornwall.'

'As a matter of a fact we did.'

'Well,' I said, 'what is it? Where is it? On the coast? In the mountains? Magaluf?' I added teasingly.

She laughed awkwardly. 'No. Definitely not Magaluf. It's just a little place inland, a nice old farmhouse, converted to our taste of course, with a small olive grove, and a nice garden and pool.'

I knew she was playing it down and I imagined what it really was: a huge estate, with a big house, a pool to die for and a working olive farm.

'Sounds great,' I said. 'Do you get out there much?'

'Oh we generally spend a fortnight there in August and then a month in the winter if we can.'

'Not much then,' I commented. I thought of the squalid places that the Rwandan families lived in. 'So it stands empty for most of the year?'

'We're just too busy with work,' was my sister's defensive reply.

There was an awkward silence and then she said quite unexpectedly, 'Maybe you'd like to go out there.'

I looked up in surprise. 'Me?' I said stupidly.

Olivia laughed. 'Yes. You. We'll talk about it some other time, but I don't see why you shouldn't.'

'Thanks,' I said, a tad inadequately, finding it hard to imagine that I would.

Our main courses arrived and we ate in silence. It was very good but my appetite was not what it usually was, and I'm afraid I left quite a lot of it.

'Do you really think Charlie will come tomorrow? What did he say when you told him?' I asked. 'He must have been as shocked as we both were.'

Olivia shrugged. 'He actually didn't say much. There was a silence when I told him and then he just said that he'd be there, and he wanted to know if I'd spoken to you. I told him that you were coming up and I was going to hold off telling you until you had arrived.'

That would explain why I hadn't heard from him.

'Why don't you text him yourself and ask?' Olivia suggested.

I felt around in my bag and brought out my phone. There was already a message from Charlie: *Hi there Jenny Wren. Guess I'll be seeing you and our dear sister tomorrow. Hope you're okay. Love C.*

I looked at Olivia. 'He beat me to it.' I held up the phone. 'A text from Charlie. He said he'd see us tomorrow.'

'To tomorrow then,' she said and raised her glass.

I did the same. But what exactly were we drinking to?

'Dessert, Jenna?' she said, but I sensed a hidden message again. Olivia was ready to go, and of course dessert would never have been on her private menu.

'No thanks,' I said brightly, even though the thought of something chocolaty had been haunting me all evening. Comfort food.

Olivia put up her hand for the bill. When the waiter came over she handed him the cloakroom tickets. It was just before eleven, but the restaurant was still alive and busy, like it was somewhere in Spain rather than England.

We didn't speak in the taxi going back. I wondered what Olivia was mulling over in her mind: Michael working late? Me? Charlie? The past? I stared out of the window at the streets and houses, the bridges and office buildings, the bright lights of life flashing by. There was something compelling about London, but it lasted only a short time for me before I was drowning in the hustle and bustle, and longing for the peace of the seashore. Mind you, the seagulls could be as noisy as the traffic!

Tomorrow. The word was already heavy with fear and pain, memories and emotions. I felt my stomach churning as I envisaged the prospect of meeting the mother who had, it now seemed, abandoned us; the mother whom I'd loved, adored and admired. I put the thoughts to the back of my mind and forced myself to think of dad. How was I going to tell him about this?

Something from the past was haunting me. The whispered rows, the way they had loved each other so dearly and then both turned away: dad to drink, mum to who knew where. Maybe that was the key: the past. Something that had never seemed quite right. And deep down inside I had never truly believed that mum was someone who had abandoned her children for the hell of it. There had to be more.

3

OLIVIA

In the taxi that took them back from the restaurant, Olivia sank back into the seat and watched, through the window, images of London sliding by. Superimposed, on top of those reflections, she saw her own and thought how pale and gaunt she looked, how tight lipped. Olivia suddenly remembered being on a sled in a store somewhere, at Christmas, while the fake scenery passed by; she had thought she was chimney high and on the way to a Wonderland. When everyone piled off, Father Christmas was waiting with a 'Yo ho ho!' and a gift in cheap paper. She'd sat on his lap (it was okay to do that back then) and he'd even kissed her on the cheek. She remembered the scratch of his beard and how she had wished really hard that her own father would turn into Father Christmas and stay that way forever.

Her father. She could hardly bring herself to say the word 'dad', a word that seemed to trip so easily off Jenna's tongue. Olivia had never felt close to him. Of course for Jenna, it was different. She adored her father and vice versa. But where had he been in Olivia's life? When she thought of him it was from afar: dad with Jenna on the beach; dad's silhouette in the studio at the end of the garden; dad on a rare occasion at the dinner table. Olivia could never remember being in his arms, holding his hand, or any other form of demonstrative contact. Some years ago she deduced that he had never felt any love for her as a daughter. Because of that she harboured intense feelings of envy for her sister's relationship with him. Because of that she had cut off all contact with him, at least as far as was possible.

She remembered only fragments of life with her mother: mum carrying her up to bed; stroking her hair off her forehead when she was upset; mum reading to her; her perfume, a song, a smile. But, by God, those fragments still had the power to hurt and that's why she kept them firmly so locked up.

And then there was Anya, who had done all those things when mum was busy, and after she'd gone. Anya had been such an important figure in her life that her image had merged with her mother's until they were so blurred she could hardly tell one from the other. Poor Anya had been only about eighteen at the time, but she had seemed so much older than her years. She had been patient with Olivia, with them all, and took the time to try and understand their erratic and often tiresome behaviour as they struggled to come to terms with their mother's disappearance.

Olivia thought about her decision not to have children of her own; it was hardly surprising, given the past. She made excuses to her parents-in-law about how busy she and Michael were with their careers, and how they intended to start a family a little later on in life, like their other friends had. But Olivia knew that she had no intention of getting pregnant. Having a child was far too much of a responsibility, and just the thought of being a mother scared her to hell. She was afraid of letting Michael down, of letting a child down. Of course it was completely irrational to think in such a way but she couldn't help it. As far as Olivia was concerned, both her parents had let her down and she had no intention of carrying that family gene into the next generation. Now it occurred to her that she and Michael had never talked about it with each other.

She supposed that she hated Cornwall because it was the place that had caused the most pain and sadness in her life. For that reason Olivia kept all thoughts of her mother and the pain of her disappearance locked away in an impenetrable vault deep inside.

So what the hell had happened to make her mother leave? Olivia lurched from blaming first one parent, then the other. Later, all the hatred and blame had been focused on her father. It was all so confusing.

Tomorrow was going to be the worst day of her life. Of that she was certain. But there was no way she was going to show her feelings. No way she was going to tell anyone that the pain of her mother leaving her had grown like a tumour inside her. She had been too young to realise exactly what had happened; but later in her life there were many nights when she couldn't sleep and had cried and cried into her pillow.

The thought of seeing her mother again was a trauma she could hardly bear to think about. She felt herself panicking and began breathing deeply. Olivia felt the eyes of her sister on her and tried to pull herself together. Jenna must never know what she was really feeling.

'Olivia?' A voice beside her broke into these thoughts and a hand brushed her arm. 'We're here.'

She looked up at the apartment windows but all was dark. Michael was not home yet. Olivia climbed out after her sister and paid the driver. She breathed in the cool air from the river before they entered the lobby. It calmed her a little.

'Are you okay?' she heard Jenna ask.

She nodded and smiled. 'Yes, I'm fine thank you.' She glanced at her watch. It was nearly midnight. Good. They could go straight to bed. She didn't want any more conversation.

Olivia followed her sister into the lift. What an odd creature she was with her well-worn clothes, her dark unruly hair and sad little face. She wanted to take her in hand; introduce her to a good hairdresser; take her shopping for clothes; show her some culture and nightlife.

'Thanks for supper. I really enjoyed it. Great place,' Jenna said as the lift sped upwards.

'You're welcome,' Olivia replied. Then she said: 'You should come up to London more often.'

Jenna shrugged. 'It's not really my scene,' she said, 'but thanks for asking.'

'I could make you like it,' Olivia replied with a smile.

'Well, maybe parts of it,' Jenna conceded, glancing down at the river below and the dancing lights of the city all around them. The lift, which was on the outside of the building, was all glass. It was quite a thrilling, heady sight.

Olivia was relieved when Jenna went straight to bed. She'd had enough family conversation for one evening.

She took a nightcap, a small glass of Cognac, out onto the balcony and sat staring in silent contemplation at the crowded city below.

Idly she wondered how she had come to marry Michael. What was it that had drawn them together but which now seemed to have so little meaning in their lives? They hardly saw each other; they were so wrapped up in their own work, in their own routine, every day. Michael was up at five thirty each morning to work out in the gym in the basement of the building, followed by a swim in the private pool. He had showered by seven and was out of the apartment by half-past, calling out 'Bye darling!' just before the door slammed shut.

'Bye', she would respond to nothing, to the silence, or not at all if she was already in the shower when he left. When they first met he would linger in the bedroom for a last kiss. When had that petered out?

It is true that it had never been a match made in heaven. They had both sort of drifted into the relationship, driven by their lifestyle, their combined wealth and the power they held in their respective businesses. In the business and social world they inhabited they were good for each other.

She lay back in the chair and closed her eyes to listen, as Jenna had done, to the sounds of the city, the never-ending clatter of life in the metropolis: traffic, sirens, machines, cars, people. Was there ever a period of inactivity? She doubted it. Yet there was also something soothing and soporific about it too. Slipping into a half-sleep, her mind journeyed back to the past.

At first Olivia was afraid of the sea, of the crabs that scuttled over the beach, of the ribbons of seaweed strewn on the sand when the tide came in, waiting to wrap itself around her legs if she went to paddle in the shallows. Jenna would take her hand and show her the rock pools when the tide was out, picking up shells with horrid slimy creatures inside them and letting the little creatures crawl across the palm of her hand. Olivia used to scream and run away and everyone laughed at her.

It was Anya who persuaded her that she wasn't going to sink into the sand and disappear; that it was quite fun to feel the sea lapping around your legs, minus the seaweed of course, but she still flatly refused to go swimming in it. It tasted disgusting anyway and Olivia always managed to open her mouth and swallow some. She would watch Jenna and Charlie as they ran into the waves and hurled themselves into the sea, swimming like fish. Afterwards they would run up the beach towards her and shake their dripping salty bodies all over her and her nice clean towel. It was so unfair; she screamed and wailed and Anya scolded her brother and sister for upsetting her. Jenna and Charlie would run away laughing and perch on the rocks like a pair of dark Cormorants, giggling at her.

Whenever they had been to the beach, Olivia would check her bed at night before she got in it, looking for pieces of seaweed, or dead crab legs or the sharp edges of broken shells. It was Charlie who often put them there and Olivia hated him for it.

There was very little she had liked about living in Cornwall, except perhaps for her mother's little café; she remembered watching her making sandwiches and serving pots of tea. It was a cosy place to be and Olivia learned to sit quietly in a corner, with a milkshake or a fresh juice. She liked the simple way it was decorated with blue and white tablecloths, little vases of flowers, whitewashed walls and old ships' lanterns for lights. She didn't recall ever going into the café again after her mother left.

When she was old enough, in the summers after her mother had disappeared, she would wander through the narrow streets of the town, looking into the shops and hoping, if she dared admit to it, to see a reflection of her mother in the windows. But of course it never happened. Instead, from the safety of the promenade, she watched the summer visitors who turned pink on the beach and stuffed their faces with pasties, candyfloss, fish and chips, and ice cream. It revolted her and she would pray that they'd be sick on the way home.

Olivia remembered a day when she must have been nine or ten, and her father had taken all three of his children to London for a day and a night to visit grandpa Moon. They seldom saw their grandfather except for once a year, in the summer, when he would take the train down to Cornwall for his annual visit. It was the first time they had ever visited their grandpa in London and she remembered how they had chattered about what to expect in the big city, with its parks and wide streets, its red buses, Big Ben and Trafalgar Square. They didn't stop talking for nearly the whole drive up there and, for once, they didn't argue with each other. Olivia had to sit in the front because she was car sick in the back; she remembered spending a lot of time looking at her father's hands on the steering wheel, counting the specks of paint on his fingers, and wishing he'd cleaned them off.

Grandpa Patrick Moon lived in a large airy flat in South Kensington; it had big windows, shiny polished wooden floors and elegant furniture. Olivia adored it instantly. They'd had dinner at a proper table, laid with candles and gleaming crockery and silver cutlery. She recalled sinking into soft plump sofa cushions, and sleeping in a bed with crisp white sheets and soft blankets instead of a lumpy old duvet; and there was instant hot water in the beautiful marble bathroom that was warm underfoot!

Jenna and Charlie were like fish out of water though, perching awkwardly on the puffy sofas, and tiptoeing everywhere because of the noise their shoes made on the wooden floors. They were afraid to talk too loudly because their voices echoed so much in the high-ceilinged rooms. It was Olivia's turn to laugh at them. She felt completely at home and it had been then that she'd fallen in love with London, the city of her dreams. She and her grandpa spent a lot of time chatting. He showed her some wonderful old books in his library, played her classical music that she instantly adored and, when he saw her examining the paintings on the walls, explained who the artists were and when the pictures had been painted. Some of them were very old and very valuable.

Grandpa Patrick was special and she was sure that he liked her best. That thought made her feel happy inside.

'When I grow up,' she had declared in the car on the way home, 'I'm going to have a flat in London that's painted all white and hasn't got any nasty cobwebs or sand or dust in it!'

Everyone laughed and Brendan had reached out a hand from the steering wheel to tickle her, which she hated. It always made her feel sick.

'Stop it,' she'd shrieked. 'I am going to live in London.'

Olivia made several more trips to the flat on her own. Her grandpa showed her his way of life, taking her to the museums and art galleries, and for tea in elegant, grand hotels; afterwards they would go for a stroll in Kensington Gardens, or to Buckingham Palace to watch the Changing the Guard ceremony.

Patrick Moon died when Olivia was just fifteen years old. She missed him very much and still did. She had been so much closer to him than she had ever been to her father. She later learned that he had left her his flat in London, and shared the capital he had accumulated with the rest of her family.

After her mother left there were long hard lingering days when the house was quiet and subdued.

Olivia had clung onto Anya, clutching at her hand, her coat, her dress; she was afraid to let go of her in case she too disappeared.

'Where's my mummy?' she remembered asking, over and over. 'Where's my mummy?'

'Hush, Olivia,' Anya would reply. 'I don't know where she is, sweetheart.'

Olivia had no doubt then that her mother would come back, out of the blue, with a smile and a laugh; and everything would be just as it had always been. She was just a child. It was natural to believe something like that would happen.

But of course Rowena never did turn up. Not after a week, a month, six months, a year. By then Olivia had adjusted to a new rhythm in her life, turning to Anya as her new mummy figure, and to Jenna and Mary-Ellen as the next best people to help take care of her.

Olivia remembered very little about that time; they were mere snatches of memory. She had no idea of the lengths her father had gone to in order to find his wife, the woman whom, he'd realised with hindsight, had been so precious to him. She didn't see the light diminishing in her brother's eyes, or the pain and confusion that Jenna had suffered. But she noticed when there was nobody around to help her with something, which made her cross and irritable.

Only later did Anya tell her about how they had all dealt with their loss.

Charlie had struggled with everything and Olivia now realised that he was the one who had probably suffered the most. He had flunked homework, disappearing to play with his football, kicking it over and over again against the garage wall; she remembered hearing him scream only once, when a dog took his beloved football and punctured it, and Anya had taken him into Looe to buy a new one. But even that couldn't bring her to feel sorry for her brother, then or now.

Her sister was always itching to get outside into the fields or down on the beach of her beloved Cornwall to be on her own.

When Olivia was eleven she had run away from home. She vaguely remembered it was after a row with her father about a trip to the cinema in Looe. She had wanted to go with a couple of friends but, because she was only ten, he had insisted that Jenna should go with them. Olivia had been adamant that she wanted to go on her own, that her older sister being there would make her look stupid in front of her friends and she didn't want to be the laughing stock of the school. But her father had refused. Olivia had stomped up to her room in tears, slamming the door shut, screaming and throwing things around in her anger and frustration. That anger gradually gave way to a clearer decision. She would leave the boring family she lived with, the dull restrictive life she had to endure, and go and find her mother and bring her back home.

So she packed a bag, one of Rowena's she found in a wardrobe, stole five pounds from Jenna's secret stash, which she had discovered after spying on her, and crept out of the house.

She got all the way to Truro on the bus. She was attempting to buy a train ticket from Truro to London when a policeman noticed her and started asking questions. Olivia refused to tell him who she was or where she had come from and he called for a car to take them both to the police station. Eventually she spilled the beans and Brendan Moon was summoned to Truro to collect his daughter.

Olivia recalled that they had driven home with her father stern faced and resolute. There had been no hugs from him or visible relief at their reconciliation, nor did he ask her any questions about why she had run away. Angry and miserable, Olivia had stared out of the window at the world sliding by and wished for a miracle.

Jenna took the hungry and sullen Olivia straight to bed. She even sneaked some biscuits and chocolate upstairs for Olivia, but she didn't mention the money Olivia had stolen.

Olivia shuddered at the thought of still living in Beach Lane Cottage, that mausoleum of a house in Cornwall, with its draughts and cracked walls, its threadbare carpets and creaking floorboards, its cranky old hot water system. It had no fitted kitchen and certainly not a dishwasher; the bathroom had been cold and cavernous and it was still decorated with ancient bits and pieces from Jenna's beach-scavenging days. The house had only storage heaters and a wood-burning stove to warm it up and a Rayburn cooker in the kitchen.

She had no fondness for the place, and life as it had been with her mother was a distant and fragmented memory. The only way she could describe what was left of those times was as an 'experience', extracts that danced around on the outskirts of her mind, and those frightening moments in the early hours when she woke with clear and painful images. She would lie awake until daylight took the images away, afraid to fall asleep again. Over the past year or so it had happened more frequently and Olivia had sought some outside help.

The therapist whom she saw every month had helped Olivia to see that she was in mourning, that because there had been no confirmed death, there had been no natural closure. There would forever be questions unanswered, doors left open; it would be best if she could face them head on and deal with the answers.

With hindsight, Olivia realised how odd it was that none of them – she, Jenna, Charlie or her father – had ever sat down and talked about what had happened and what it meant to each of them. Their father had not encouraged discussion about their mother's disappearance, and stifling the natural healing process had done more harm than good.

She felt it had made freaks of them all. In her teenage years she had thought of her family as boring and creepy; if the truth were known, Olivia was still of that opinion. She reckoned that her sister, with her sensible, stoic façade, was an emotional wreck. Wasn't that why she had never managed a long-term relationship? Wasn't that why she continued to hide down in Cornwall, why she remained in the old home with her father? Had nothing changed for her? As for Charlie, he'd just gone off the rails without any parent to guide him. Even she had been aware of how estranged Charlie and his father were. They all had demons to fight, but she hadn't turned into an alcoholic, or hidden herself away, or thrown all caution to the wind and dropped out of life. She had been determined to make the best of every opportunity.

Olivia heard a car door slam in the street below. Michael? She quickly went back inside, put down the empty cognac glass in the kitchen and headed for the bedroom. She undressed and went into the bathroom to wash her face and brush her teeth. As she got into bed she heard the front door open and close.

The clink of glass and a bottle from the kitchen told her that Michael was having a nightcap too. On impulse she got out of bed, put on a wrap and went to join him; but the glass doors onto the balcony were closed and she could see he was on his phone, his head turned away from her.

She lay in bed waiting for him but finally drifted off to sleep.

4

JENNA

It was hot in her room in Olivia's apartment, and Jenna couldn't sleep. She'd pushed the sliding doors to the balcony slightly apart but was distracted by the noise of London, which seemed to go on all night: the distant sirens, the traffic below, a boat horn, loud voices as a group passed by on their way home.

Jenna wouldn't have slept anyway. For the first two hours she had tossed and turned. Her nerves tingled with the utter immensity of the day that was slowly approaching; her thoughts were scattered all over the place, one minute in the past, the next in the present, wriggling and tumbling like eels in water. Sleep was impossible. She sat up and slid out of bed, reaching for a glass of water on the nightstand. The soft white curtains billowed in the breeze and cast shadows across the room. It was too cold to sit on the balcony so she perched on a cupboard by the window.

Across the river a fog or mist was building up but the sky above it was still clear and she could make out a few stars through the light pollution that covered the city. She thought of Cornwall and how different it was down there: the utter darkness all around at night and the soothing sounds of the sea, or an owl hooting, and her own breathing.

She climbed down and went to the wardrobe to get something out of her satchel. It was an old shoe, probably a seventies vintage, rope soled and open toed, with a green canvas strip across the toes and around the ankle. It travelled with her wherever she went – her Cinderella shoe, the one that would one day find the right foot to fit again. How close that moment was now.

About six months after Rowena disappeared, Brendan became angry. He had brought in someone to put Rowena's belongings in bags and take them away. Jenna was too frightened to ask him to stop, so the night before it was due to happen she had sneaked into her mother's room and found a silver-framed black-and-white photograph of her mother on the beach; she also discovered a few other loose ones in a drawer. The shoe had come into her possession unexpectedly. When Jenna arrived home from school later the next day, after the purge, she saw it lying in the driveway, fallen from a plastic bag. She hid it in her school bag and kept it.

Another month passed by. The bedroom that her parents had once shared was gutted. The carpet was ripped up, the cupboards stripped out, the walls painted.

Brendan moved back into the room and began a short period of trying to be a father to his abandoned children.

It didn't last very long. After six months he started drinking again and began to spend more and more time alone in his studio. Anya looked after them almost single-handedly, and Jenna helped. It was a time when she hardly ever went to the beach, a time that she most keenly felt the absence of her mother.

The only good thing to come out of it all was that they discovered that Brendan was painting prolifically, and his work was in demand. He seemed to have invented a whole new approach. His new canvases were covered in strong bold images bordering on abstract – seascapes and landscapes, weather patterns, the seasons; all executed in a wild but vivid manner. What he was experiencing in life he was transferring to the canvas. For Jenna it mirrored not only their environment – wild and desolate, stormy and chaotic – but also their lives. The canvases were selling like hotcakes.

It was incredible, she recalled, how one person's art, created out of a mire of misery, could become another person's pride and joy.

She took up the shoe and pressed it to her face. Although she knew it had once belonged to her mother, it gave no clues to the mystery that might unravel tomorrow. And she knew that deep down inside they all wanted the answer to the million-dollar question: Why?

5

CHARLIE

'Charles Edward Moon, you stand before us today to hear the charges brought against you by the Crown Prosecution: firstly of unlawfully possessing Class A drugs and secondly of unlawfully selling these drugs to other parties. You are ordered to appear at this Court on a date to be notified. Until then you have been granted police bail. You must abide by the rules of your bail, which your lawyer will convey to you.' Charlie heard the hammer hit the gavel, and he and his lawyer left the courtroom.

'Bail?' said Charlie turning to him outside. 'You worked it. Thanks!'

The lawyer shook his head. 'Wasn't me,' he said grimly. He unfolded the bail conditions and read them out.

'Report to the police station in Vauxhall every Monday, and you must appear in court when required. You better make damned certain that you do,' he warned. 'A letter will be sent to you regarding the date of your trial, or I will be in touch about this. I would like us to meet at least once before that date. Here are my contact details.' He fished in his pocket and produced a card. 'Be a good lad and don't get into any more trouble. In particular, don't go anywhere near even a sniff of a drug or a dealer.'

Charlie twisted his face and replied, 'What sort of man do you take me for?'

The lawyer grimaced, then turned and headed off towards his next client.

Charlie sat down on the bench alongside the wall and speculated on who might have guaranteed bail for him. Jack Solomon, his boss? Possibly, but he doubted it. Dad? Olivia and Michael? Charlie laughed at the idea of any of them doing such a thing. So who then? He realised he was shaking. This was serious. The odds of him ending up in prison were high. And what stretch would he be looking at? He reckoned somewhere between three and five years. Last time, a long time ago, it had been a fine and a warning; he was reminded that if he were arrested again and found guilty, he could serve a term in prison. It was all very well for the lawyer to tell him not to worry and to favour pleading guilty. Charlie favoured pleading the very opposite.

But he would worry about that later. Right now he was free. Forget work; he had most probably been sacked anyway. A drink was what he needed. He set off for the Club.

When Charlie was a child it seemed to him that he hadn't counted for much as far as his father was concerned. Brendan was verbally dominant, usually tanked up on alcohol and excessively belligerent. Charlie realised from an early age that his father merely tolerated the children, except perhaps for Jenna. This was mostly because Brendan had never understood why Charlie would rather kick a football around on a beach, whereas Jenna and he were happy to get down on their hands and knees and study the things that lived and grew on it. He didn't get why Charlie wanted to fly a kite rather than examine the contents of a rock pool and hunt for shells and stones, or mess around on a surfboard instead of catching fish.

Charlie realised with some resentment that his father

was different with Jenna. They were like shadows of each other, seashore scavengers hunting for what the sea and the sand gave up, scrabbling and searching for its bounty.

Charlie's earliest memories of Cornwall were around the age of four, listening to Olivia, his baby sister, screaming after they'd all been put to bed. The best thing about it, if you could say there was a best thing, was the sound of his mother's soothing voice in the nursery, even if it was for Olivia and not for him. How he'd wished she would come to him; he longed to feel her cool hand stroking his forehead, her gentle voice lulling him to sleep. Instead Charlie would bite down on the ear of his scruffy old toy rabbit to stop himself from crying and he would will himself to sleep.

You could say the damage began that early. Charlie developed a tough outer edge that never betrayed the loneliness and sense of abandonment he felt inside. As time passed and he grew into a young man he never allowed anyone to touch his heart. Not ever.

It was actually a great relief for Charlie when he was packed off to boarding school at the age of nine, more than a year after his mother had left. He was not afraid of being thrust into such a competitive environment. Charlie had already learned survival techniques. He wasn't a mean kid, but he looked out for himself above everything else. He believed he was the only one who ever would or could.

Jenna and his father had delivered him to the doors of Cunningham Moor on his first day. Charlie had been quiet and sullen, wanting to make it as hard as possible for them. They tried to get him to talk in the car but he refused to respond. Why should he? He presumed they were happy to be sending him away so that nobody would have to deal with difficult old Charlie any more. Nobody, particularly his father, would have to make the effort to play with him, or read to him, or help him with his homework.

He'd waited, head down, kicking at the gravel as his father unloaded his trunk. Several other boys were milling around the school, the sound of their laughter and chattering a painful discord to Charlie's ears; there was an inkling of interest there too and he shot them a surreptitious glance.

'Come on then, old chap,' his father had said, tousling his hair, 'let's go and see where they're putting you.'

They'd climbed the steps and entered through the large wooden doors that had been thrown wide open for the returning hordes of schoolboys and their parents.

Two masters stood in the entrance hall, each with a clipboard and an alphabetical sign to indicate which side the pupils should queue. 'M' was to the left so that's where Charlie headed, shuffling along towards the master.

'Moon, ah yes, new boy,' the master noted. 'You'll be in Heron House, second dorm, bed three. There are four houses here: Heron, Curlew, Falcon and Lake. They started off with Lake, named after the founder of Cunningham Moor; then they added Heron, Curlew and Falcon, after the founder's love of birds.' He paused and smiled down at Charlie. 'You'll like it here. Heron House, through the doors opposite, across the courtyard, house on your right.'

Charlie, Jenna and their father followed the directions and ended up in front of a two-storey redbrick building covered with white rambling roses. Inside they were ushered upstairs and along the corridor to the dormitory where Charlie was to spend his first term. There were four beds in the room, which had tall sash windows and was light and airy. A screen between each bed provided some privacy, and each pupil had a lockable bedside cabinet and a small wardrobe. Through a door at the end of the dormitory was a bathroom with a shower, two toilets and two sinks. It felt warm and comfortable. It didn't smell too bad either, Charlie remembered thinking.

Rather than wait for Charlie's trunk to arrive in the dormitory, they'd decided to go down to the school refectory, where tea was being served to the new boys and their parents.

'Why don't you go and say, hello?' his father said, seeing Charlie looking across at another boy of about the same age, with his parents.

Charlie shook his head. He wasn't about to do anything that might make his father feel better about leaving him.

Brendan sighed and rolled his eyes at Jenna, but she had more sympathy.

'Let's leave dad to chat to the parents and go and have a look around, shall we?' she suggested.

Relieved, Charlie nodded and they hurried out into the fresh air of the grounds. He liked what he saw immediately: a football pitch and a rugby field. They wandered over to the main cluster of buildings and looked in through the windows of some single-storey classrooms, and into the ground floor of a large performing arts centre. Everyone they passed, pupils and adults alike, smiled and acknowledged them, and Charlie couldn't help but be drawn into the general good feeling of the school.

'I'm sure you'll like it here, Charlie,' Jenna said encouragingly.

'Maybe, whatever,' he'd replied, but he'd found himself

wondering who else would be in his dormitory room.

'How long are you and dad planning on staying?' he'd asked.

Jenna had smiled. 'Not long I don't suppose. Dad will probably have a word with your housemaster and I expect we'll be off after that. I'll miss you, Charlie. You'll be okay, won't you?' There had been a touch of anxiety in her voice.

'Yep,' he'd replied. He was going to miss Jenna, but at the time he'd found himself wanting them to leave so that he could just get on with the job of settling in and seeing how things worked. Charlie and Jenna had given each other a quick hug, then walked back to the refectory and found their father deep in conversation with the art master.

'Charlie, say hello to Mr Franklin,' he'd instructed.

Charlie had held out his hand and shaken the art master's own. 'Good afternoon, sir.' He hadn't felt like responding so politely, but he wasn't going to let himself down.

'Good afternoon, Charlie, and welcome to Cunningham. I hear you're in Heron House. It's a very fine house, you know, and I say that because it's mine too. We teachers are allocated to the houses too! I look forward to seeing you at your first art lesson.' Then he'd said goodbye and gone to speak to some other parents.

'Good start, eh?' his father had said.

Charlie shrugged. 'I suppose so.'

'Let's go back to the dormitory and see if Charlie's trunk has arrived,' Jenna had suggested, seeing the exasperated look in her father's eyes.

Charlie had watched them leave from the dormitory window, his eyes following as they walked back towards where the car was parked. Then they'd gone out of sight, behind the main building wall. He'd drawn in his breath and turned to find another boy standing on the threshold of the door.

'Hi,' he'd said, 'I'm Moon, who are you?'

'Grant. Fancy kicking a ball around?'

Charlie had grinned. It was going to be all right.

Charlie soon discovered that boarding school meant he could breathe again. He had lived his first nine years of life at home, in a perceived atmosphere of neglect, loneliness and confusion. Apart from missing Jenna, the proximity of the beach and the sea, and the wildness of the Cornish coast, he was grateful to be free of the agony of life at home, and his father's moods, and he found within him a spirit that was verging on wilful.

Luckily he excelled in most of his schoolwork, thanks to his sharp and retentive memory, but he found it hard to make himself concentrate on pretty much anything for longer than the blink of an eye. Just when the teachers thought they had his attention, he would do something stupid.

It was because of that flaw in his nature that Charlie didn't quite complete his time at Cunningham Manor. Thankfully, though, he had already sat his A-level exams when the school had no choice but to expel him after cannabis was found in his locker. He and some friends were going to celebrate the end of their final term before they dispersed to various universities and far corners of the world. Charlie had his eyes set on a London University.

The school had the strictest rules about drugs but because it was also a criminal offence, they were duty bound to report the matter to the authorities. The police were called in and Charlie was cautioned. That step had been taken to protect the pupil in question, but it was also to warn the rest of the school of the consequences if they should act as Charlie had done.

The headmaster phoned Brendan. He suggested he took his son home and made sure he understood the implications of using and being in possession of drugs, for the sake of Charlie's future.

Charlie didn't intend to wait around for his father, nor did he intend to spend a miserable summer at home, waiting for his results. Instead he climbed out of the dormitory window and escaped.

With little difficulty, he hitched a lift to Newquay, on the north coast. He spent a couple of months hanging around with the surfing fraternity and working in a bar, and narrowly escaped arrest after the bar was raided by the police searching for drugs.

In August Charlie had to go back home to get his A-level results. Jenna was away in Plymouth, and Olivia was staying with a friend and her family when Charlie arrived.

Charlie had one almighty row with his father, who made it quite clear that he thought his son was a complete waste of time. He didn't even congratulate him when Charlie opened his envelope and discovered he'd earned himself an A in three of the exams.

Miserable, angry and confused, Charlie crammed his bag with everything he wanted and needed from his room in Beach Lane Cottage and went back to Newquay.

Although the London University had offered him a place in the autumn, reading mathematics and economics,

Charlie wasn't ready to take it up. There was too much pent-up madness in him to allow him to concentrate on academic pursuits. The university agreed to defer the place for a year, and Charlie went travelling, talking and charming his way around India and the Far East, with his long blonde hair in a ponytail, a goatee beard and an earring. He bartered in the markets, lived with the locals in the high mountain passes. He spent the last few days of his time in India on the beaches of Goa, sleeping in shacks and cooking fish on a fire on the sand. He didn't want to leave.

But England beckoned him back as the year sped towards the start of the university term. On home ground again, he found himself a room in Vauxhall in south London, a stone's throw away from the station. At night he would lie listening to the trains chugging in and out, and dream of the beaches of Goa.

For four long years he knuckled down and studied mathematics and economics. He came out of it with an honours degree, but only Jenna was there to see him graduate. His father was busy working on a big commission.

All along Charlie had his mind fixed on working in the City. He'd heard about the money people earned in bonuses, and he trawled the Internet for information about trading room floors. During his studies he started gambling to understand how odds worked. He read about probabilities and discovered that he possessed the uncanny instincts of a winner.

Charlie had tracked down an old friend from Cunningham, who invited him to join his Club. There he paid attention to the brash, City stockbrokers discussing the day's trading and boasting about their successes to each other.

He soaked up the tales of insider trading and the devious manipulation of share prices; he overlooked the red faces caused by excessive drinking and the tales that highlighted their competitiveness and greed. It didn't matter to him that they were shallow, egotistical moneymakers; the point was that they were successful and rich, and Charlie himself was being slowly seduced by the macho-culture of the City. He memorised the names of the companies they talked about, and the deals they had made; and he made sure he knew the day's trading patterns and indexes. They grew to like Charlie Moon, with his happy-go-lucky manner, his easy friendliness and his quick mind.

By the time Charlie had graduated he was desperate to find a job in the City. One evening, while out drinking with a group of City guys, he found himself singled out by an investment banker, Jack Solomon.

'I've been listening and watching you,' he told Charlie. 'You intrigue me because you're different to the others. There's something street-wise about you, despite being well educated. I could do with someone like you on the trading floor at the moment, someone smart and canny. I get too many university graduates who know it all on paper but struggle with the reality of it all. They lose me money.' He handed Charlie his card. 'Make an appointment with my personal assistant and come and see me. We'll have a chat and I might be able to find you something to do.'

A few days later he was hired as an assistant on the trading floor. Jack Solomon wanted to see what he was made of before he committed him to anything better.

Charlie Moon was twenty-five years old, on the road to earning the money of his dreams, wining and dining in the best London restaurants and generally having the time of his life.

Charlie perched on a stool by the bar, in the Club, and ordered a glass of merlot. He took a collected look around. Not many in yet, at least not anyone that interested him. He took a cigarette from the almost-empty packet of Marlborough and made his way to the back of the Club. He pushed open the fire door and stepped onto the metal landing outside. It was still light, even though the inside of the club was dark and dim as though it were night already. It suited the pond-life that inhabited it, those who lived under the surface of the real world, emerging like vampires after dark, sucking up the vulnerable and the needy. He should know; he was one of them. Feeding the workers the habit they needed to keep them alive, those hard-core movers and shakers of the City world, with its stock market, its shares, its futures and pensions, its hedge funds. It was easy to burn out early without a little something to keep you going. And so he had immersed himself in the seedy underworld of the Square Mile.

Eventually he'd grown to despise the very thing he'd thought he'd wanted: the hedonistic lifestyle, the money. He began to draw back from the unsavoury and sometimes twisted behaviour of his colleagues, struggling with the sudden revelation that he might be selling his soul to the devil.

Along with the drugs charge and the impending trial, the news about his mother had shaken the core of his world and his feelings. The past had come flooding back, and with it all the black thoughts that he had buried in the deepest recesses of his mind.

Charlie felt his hand beginning to shake. Of all the things he had done in his life, he was sure that tomorrow's event was going to be one of the worst. He wondered why he had agreed to it at all. He supposed it was a morbid sense of curiosity, a sense that he might find closure? Or settle an old score with a woman who had abandoned him, and whom he had once called mum.

Charlie thought about his sisters being together this evening. Olivia had magnanimously invited him to join them but he had rejected the invitation. It would have been okay spending time with Jenna, but not with Olivia. Oh no, not her or her pompous and hypocritical husband, Michael.

He went back inside, ordered another glass of wine and took his place again on a stool at the bar. Jack Solomon appeared and came over. His face was grim and unfriendly.

'No thanks,' he said when Charlie offered him a drink. 'I don't want to see you again, Charlie. There will be nothing owing to you from the company. And don't be stupid enough to come back into the office either. Security has been warned not to let you in. It's probably for your own good, otherwise you might be in danger of being lynched.' He went to walk away but turned back. 'If I were you, I'd leave the Club right now, before anyone else sees you. I can't vouch for your safety if they do, though. You've disappointed a lot of people, Charlie. You've broken the code and they'll make you pay.'

Charlie downed his wine, slapped some money on the bar and left through the back door. He wasn't going to argue with Jack and he was grateful for the warning. But what a bunch of hypocrites they were.

Still, he felt vulnerable as he stepped into the streets. It was once a place where he was completely at ease; now he knew people were out to get him: dealers and traders, not only in the City world but also in the drugs world. He hurried to the nearest station and got a cab to Vauxhall, to his safe house.

6

THE MEETING

Charlie was already there, waiting by the reception desk when Jenna and Olivia arrived at The Savoy the next morning.

Jenna rushed straight over and hugged her brother. Olivia hung back. She and Charlie eyed each other like wary foxes.

'What do you make of today then?' Charlie said to Jenna, ignoring Olivia and her look of disdain.

Jenna shrugged. 'I don't know. I'm scared. Are you?' The feeling in her stomach, the churning apprehension, was the worse she had ever experienced.

He shook his head. 'Curious but not scared.'

'The Moon family,' a voice suddenly interrupted them. They turned to see a tall silver-haired dapper-looking man in a pin-stripe city suit approaching them.

'Yes,' Olivia replied, taking charge. 'And you are?'

'Albert Findlay, Mrs Moon's lawyer.' He shook their hands in turn.

'I would like to thank you for agreeing to this meeting. I realise the request must have come as an enormous shock, and the circumstances of it will become clear as the meeting progresses. I hope you will manage to stay and hear everything that has to be said. I would urge you to do so. Now, please follow me,' said Albert Findlay, implying that asking anything at this stage was out of the question. He led them down the stairs to the lounge area, and turned left along a corridor to the meeting room. Inside they found a table with three chairs on one side and a single chair on the other. Behind the single chair was a door.

Albert Findlay indicated that they should sit. A moment later the door opened and a woman in a wheelchair was pushed into the room.

The three Moons stared curiously. She was covered to the waist with a blanket, and she looked ill and frail.

Jenna felt confused. She looked at the woman standing behind the wheelchair, a nurse? Something stirred in her mind, but it wasn't a memory of her mother.

Olivia had paled. She was grasping something that Charlie and Jenna had not yet grasped.

They saw the hand that rested on the arm of the wheelchair move slightly, and Jenna caught sight of a silver wedding ring. She gasped.

At that point, Albert Findlay spoke.

'My client, Mrs Moon, has asked me to apologise for shocking you in this way. She has an inoperable brain tumour; she finds speech very difficult.'

Olivia opened her mouth to speak but Albert Findlay raised his hand and smiled. 'Please allow me to finish and then you may have your say. My client would like you to stay and to hear what I have to tell you on her behalf. She has only a short time left to live, but she is not here for sympathy. It's simply that she feels the time for explanation has come. She feels it is only right that you should understand everything about her disappearance. She is not looking for reconciliation; she merely wants to see you all for the last time and to try to help you to make sense of it all. After this meeting, she will return to the hospice and you need never to see her again. Do you agree to stay, all of you?'

Jenna turned to Olivia and was shocked to see the expression on her face. It was one of utter horror. She tried to grasp her hand but Olivia snatched it away.

'I do,' said Charlie carefully and coldly, his eyes on the woman in the wheelchair. 'I want to know exactly why she left us.' Until this moment, when it had been absolutely confirmed to him that this woman, or what was left of this woman, was his mother, he had accepted the possibility that something awful could have happened and that she might be dead. He had always wanted that fact confirmed so that he could allow himself to grieve and properly forget. To discover now that his mother had been alive all along, and had in fact abandoned them, filled him with cold rage. Her illness meant nothing to him; what mattered were the past and her explanation.

'What about you, Jenna?' Albert Findlay asked.

'I…I don't know,' Jenna replied wildly. 'I don't know.' Part of her wanted to escape, to run out of the room, out of the hotel, away from London.

He smiled sympathetically. 'It's difficult, I understand, but it may help in the long run.'

'Help!' scoffed Olivia. 'Help what? We'd already got over her abandoning us and got on with our lives for the last twenty-odd years; why should today make any difference? As far as I was concerned she was long dead and forgotten.' Olivia was angry. Being presented with this situation made it difficult to shower the hatred she felt, over someone with such a disadvantage.

Despite such harsh words, Albert Findlay nodded with a practised understanding. 'Your mother accepts that none of you has any reason to be here and that you all have every reason to be angry. However, having come this far today, could you not just extend your stay a little longer and hear me out?'

Jenna was twisting her hands like a child; she was unable to look again at the person they were calling 'her mother' in the wheelchair. She wanted the nurse, or whoever she was, to wheel her away. She wanted it all to be a joke and their real mother to emerge through the door opposite. This simply wasn't fair.

'All right,' said Olivia suddenly. 'I'll stay and hear what she has to say to us all.' She turned to her brother and sister. 'And by the way, in case you hadn't already realised, her nurse is our old au pair, Anya.'

Jenna and Charlie looked in amazement at the nurse who stood behind the wheelchair.

'Oh my God,' said Jenna, recognising her now, despite the huge gap in years since they'd last seen her. How had she not recognised those mesmerising eyes?

'Hello Jenna,' said Anya. 'And Charlie.'

Charlie shook his head. 'This is like some bloody horror movie!' he exclaimed. 'Can someone please tell us what the hell is going on?'

'Anya to the rescue again,' said Olivia with a hint of sarcasm. 'How apt.'

'Stop it,' cried Jenna. She turned to the lawyer. 'I'm sorry, but it's not what we expected.'

'No,' said Albert Findlay. 'I'm sure it's not. Mrs Moon is going to leave us now, to avoid causing you any further distress. If you will allow me to read the letters then my job here will be done and we can all go.'

'Letters?' said Olivia. 'What letters?'

'Your mother has written each of you a letter. She has also written one that explains why she disappeared.'

'As if a letter will help!' Olivia responded bitterly.

'I don't want her to go. She can stay and see this through with us at least,' said Charlie, staring unflinchingly at the pathetic figure of his mother in the wheelchair. Yet somehow he couldn't reconcile them to be one and the same. A flicker of pain interrupted his show of indifference.

Olivia didn't agree. 'No', she said, 'I'd rather she went.' She, like Jenna, had been unable to look at the frail figure in the wheelchair. She too had wanted to be presented with the mother she vaguely remembered but only so that she could hate her all over again.

Jenna forced herself to look. How she longed to be gazing at the gentle willowy figure with long blonde hair, and the smile she remembered in her dreams. But if this were to be the last chance of seeing her mother, whatever she looked like, then she would never forgive herself for letting the opportunity go. Her eyes slowly settled on Rowena. She took in the thinning hair, the wasted body. How could this have happened to someone who had been once been so vibrant, so sweet and so beautiful? If this was divine retribution then it was as vile and callous as retribution could possibly be, not only for Rowena but also for them all.

'I'm so sorry, mum,' she heard herself say and stifled a sob. Olivia and Charlie were looking at her with astonishment.

Once again she saw the hand lift in acknowledgement and Jenna realised that if Rowena still bore any feelings for her children then this must be an incredibly hard thing to do.

'Sorry for what?' said Olivia. 'She left us, remember?'

Jenna ignored her. On impulse, she got up from her chair, went around the table and approached the wheelchair. She crouched down in front of Rowena, level with the half-hidden face and covered her mother's frail hand with her own.

'I'd like to hear what happened. We all would really. It's just all the terrible feelings that have churned up again and we can't think straight.'

There was a sudden choking sound from Rowena; her body heaved and then Jenna saw the tears. She stood up quickly, shocked at the reaction she had provoked.

Anya bustled Jenna firmly but gently out of the way and fussed around Rowena for a few moments. Oxygen was administered, the distressing sounds diminished and Rowena settled again. They saw Anya listen intently to something Rowena was trying to tell her; she relayed this quietly to Albert Findlay.

He cleared his throat. 'My client, your mother, has told us that she will stay. She says that you are all so brave that she must see this through with you, whatever your reactions, whatever may be said.'

Jenna sat down again and was amazed when both Charlie and Olivia each took a hand in theirs. It was their first ever act of sibling solidarity.

Albert Findlay took up the papers that lay on the table in front of him.

'Firstly, my client, Mrs Moon, would like me to read to you the explanation for her disappearance. This is her testimony, her letter to all of you.

My dearest children, if I may be allowed to make this claim.

You are brave and generous and I cannot wish for more than that today. I know you must wonder why it has taken more than twenty years for me to find the courage to give you the details you are about to hear. I confess that it is because of my illness. Without this certainty of death in the near future, I might have carried on and you would be none the wiser until some time even further in the future.

Let me begin at the beginning, when I was young and vulnerable and had the world pulled from under my feet.

When I was eighteen, and I had finished school, I went with some friends to travel around India. While we were there we met a group of Indians about the same age as we were, and we hung out with them for two or three months. They showed us their country – the city, the beaches, the markets, countryside and the people. We grew to love it.' Already Charlie could hardly believe what he was hearing; it was his life! *'But it turned out that they had deceived us. They had befriended us because they wanted to use us to smuggle drugs to England. I know, it sounds like a setting for a movie but believe me it happened. The gang's mastermind was an Englishman. He had recruited our friends, paying them well for their work. Unwittingly, I carried the drugs home to England, and that's where it all began. Men from the London drug ring broke into where I was staying on the night I returned and threatened to kill me if I ever told anyone what was happening. They took their stash from my bag. I hadn't even known it was there. It might be difficult to believe but it was true. But that wasn't the end of it. They approached me again and again and forced me to carry out work for them, collecting drugs and making cash* drops. I had never taken drugs in my life, not even a puff of marijuana, but one night they held me down and forced me to take heroin. I had nowhere to go, no one to turn to except the Confessional. You remember I'm a Catholic. The priest was concerned for me, for my safety, my soul, etc, etc but there was nothing he could do. He urged me to give myself up to the police. I knew he was right but I was too scared.

One day, out of the blue, I was having a drink in a pub in North London, far away from my usual patch, and I overheard two detectives talking about a drug ring. I couldn't believe my ears. They were talking about the one I was involved with. I just took the bull by the horns and approached them. At first they laughed at me and told me to get lost, but I wouldn't leave. I just kept on talking and they finally realised I was telling the truth. They smuggled me into a police station to take a statement and then offered to put me in the Witness Protection Programme so that I could testify in court when the gang was arrested. I was terrified, but I agreed. I knew what it meant; I would have to change my identity and leave every aspect of my old life behind. But I was prepared to do anything to get away from the awful life I was trapped in.

After the trial, which was dreadful, with people shouting death threats at me in the courtroom, I was given my new papers and identity and, despite being told to go abroad, I went to Cornwall, where I had lived as a child. After a year of moving from one place to another, never daring to stay anywhere for too long, and always looking over my shoulder, I met and married your father. He often wondered about me, where I'd come from, who my parents were. I told him they were both dead, which they were by that time. I saw from the papers and television that the gang had been put away for a long time. I relaxed a *bit then.*

But it all caught up with me again, years later. There had been a drugs bust not far from where we lived along the coast, and I was contacted by the police. One of the gang that had been arrested had done a deal and he'd mentioned that the people I'd worked for had traced me to Cornwall. If they found me, they found all of us, and I just couldn't take the risk of anything happening to you. So I left. I had no choice. I begged the police to help and I was put into yet another Witness Protection Programme. But this time I had to leave the country. It might have seemed like the wrong decision, but I thought it was safer to go alone, and leave you in Cornwall.

I went to Australia, as far away from you all as was possible. I immersed myself in a new life down under. I started a business there.

I earned enough money to employ people in England to keep an eye on you and I paid for security to continue to protect you. I wanted to know what you were doing, how you were all managing. I've followed your lives almost since the day I left.

When I was diagnosed with a brain tumour, I decided to put things in place for your inheritance and your protection. The company has been sold and the money will go to you all equally. It's up to you whether you accept it or not.

Albert Findlay paused and placed the letter on the table. 'Mrs Moon would now like me to read the letters she wrote to each of you.'

They were not quite ready for this next round as they were still trying to take in the revelations they had just heard.

'Can we have some water please,' Olivia asked. Despite

her cool appearance, it was harder for Olivia, than her brother and sister imagined, to sit in front of the mother she had once been so close to.

Anya arranged for glasses and a jug of iced water to be brought; all three sipped at it.

'May I continue?' Albert Findlay asked. One by one they nodded, too stunned to be able to collect their thoughts. Even Olivia, the cynic, was knocked out by what she'd heard.

'The first letter is addressed to Jenna.'

Jenna squirmed uncomfortably, wondering what on earth she was going to hear. She was still reeling from the facts contained in her mother's letter.

'My dear sweet Jenna

You are a wonder to behold. I've seen you grow up, although you never knew it. I've seen the kindness and generosity of spirit you show in your work and to others, to your father, to friends, and to your brother and sister. I've seen the ups and downs of your life.

There are some things I want to tell you. Some you will not find kind, but that are important for your future.

First of all, I would like you to hear the truth about Mary-Ellen. I was grateful for her help and kindness towards the family after I had gone. It seemed inevitable that a relationship would develop between her and your father. I didn't know that they were having an affair when I was still living there and deceiving us all. With hindsight, I suppose your father had to turn to someone else who wasn't always tired and tetchy. But I'm afraid it gets worse.' Jenna and Olivia exchanged a brief glance, and Jenna saw Olivia's eyebrows lift slightly at her.

'The Blue Moon Café has always been in my name, Rowena Moon that is, and so has Beach Lane Cottage. That has never changed and for some reason your father has never attempted to alter the situation. On my death they will both pass to you but I know that Mary-Ellen has been expecting to get something from it too. That might seem fair but for one flaw. Mary-Ellen has been deceiving both you and your father with a fisherman in Plymouth. As far as I am concerned, she does not deserve to get any part of the house or the business, which I know you care for so well.

But Jenna, I have watched you from afar and I think that you are living a life that is stifling your talents and abilities. You are tied to a place that is holding you back when you should be blossoming. You care for your father, which is admirable, but he must learn to look after himself and let you go. You're like a trapped butterfly and the air in your jar is running out. You think you love the house where you grew up but ask yourself honestly: is it really what you want for the rest of your life? Deep down inside don't you yearn to chase the stars, to break out and reach for new horizons, to experience the length and breadth of life?

I plan to sell both places and set you free. Don't be scared or angry. Your father will be fine. Think of yourself for a change and embrace the opportunity. Go ahead, Jenna Moon, spread your wings and fly. God bless.

There was silence as he finished reading and put the letter on the table. But then Charlie began to clap, a slow handclap. 'You know it's true, Jenna,' he said, turning to her. 'You need this chance to do something for yourself.'

Jenna felt as though a boxer's training bag had slammed

against her. Everything she knew and loved was being taken from her. Why would her mother be so cruel? Why? She looked wildly around her, at her siblings, at Albert Findlay.

'I don't understand,' she said desperately. 'I'm happy the way I live my life. I don't want to change.'

'No you're not,' said Olivia. 'You know you're not. Not really. Not deep down inside. Think about it. Go on, I dare you. Actually think about what you really want from your life, which, incidentally, isn't your life at all. It's dad's life and Mary-Ellen's, the deceiving bitch.' She smiled. 'I can't wait for her to receive the news that she'll get nothing.' She looked across at her mother. It was not as hard a thing to do as she had imagined. How bizarre that she was beginning to enjoy a meeting she had imagined would be traumatic. It was like listening to an author setting the scenes for a novel.

'I'd like to read your letter now, Olivia,' said Albert Findlay. The room fell silent again, leaving Jenna reeling from her own letter, and trying to concentrate on her sister's.

'My dear sweet Olivia

What a difficult child you were and how I loved you. My youngest child and, I admit, the one I favoured, the one I spoiled. I couldn't help it, despite the exasperation you caused us all. Leaving you was the hardest because of the way in which you had come to depend so much on me. I ached for the pain I would cause you.

From afar I saw how you craved something more from life than dull old Cornwall, how you longed to get away. I was proud of the way you were determined to do well at school. I watched you climbing the ladder and finally achieving your dream: a beautiful apartment in London, a good job, a fabulous lifestyle with a high-flying husband. Well done, my darling. Well done.

But are you truly happy, Olivia? I suspect not, surrounded though you might be by your achievements, your trophies. Are these the be all and end all of your life?

I'm going to tell you the unthinkable now and it will hurt. Believe me, I do it out of love, though love sometimes must be cruel to be kind.

Michael is having an affair with his colleague Heather, and he plans to leave you. He is no longer enamoured by your life together. Don't ask me how I know all this? Just know that I do.

I want you to do what you are best at; act with your head and not your heart. The apartment is yours and you must act quickly. Give Michael nothing. There is nothing he deserves. But do it now. Don't wait for him to leave you. Be strong, my sweet little Olivia, with the resolve that you are so good at. Like Jenna, you deserve so much more. God bless.

Olivia was paralysed by the shock slowly creeping through her. All the deepest fears and suspicion she had been harbouring had been released. The late nights, the secret phone calls, the cool way in which Michael treated their relationship. Why? What had she done to push Michael away to someone else? She was the perfect wife, the perfect host, the perfect partner. They both worked so hard. Yes, their relationship was not as it had been when they were first married. She was often asleep when he arrived home late, exhausted from a series of long days of negotiations with an author. He got up early in the mornings to train and then they both rushed their separate ways to work. At the weekends she went to the gym and went shopping with friends. She and Michael would meet in the evenings for dinner, usually with a group of his friends. Sometimes their work took them away. She had to admit that their lives had gradually taken different paths and they had grown apart. For the past few months they had been nothing more than companions in their apartment. They both went to bed with a good book, and neither had any desire to make love. Olivia had thought of planning a holiday for them, so that they could try and repair the damage that had been done, but somehow she never found the time. It hadn't occurred to her that Michael might not want to repair it. But now the unthinkable was about to happen. Michael was going to leave her. Her mother was absolutely right; she had to be one step ahead.

'Get away from the creep,' said Charlie. 'You know it makes sense.'

Olivia gave him a withering look, but she was shaken to the core.

'What Michael has done is unforgivable,' said Jenna quietly, as much to herself as to Olivia.

Olivia looked across at her mother. How could she know these things? But somehow she knew it was true.

Albert Findlay spoke again. 'The last letter is, of course, for Charlie.'

Charlie slunk down in his seat as if to try and escape the home truths that were about to be aired about him in front of everyone.

Dear darling Charlie
I remember how you never made any fuss when your father

94

and I spent so much time with Olivia because of her demanding behaviour. What a sweet little introvert you were, clutching your rabbit, muttering funny things.

I hadn't realised just how hard it was for you in those early days, unable to connect with your father, ignored and finally abandoned by your mother. When I learned you had been sent away to boarding school I feared for you but in fact you thrived. Yes, you were headstrong and rebellious, but it suited you. I guess you were happier away from home than in it. But it saddened me to see the relationship with your father deteriorate even further.

And then you really went off the rails. Teenage rebellion was one thing, but my heart sank when I saw you being sucked into the world of drugs. A world I was only too familiar with. I was terrified for you.

Charlie, now that you know what happened to me, I beg you to break free. Get out of that world, get out of all of it and start doing something positive with your life. My only consolation is that you are not a hardened drug user yourself. That much you've resisted, which proves you have the strength and willpower within you to do this.

You are facing a court appearance and the strongest possibility of being sent to prison. I urge you to think clearly about this and your future.

Whether you receive a custodial sentence or not, I want you to think about what your activities are doing to you and to those on the receiving end of it.

Change the path you're on, because it's a path of self-destruction. Turn your life around, become a mentor, a drug counsellor, a therapist. Become something that will enable you to give back what you are taking away.

I don't want to die knowing that you are on a path of self-destruction. Let your family back into your life before it's too late. You must all help each other now. Reconcile yourself with your father. Make up for lost time. Don't leave this world with things undone. Hear me, Charlie. Please hear what I'm telling you. Good luck and God bless.

Now it was Charlie's turn to get a reaction. It was Olivia who began that slow clapping that Charlie had given Jenna.

'Nice try, but I don't think our brother's got it in him.' Charlie knew she was goading him, but this time he might be prepared to challenge her. He looked across at the woman in the wheelchair and for the first time he saw his mother, someone who cared about him. But he couldn't make sense of it.

'You can do it Charlie, and we will help, won't we, Olivia?' said Jenna, turning to her sister.

Olivia shrugged. 'As long as he has the will to do it, I suppose. But if Charlie is convicted and given a prison sentence, we can't influence what might happen to change his mind.'

Albert Findlay interrupted. 'I think that if Charlie can get his lawyer to persuade the court that he is going to get out of the drug world and begin what his mother has suggested, there is a chance he will receive a fine and a suspended sentence, with penalties attached.'

'Then it's up to you, brother,' said Olivia.

Charlie was lost for words. It wasn't that easy.

'All of you have the chance to make the choices on offer a fixture in your lives,' Albert Findlay told them. 'You may decide not to but if you do decide to follow them then you will find that all the help and guidance you need will be there whenever you need it. I won't go into detail just now but as soon as you have committed yourselves, everything will be put in motion and all will become clear.'

Rowena raised her hand and Albert Findlay bent down to hear her speak.

The Moon children sat silently, wrapped in their own thoughts, their own reactions and their feelings about the contents of those letters.

Albert Findlay stood up again and cleared his throat.

'Your mother is going to leave now. She wishes each of you well in your lives and the choices you make, and thanks you for coming today. She is unreservedly sorry for all the sorrow and emotional turmoil her disappearance caused you, but hopes that you can now see that she had no choice if she was to protect you from things that could be much worse. If you have any further questions you will find a phone number on your copy of the letter.' He pushed some papers across the table towards them. 'I'll need a signature from each of you.'

When Albert Findlay had finished speaking, Anya released the brake on the wheelchair and wheeled Rowena Moon out of the room.

Jenna panicked as Anya and her mother disappeared from the room. It just couldn't be possible that, after this sudden return to their lives, she was simply going to vanish for a second time.

'I agree to everything,' she said to Albert Findlay, then leapt up from her seat and ran from the room.

At the front desk she asked whether anyone had

seen a nurse pushing a wheelchair leave the hotel but nobody had. She ran to ask the doorman but he hadn't seen them either.

She returned to the desk and asked if they knew a Rowena Moon?

Again the response was negative.

'You must do,' she cried, 'she booked a meeting room with you.'

The receptionist smiled apologetically. 'I'm sorry, but there's no one listed under that name.'

'Findlay then, Albert Findlay?' Jenna persevered. She realised she'd been stupid; her mother wouldn't have signed in as Rowena Moon.

Again the receptionist checked her screen. 'Yes,' she said, 'there was a booking in that name.'

'Oh what does it matter,' said Jenna, suddenly defeated. 'She's long gone now and he won't tell me where she is.' The receptionist looked at her sympathetically.

She wandered over to a sofa and slumped down on it.

'Excuse me,' said someone quietly in her ear; she looked up to see the concierge. 'I saw the woman you're looking for, the one in the wheelchair. She left by the river entrance.'

'Oh', Jenna responded, but still without hope. 'Do you know where she was going?'

'Not exactly,' he said, 'but I did hear a postcode mentioned; NW8, I think it was. Any help?'

'I'm not sure, but thanks anyway. You're very kind,' she added, appreciating that he was probably speaking out of turn.

Was it any help? She had a postcode but no address. She had to think. Hadn't Albert Findlay mentioned a hospice?

Surely there would be only one in NW8?

She went back to the desk to ask for a phonebook.

Charlie had watched his sister rush from the room.

'Should we go after her?' he said to Olivia, but it was said half-heartedly. He was completely fazed by the massive revelations during the meeting and confused about what to do next.

Olivia shook her head. 'No, we'll call her later. We should finish up here first.'

Charlie shrugged. 'Okay.'

'Do I take it that you both acquiesce to your mother's wishes?' Albert Findlay asked.

'I do,' said Olivia, her mind already racing with plans, despite the initial shock.

Charlie was hesitant. 'I'm not sure,' he said. 'I don't know if I can fulfil her wishes.'

Olivia smirked. 'I knew you didn't have it in you.'

Charlie ignored her and looked up at Albert Findlay. 'It's not because I don't want to, but if I go to prison, what then?'

The lawyer smiled kindly. 'Perhaps if you agree to her help, you might find things become clearer and easier.'

'I'll take your word for it,' Charlie responded,' but I can't see how she can influence anything.'

'Look, I'll sign,' said Olivia. 'I need to go.'

The lawyer pushed a document towards her. 'This document is regarding the terms and conditions of your inheritance.'

'Oh it's not about the money,' Olivia interrupted, feeling a little uncomfortable. She longed to get away from her brother and extract herself from the awkward situation.

Albert Findlay smiled kindly. 'That may be so,' he said. 'Nevertheless, the money is your inheritance, all three of you, and is part of the, ah, deal, if you like. Once you have it in trust you may apply for a release of funds, as long as it complies with the terms and conditions.'

Despite his reservations, Charlie picked up the document in front of him and read it through. It was difficult to ingest all the information though; his mind was all over the place, like a racehorse stung by a hornet.

Olivia leaned forward almost impatiently, took a pen from the desk and, with an exacting flourish, signed the document.

She looked over at Charlie. 'Well?' she said. 'Are you going to meet the challenge?'

He hesitated for a moment but then he took the pen she was holding out to him and signed.

'What about Jenna?' he asked.

'Don't worry about your sister,' said Albert Findlay, 'I'll make sure the document gets to her.'

'Well,' said Charlie. 'It's done then. Now for some life-changing experiences.' There was a hint of sarcasm in his voice. He looked across at his sister and caught the hard steely edge of anger in her eyes.

Oh dear, Michael's in for it, he thought with a sense of glee.

7

ROWENA

It was never going to be easy, but the depth of pain and sadness she experienced when confronted with her children had overwhelmed Rowena.

When Jenna, her dear clever Jenna Moon, had approached her with such compassion she thought she would die right there and then from the intensity of her feelings. Well why not? She had nothing left to live for. All that mattered in the world to her, and always had done, were her children and they would soon be lost to her for good. Life could play such cruel and bitter jokes and she had prayed constantly that they would never suffer the same misery and regrets that she had.

Now Rowena was prepared to make her peace with God, to receive the last rites from a Roman Catholic priest; she prayed she would die with some element of dignity, and with hope for her children.

Everything was in place. As soon as she left the meeting she was to be taken by her nurse to the hospice to live out her final days, surrounded by caring strangers.

In the ambulance taking her to the hospice, Rowena saw nothing of the road ahead. Her eyes were closed; she was remembering how her children had looked for the first time in twenty-two years. The photographs that had been taken secretly on her behalf as they were growing up had never truly revealed their personalities, and she was determined that the precious moments in that meeting, when she had seen them, heard them, and watched them with each other, would not be lost in whatever time she had left.

Rowena's mind often turned to the past. It was all she had left now. In all those years, she had never let a day go by without thinking about her children, receiving reports on their progress through school, college, work and life in general. The good thing about financial success was that she was able to employ someone to watch over her family and bring her detailed reports. A permanent private detective, if you like. Perhaps it was spying, but it was for good reasons and no harm had come to them.

She had left a family that was only just beginning: her sweet little Olivia, her strange little Charlie and her firstborn Jenna, mature beyond her years. It had broken her heart to leave them. The first couple of years of her new life in Australia had passed in a blur of chronic depression; she had hardly cared if she'd lived or died and it had been a struggle to get up every day. Her health had begun to deteriorate as she paid little attention to eating or taking care of herself.

Fortunately for Rowena a concerned but elderly neighbour had offered her an olive branch, sensing that there was something deep within that was causing the misery and self-destruction. Rose had persevered with Rowena, not giving up when the unhappy woman told her to go away. Eventually she had managed to get Rowena to speak about her pain. Rowena was careful never to use names or places, and Rose never asked for details. With Rose's help, Rowena had fought her way back from a mental breakdown. Rowena had been eternally grateful to that dear lady.

After a long while and with great perseverance, the pain had begun to subside enough for Rowena to rejoin the world. She found employment in a new profession, and gradually began to build a new life.

But as Rowena gained physical and mental strength, Rose's own health deteriorated. She had no relatives to care for her but Rowena made sure her old friend had all the support she needed. Just a few weeks later, Rose died peacefully in her sleep, in her own home, surrounded by the remnants of her life and with Rowena holding her hand.

Rowena was devastated when Rose died. She had lost the only true friend in her life, the only person she felt she could completely trust and depend upon. Now she was completely alone.

Not surprisingly, Rose had left everything, including her house, to Rowena. Rowena moved into that lovely old house and spent the next fifteen years as a virtual recluse.

To observe her children from a distance was sometimes torturous but she was grateful to have the power and the resources to be able to do it. Perhaps a complete break would have been better but Rowena couldn't do that.

So they had grown without her, without her love and nurturing, without need of her. Twenty-two years was such a huge gap that the short time she had been actively their mother probably counted now for little in their lives. Her 'spying' on her family had also been because of her anxiety about their safety, an anxiety that never left her. A substantial amount of money had been spent on ensuring they were cocooned and protected by an invisible army, and she never let this slip. It cost her a fortune and this was why she was so ruthlessly determined to excel in her business life. Their lives depended upon her success.

Rowena had always been good at business, making the Blue Moon Café a profitable success in Cornwall. She knew how to make things work, how to increase profits, how to look for the next expansion or improvement that would benefit the business. In her new life she began to look for opportunities and found many without even having to try. She worked doggedly, learning the tricks of the trade, what made the customers tick, familiarising herself with every aspect of the transportation business so that she knew how every cog fitted with the next to make it all turn smoothly. Nobody from any department could pull the wool over her eyes. She was ruthless and determined, but not for herself. It was all for that distant family who, although they didn't know it, needed her protection.

As the business grew she retreated further and further into the background; she was still in control but not actively or visibly in charge. A team of trustworthy and able employees kept the wheel turning.

She enjoyed life as far as she was able to in the world that was on offer. Pursuits like riding kept her physically and mentally in good shape; she enjoyed good food and wines; and she had a few trusted friends who respected and never questioned her slightly eccentric desire to live a reclusive life. There were no relationships, no partners. Despite her new identity, Rowena continued to consider herself married to Brendan.

She had not set foot in her home country since the day she left. It was simply not possible. Then something sinister had happened to undermine that resolution, and suddenly just a few weeks ago, she had found herself back in England, in a top-floor suite in a London hotel, looking out across the Thames on a misty morning, with the sun trying to push through the grey clouds in the east; and she thought about the inoperable tumour eating away at her life. She had imagined Olivia waking in her apartment and making tea, which she would probably take out on the balcony; she'd want to enjoy a few moments of peace before the morning's routine began. She knew Olivia ran every day around the dockland area where she lived, then walked to Canary Wharf to take the riverboat along to Blackfriars Pier. A nice way of travelling in London, Rowena had thought, much nicer than spending half of your life boarding metal tubes that sped you through the windy dusty maze of tunnels deep below the streets of London.

Rowena liked the way the fog softened the sharp edges of the office blocks and towers on the opposite bank, smudging out the myriad cranes that loomed over London like metal giraffes, and leaving the soft outline of the dome of St Paul's Cathedral as a gentle and welcome sight. It reminded her of Cornwall, of the mist weaving its way through the hills as it rose up from the sea; she recalled eerily the sound of voices, and the surf crashing onto the rocks and beaches, had carried through the damp blindness.

She often indulged in memories of Cornwall, of running the Blue Moon Café and handling her sometimes difficult, but creative, husband. Rowena also remembered with great sorrow the deterioration of that relationship. She thought of Brendan's black moods and depression and how he had turned to alcohol to help him; the utter wretchedness she had felt trying to juggle three young children, a business and a husband who was no longer a part of their lives. Thank goodness for the 'inheritance', which had been part of the reward for her role in the arrest and subsequent imprisonment of the drugs gang, and used to pay for the employment of an au pair, a girl who had saved her family once, then re-appeared years later, into her life again.

A flicker of a smile passed over her tired face as she recalled yet again the events on the night that her darling Jenna had arrived. Her thoughts tended to dart from one moment to another these days. It was as if she were a juggler, frantically trying to keep china plates up in the air so that none would have a chance to fall and smash into fragments that she could never piece together again.

It had been the best time of her life with her husband; newly married, expecting their first child, still exploring the mystery of each other. They found the house they were to buy, Beach Lane Cottage, halfway down the steep lane that led to the small beach, quite by chance.

Rowena had been in Looe for the summer, taking casual work as a waitress in the cafés, or working for a short spell as a deckchair attendant. She'd spotted Brendan right away. A group of young artists had booked a table for a rather rowdy lunch in a café that overlooked the beach. He had just seemed to stand out from the crowd, with his unruly dark hair, his almost ruggedly handsome face, his tanned and strong muscular body, which was quite a contrast to the trend for the thin and wasted seventies boy look. His flares were well fitting, as was his t-shirt, and it made him look so damned attractive. She had wandered casually over to their table, prepared for the taunts and jibes she was used to from the boys that came to Looe in search of a holiday fling. She remembered being oddly moved when Brendan had taken a pair of glasses out of his leather shoulder bag to look at the menu. It grounded him, made him seem different and rather safe. She could hardly take her eyes off him.

'I'd like a bit of the other,' sniggered one of the group when she'd asked him what he would like. Rowena had rolled her eyes and smiled with a long-suffering look.

'Fancy a good time tonight, darling?' said another.

She had been about to throw back a sharp retort when Brendan had looked up at his friends with a serious look on his face. 'Let's not sink to those sort of depths eh? We're not here on a holiday jaunt, we're here because we're serious artists, right?'

There was a pause followed by a couple of mumbled apologies. Brendan had then looked directly at Rowena for the first time. 'Please accept our regrets for this rocky beginning. If you would be so kind as to bring us a bottle of your best house wine and some tumblers, and a nice big plate of whitebait for us all to share, we shall promise to be on our best behaviour. In fact,' he'd added with a twinkle in his eye, 'we're much easier to handle after a glass or two.' Rowena remembered how her insides had simply melted. She'd burst back into the kitchen, ranting and raving about having found the one, and that was how it had all started.

That had been in June; by September she was completely smitten. They both were and so Rowena had decided to settle in Cornwall, hoping it would turn out to be the place where she could hide and live a new life.

They were married in a small church just outside Looe. Just four other people were present: Brendan's father, Patrick, who had come up from London, two artist friends of Brendan's, and Rowena's friend, Mary-Ellen.

And so she became Rowena Moon. Patrick Moon

had treated them all to lunch in a lovely restaurant on the cliff-tops, and afterwards she and Brendan had gone back to the little seaside flat they were renting, as husband and wife. Their silver rings had been engraved with their names. Rowena's dress was a white and purple medieval affair, with long pointed sleeves and a tight bodice. Instead of the usual flower-covered headband, she had made one with moons and stars. It was the ultimate hippy wedding; the ultimate happy day; and they were a blissfully happy couple.

A few days later they were out walking along the cliff path, a few miles outside of Looe. As they wandered down the lane towards the sea, they found Beach Lane Cottage, a four-bedroom, whitewashed house with an overgrown garden that was full of roses and herbs. There was a glasshouse that would be just right as a painting studio. It was perfect, if a little dilapidated, and it was for sale.

'I would love to say,' Brendan began sadly, 'that it's meant for us but we can't afford it.'

But Rowena had a little nest egg tucked away, left to her by her deceased parents, or so she said. She insisted they use it for the cottage and he had agreed, promising to pay her back when he became rich and famous.

Beach Lane Cottage really was just right. Not too big, not too small. There was a cooking range in the kitchen, a wood-burning stove in the living room, and plenty of coal in the bunker and wood in the shed. Brendan set about adapting the glasshouse for his studio. The light in it was fantastic. In the summer it was a glorious place to work, with the views south across the sea, the rolling and steep hills behind them, and the clear blue sky above. Blinds were added to keep the sun off.

The rocky beach was just a stroll away. It was an evening on that beach that she remembered now, just over a year after they'd moved in and nine months after she had discovered with joy and some trepidation that she was pregnant with their first child.

Jenna was a week late and she and Brendan had used their evening strolls on the beach to try to bring the baby on. That particular evening the tactic had worked but there had been no time to run back and call for an ambulance. It all happened too quickly for that. She and Brendan had delivered their precious baby themselves. She lay on Brendan's jacket, on the sand, with the tide coming in. Brendan had used his penknife to cut the cord, first dousing it in the whisky he always carried in his hipflask. Brendan had hurried with their baby girl, wrapped in his coat, back up to the house to call for an ambulance, while Rowena waited on the beach, with the sun going down. Thirty long minutes later she was reunited with her daughter in an ambulance and they were all on their way to the hospital.

Brendan had chosen the name Jenna. He'd said that Jenna Moon was a good Cornish name and a beautiful one too. How happy they'd been, in those early days, watching their firstborn blossom and grow. It broke her heart to think that it was because of the consequences of her life, that their joy had been broken apart.

8

JENNA

The taxi had dropped Jenna off near the hospice. The rain was relentless and Jenna had taken refuge inside a phone box, sheltering and shivering, from the cold and from sheer apprehension. Her body was tense with emotion and she ached as though she had flu.

Across the road stood a large double-fronted Victorian house with a sweeping driveway. Just a door separated her from her mother, but for Jenna it might as well have been the Berlin Wall. But despite her anxiety, Jenna knew that she had to see her mother again, to try to find some form of closure.

She believed that her mother's emotion upon seeing her children was genuine. There was no doubt about that. She accepted that her mother had done only what any mother who loved her family above all else would have done: sacrificed herself to protect her loved ones from harm.

Yet they hadn't escaped harm, had they? The mental damage that her disappearance had caused would always be with them. Jenna had grown up carrying around a sense of loss, a sense that there she was somehow incomplete. She was unable to form strong attachments to people, men in particular; she feared they might let her down or, worse, she would let them down. The fear was especially acute after the episode with Chris; that had convinced her that she wasn't worthy of love.

It was some comfort now to learn that all through their

lives their mother had been an invisible presence, watching them grow. At least she hadn't simply disappeared and never given a thought to them again.

Rowena's letters had presented a few home truths. If Jenna were absolutely honest with herself she would agree that sometimes she felt stifled living with her father, but to give up Beach Lane Cottage was unthinkable. She loved that place. It meant so much to her.

Jenna had suspected for a while that Olivia was unhappy, with Michael and with her life. It didn't take a genius to work that one out, even though she saw her sister only occasionally.

As for Charlie, well something had to give eventually. Surely he couldn't have sustained the life he was living for much longer. She was anxious for him and the impending trial and had decided to give him as much support as she could. She hoped he would take note of everything his mother had mentioned in her letter to him.

A crack of blue had appeared in the sky above the hospice. The rain had stopped and puddles were gleaming in the sudden burst of sunlight. Jenna watched a flock of starlings swoop and turn together over the rooftops. Their movements reminded her of the changing patterns in the kaleidoscope tube she'd played with as a child, pushed hard into her eye to block out the real world, the world where things could so easily be lost.

She stepped out of the phone box and quickly crossed the road.

Her mobile vibrated in her pocket. She had switched it to silent while in the meeting. It was her father calling.

Later dad, she said to herself. No time to answer now.

She switched it off completely. No more distractions.

Her heart was hammering wildly against her chest as she opened the gate, walked up to the front door and hovered outside uncertainly. Despite the warmth of the sun her whole body felt frozen and she simply couldn't find the courage to raise her hand and press the bell button. A sound behind made her turn and she saw another woman approaching.

'Have you pressed the bell?' the woman asked in a cheerful voice.

Jenna shook her head and the woman reached across her and pressed it before Jenna could say no, or stop her.

'There,' she said smiling at Jenna. 'Someone will be here in a jiff.'

She continued to smile at her and Jenna slowly began to relax.

'Do you have someone in the hospice?' the woman asked.

Jenna nodded. She was not yet relaxed enough to speak.

'Me too,' said the woman. 'My mum. She's got bone cancer. It's a lovely place,' she added, looking up at the building with fondness. 'Is this your first visit?'

'Yes,' Jenna managed to reply.

'Well everyone's so kind and, as I said, it's a lovely place.'

Then the front door opened and Jenna found herself swept inside. The other woman followed.

'Hello Theresa,' the woman said.

'Hello Isabel, you go right in to see your mum, she's expecting you.'

The woman who had answered the door turned to Jenna and held out her hand. 'Hello dear, I'm Theresa McCann, matron of this hospice. I don't recognise you,' she said. 'Who have you come to see?'

Jenna was looking around at the interior of the hospice; she took in the Victorian tiled entrance hall with the sun filtering through stained glass and casting patterns the colour of rubies and emeralds on the floor, and the large vase full of flowers on a hallstand. Isabel was right; it did seem like a lovely place.

'Mrs Rowena Moon?' said Jenna, taking Theresa's hand and shaking it.

'Oh yes, Mrs Moon. But may I ask who you are?'

Jenna was almost afraid to say the words but she took a deep breath. 'I'm her daughter Jenna. Jenna Moon.'

Theresa looked puzzled. 'A daughter? I didn't realise that Mrs Moon had any family. She's never mentioned it. I'm sorry,' she added as she noted the distress on Jenna's face. 'Look, why don't you come into my office and I'll speak to the nurse.'

Jenna followed her along the passage towards the back of the house into a small but bright room overlooking a garden. A window was open and she could hear the sound of a fountain outside; a soothing sound, she thought.

'I'm not surprised she hasn't mentioned us,' she said. 'By us I mean that there are three children. It's a long and complicated story but that doesn't matter now. We lost mum a long time ago and now I've found her I just can't let her go again.' Her voice wavered and Theresa put a hand gently on Jenna's arm.

'Why don't you wait here and I'll go and see what I can

do. I'll have some tea sent in for you.'

Jenna idly stirred her tea while she waited for Theresa to return. Just over an hour ago, the mother she hadn't seen for twenty years had been right in front of her; but the woman she had seen had borne no resemblance to the mother she remembered. How cruel life could be, to return her to them and then to be told that she would leave them once again, but this time she could never ever come back.

Theresa returned. She sat down and seemed to compose herself.

'She won't see me, will she?' Jenna said before Theresa could speak.

'I'm afraid not,' Theresa replied apologetically.

Jenna shook her head fervently. 'I know it's not what she really wants. Is she still trying to protect us?'

Theresa had no idea what Jenna was talking about but she smiled sympathetically. 'I'm sorry, my dear, you must be disappointed, but I'm afraid my responsibility is to my patients. But her nurse is coming to speak to you.'

'Anya!' said Jenna, who had forgotten about her. There was a knock at the door and there she was.

'Hello Jenna,' she said gently and her voice and other familiarities came flooding back to Jenna.

'I'll leave you two alone for a moment,' said Theresa and quietly left her office.

Jenna and Anya stared at each other for a moment, full of mixed emotions; then they both reached out at the same time to hug each other. Once Jenna started hugging Anya, she couldn't let her go. Anya rubbed her back soothingly and for a moment Jenna was a little girl again.

'Have you always known about mum?' she asked, 'I

mean about why she went away?'

Anya put Jenna at arm's length. 'Not officially, no, but I did overhear your parents talking to one another about her past catching up with her, and later on I put two and two together.'

'So dad's always known?' said Jenna incredulously.

'I suppose he must have.'

Jenna felt like screaming, not with anger but with the pure agony of pain and betrayal. Tears brimmed in her eyes and she buried her head in Anya's shoulder and sobbed. Anya held her until her crying subsided.

'Don't blame your father,' she said. 'It wasn't his fault that Rowena was mixed up in something so complicated. I don't think he wanted her to leave without you all, but it must have been an impossible situation.' Anya knew she was being more generous than Brendan deserved.

'Will mum see me?' Jenna sniffed.

Anya smiled. 'Yes, but you must give her time. She didn't expect any of you to want to see her. She's very weak and I'm afraid the emotion of the meeting has completely shattered her.'

Jenna nodded, trying to understand. Now she was so close, she wanted to see Rowena with all her heart.

'How did you find her?' Jenna asked.

Anya smiled. 'I didn't. Rowena found me. I went back to Norway to train as a nurse and ended up working with the terminally ill. I came back to London only a year ago to complete a training course at Guy's Hospital. I'd written a presentation for a conference about nursing patients thorough terminal illnesses and your mum found it on the Internet after she was diagnosed. She got in touch and I agreed to become her nurse.'

'That's such a coincidence it almost isn't, if you see what I mean,' said Jenna.

'Yes, you could look at it like that, couldn't you? I couldn't quite believe it when she first got in touch. I don't suppose I'd thought about her for so long and then she suddenly popped up in my life again, but for such a sad reason.'

Jenna nodded silently.

'Are you staying in London?' Anya asked.

'Yes, at Olivia's, but I was planning to go back to Cornwall tomorrow. If mum won't see me then there's no point in staying.' Her voice broke.

'I'll see what I can do. Why don't you stay for another couple of nights? Rowena just needs a little bit of time, but time is not something we have a lot of to spare.'

'Will she die soon?' Jenna asked, needing to know the answer, however hard it was.

'Soon, yes. I can't say when, it may be a matter of weeks, days maybe.'

'Oh God, Anya, I must have some kind of reconciliation with her before she goes,' Jenna cried in anguish.

Anya put her arms around her. 'It's okay, I'll make sure you do.' She wrote a number down on a scrap of paper. 'It's my mobile. You can speak to me, or text me, whenever you like and I promise I'll let you know what's happening.'

Jenna nodded. 'Yes I will. Even if I can't stay at Olivia's I'll find somewhere.'

'Oh Jenna, it's so lovely to see you after all these years. I missed all of you so much when I went back to Norway. I worried about you all too. Did you know that Olivia and I got in touch with each other again?'

'Yes,' said Jenna. 'I was a bit envious when she told me.'

'Time passed so quickly. What with my training, and then working long shifts, I didn't seem to have time for anything else. I'm sorry I didn't stay in touch more regularly.'

'Didn't you get married?' Jenna asked, suddenly intrigued to hear about the in-between life of an au pair she had known for such a short time. She had imagined her with a string of golden-haired children, and a strong Norwegian husband.

Anya shook her head. 'No, I'm an old spinster now,' she laughed. 'But maybe someone will come along. What about you, do you have any men in your life?'

'No', said Jenna, shaking her head vigorously. 'I find it hard to trust in relationships. But you, you're no spinster. Look at you, any man would snap you up.' It was true: Anya was older of course, but still a striking woman with the beautiful blue eyes Jenna had always been mesmerised by.

'Oh Jenna, you poor girl,' said Anya, getting a hint of the depth of damage that had been done by Rowena's disappearance: broken trust and an inability to form relationships.

'Don't be sorry for me. I don't care. I like my work, as you do, and I'm happy in Cornwall. It's part of my life, a fixed part of it, and I don't want it to change.'

'Your mother thinks otherwise. She thinks there's more to you than Cornwall.'

Jenna shrugged. 'Well, we'll see, but I have travelled you know. I went to Africa to teach at a school for three months. Surely she must know about that?'

'Maybe she does but perhaps she thinks you can do so much more. Anyway, you must tell me all about it sometime. But I have to get back to Rowena now.' She hugged Jenna and kissed her on the cheek. 'Take care, little one, and call me whenever you want to.'

'Anya,' Jenna said. 'I'm so glad you're here…again.'

Outside the hospice Jenna started walking and didn't stop. She wandered blindly, unaware of where she was until she stumbled and a passer-by came to her aid.

'You all right, love?' the man asked.

Jenna nodded. 'Fine thanks, just lost my footing on these paving stones,' she said. 'Oh, tell me about it,' he said. 'It's about time the council did something about it!'

Jenna smiled wanly. 'Yeah.'

She was relieved when he carried on and left her, alone again.

She sat down on a garden wall and groped in her bag for her phone. She switched it on, dialled a number and waited with shaking hands.

'Charlie?' she said as he answered, her voice wavering.

'Jenna! Where the hell are you?'

'I don't know,' she answered truthfully. 'Somewhere in north London, near Primrose Hill. Not my patch,' she added with an attempt at humour.

'Get a taxi back to the hotel. I'll meet you there.'

'There doesn't seem to be any around,' she said. 'I could find my way back on the bus or tube I suppose.'

Charlie was alarmed by the lost and distant tone of his sister's voice. He thought quickly.

'Okay, find the end of the road you're on, and give me the name and the postcode.'

'Why?' Jenna asked but she stood up anyway and headed towards the end of the road.

'Just do as I say,' he urged her.

'Okay, I'm doing it.' He heard her breathing as she hurried along. 'Right, I'm on Rydal Street in NW9.'

'Stay there and don't move. I'm coming to get you, but I might be a while.'

'No Charlie, you can't, it's too far. I'll find a station and get myself back to central London,' Jenna protested.

'You could be wandering around for hours. Stay right there and wait for me. Promise?'

'Taxi!' she suddenly heard him yell and then he was giving the driver the location. 'I'm on my way,' he said. 'Don't go anywhere.'

Feeling relieved that Charlie was coming Jenna relaxed. She looked up and down the tree-lined street. The kerb edge was dominated by an endless stream of parked cars and the plane trees that London seemed to have an epidemic of; they had originally been put in to soften the streets and offer leafy shade, but many were now trimmed to within an inch of their existence to keep the growth of their roots under control. They looked sad and bare and unable now to fulfil their function of providing shelter. The rain clouds had well and truly passed on and the lunchtime sun shone brightly in a clear blue sky, drying the raindrops and shrinking the puddles. If she looked up, above the skyline of London, she might have been anywhere, Cornwall even. If only she were.

'Oh mum,' she muttered. 'Oh God.'

9

ROWENA

Wracked with pain and confusion, Rowena glided in and out of a deep sleep, a sleep induced by Anya administering morphine, the only thing that truly released her from her agony.

She was unaware that her daughter had found the hospice and that Anya, under previous instructions, had turned her away.

Theresa McCann slipped into the room and spoke quietly to Anya. Rowena was oblivious to what they were saying.

'The poor lass was very upset. Shocked even. But I hadn't realised that Mrs Moon had a family.'

Anya nodded briskly. 'They've been estranged for many years. She went today to make her peace with them and settle some financial matters.'

'Well it's the patient's wishes that are our concern. She looks very peaceful,' she said, turning to the bed where Rowena lay, her face relaxed from the pain relief.

'Yes,' said Anya. 'I don't think it will be too long for her now. The pain is getting worse, the bouts longer.' She looked sadly at Rowena, who had stopped tossing and turning. The morphine was working deeply now and it dulled the edge of pain so she could rest. Poor woman, Anya thought. How brave she'd been this morning, confronted with her children. What a shock it had been to hear of her past and the terrible circumstances in which she'd had to live her life.

'She's been through so much,' said Anya. 'She's had a terrible life really, separated from her children; she was forced to leave the country. And now this.'

Theresa shook her head. 'I'm sorry to hear it,' she said, 'but the hospice is here for her now.'

'Yes,' Anya agreed, 'and she's very grateful for it, I know that.'

Some time later Rowena woke in pain from her drug-induced sleep and Anya put a little more morphine through her drip. With the pain dulled again, she lay for a while, revelling in the peace she felt. A shaft of sunshine fell through the gap in the curtains and warmed her face, which was cold and clammy.

'How are you feeling?' Anya asked, coming to the bedside.

Rowena managed to smile. 'Okay,' she whispered huskily. How could she be anything else after having seen her children for the first time in nearly a quarter of a century.

But speaking didn't come easily and it was an effort to join the words together. Anya hesitated for a moment before telling her about her daughter's visit. 'Jenna was here earlier. I sent her away, as you requested,' she added hastily.

Rowena nodded. 'Best.' Anya knew she was trying to tell her that no good would come of it. She didn't answer. It wasn't her choice.

'You?' Rowena challenged her. She was asking Anya her opinion.

'It's not up to me,' she began, 'but if you do want my comment, I don't think it would do any harm either. It took a lot of courage for Jenna to come here, and she genuinely wants to see you.'

'Selfish?' Rowena breathed, meaning her decision to turn them away.

'You have every right to feel the way you do.' Anya understood what she meant.

Out of them all it was Jenna she had thought might come after her. Olivia was still too angry and resentful. Charlie was indifferent; he hadn't yet worked out how he felt. Who could blame him, or any of them?

Rowena started to cough.

'That's enough now, you're getting anxious. Here, breathe into this.' Anya gently placed an oxygen mask over Rowena's face and she took some welcome breaths of it. She began to relax again and breathed a little more deeply.

'There now, lie back and rest and don't worry. If she really means to see you she'll be back and then we'll see how you're feeling.'

Rowena nodded. Exhausted, but calmer, she closed her eyes and slept.

10

CHARLIE AND JENNA

Charlie arrived in the taxi at Rydal Street, where Jenna was waiting for him, about forty-five minutes later. He asked the driver to take them to Albert Findlay's office so that Jenna could sign her document.

They sat for a while in silence. Charlie sensed that Jenna was finding it difficult to speak about what had happened, so he rambled on about signing the documents and about how odd it felt to find himself agreeing with the sentiments about his life with someone who was supposed to be his mother but who didn't mean a thing to him. 'What do you make of that?' he asked, but without expecting a reply. It was all just small talk. He chuckled, as he recalled how his sister Olivia had squirmed, how she couldn't wait to get away from her tainted brother. Even that didn't evoke a response, but he wasn't going to give up. She needed to talk.

'Come on, Jenna, tell me what happened?' He decided the direct approach was worth a try.

'She wouldn't see me,' she said simply. Then she turned to him fiercely. 'But I'm not giving up, Charlie, not now. She's not going to slip away from us a second time. I spoke to Anya and she's promised to make it happen.'

Charlie shook his head in disbelief. 'I can't believe it turned out to be Anya who has been looking after her.'

'Well I'm glad,' said Jenna. 'It's almost as though it was meant to be, these things coming full circle in our lives.'

Charlie shrugged. 'I don't know about that. Is it worth

it, Jenna, or should you let it go? We've got our closure now; we know what happened. Can't we just leave it at that and get on with our lives? I mean, look how upset it's making you.'

She shook her head. 'Oh no, I can't let it go now. I must see her.'

'Well okay, if that's what you need,' he said.

'Don't you want to see her too?' she asked, puzzled by his lack of interest. It was his mother too. Why didn't he feel as she did?

He smiled gently. 'Look, Jenna, I can hardly remember what it felt like to have a mother. I've managed without her for twenty years or so. Why would I need her now?'

'Because she needs us!' was her prompt reply. 'And because, no matter what, we're family.'

'Oh Jenna, you're too kind and generous. All I can think about is where was she when we needed her!'

'But we know why she left us now. She had no choice. She did it for us.'

Now it was Charlie's turn to clam up. He turned away from her. It was a revelation he just didn't need or want to face. It didn't matter anymore. 'If it's the truth,' he said at last with bitterness.

'Of course it's the truth. Albert Findlay's a man of the law!' She replied with surprise. What was wrong with her brother?

He shrugged. 'I suppose so.' He was thinking of some of the dodgy solicitors he'd come across in his time.

'Why did you sign the document then, if you don't feel anything?' Jenna asked. 'So you can get your hands on the money?'

'No!' he protested, swinging back to her. 'No, I happen to agree with her. My life is a shambles, but I also happen to feel that she owes us big time.'

She looked at him in wonder. 'I can't believe I'm hearing you say this: a) that you can really put the past behind you and live a life without drugs and b) that you can view the money as something she owes us.'

He grimaced. 'Well, a) I can try and b) I don't. They're the answers you're looking for. Maybe I'll have plenty of time to think about it all soon, behind bars.'

She softened a little when he mentioned the trial looming over him. 'And after that?'

'I'll leave London for a start. Maybe I'll go back to Cornwall. Who knows?

'Not to Newquay?' she said, looking worried.

'No, not to Newquay,' he agreed. 'Back to Looe, I guess, for a while, until I decide what to do.'

She looked fondly at him. 'Don't worry,' she said, taking his hand. 'I'll be there for you.'

He pulled away from her.

'What?' she said in surprise.

'There you go again. Offering to help me. It could be a long time in the future and you'll have a long wait. What about you helping yourself for a change, like mum said?'

Jenna laughed. 'Maybe it's not in my nature to be any different.' She suddenly felt an overwhelming sense of claustrophobia from the city buildings hemming them in as they got closer and closer to the centre of London. She felt an incredible urge to return to Africa, with its wide-open space and sky, just like in Cornwall. 'Let's take a boat ride,' Jenna said, putting her arm through Charlie's as they left Albert Findlay's offices. 'I need to feel some space around me.'

'Great idea,' Charlie agreed, not wanting to talk or think about the court case anymore. 'We're not far from the pier.'

'Can we walk there? I don't have the energy for the underground,' Jenna said anxiously. She couldn't bear the thought of being trapped in that claustrophobic environment.

'Of course we can walk.' Charlie felt oddly at ease talking so intimately with his older sister. He recalled the old days, when they'd been close, before he was packed off to boarding school.

'I called Olivia while I was waiting for you,' Jenna told him.

'And what did she have to say? She certainly didn't engage me in any conversation about her movements or anything else she might be planning. We signed. She left. Oh, I lie; she said, "Goodbye, darling brother, mind you do as mummy says'."

Jenna laughed at him. 'I asked how she was feeling, but she didn't give much away as usual. She just said she was fine. Poor Olivia! It was tough finding out about Michael in that way. No wonder she rushed off. She's got a lot to deal with. I'll go back to her apartment later,' Jenna said. 'I'll see if I can help. I'm supposed to be going back to Cornwall tomorrow but, after what Anya said, I think I'll stay in London.' Jenna wanted to stay, not only because of her mother, but also because of the revelations about Mary-Ellen's deceit! How was she going to explain that to her father?

'I'll come with you,' her brother announced.

'Oh,' said Jenna warily. 'I'm not sure how Olivia will feel about me taking you back there.'

'Well then, we won't give her any choice,' he said with a low laugh.

'Do you really mean it about not seeing mum, even though she's dying?' Jenna asked as they sat on the top deck of the riverboat with the wind on their faces. They passed under a low stone bridge and her voice sounded oddly hollow.

Charlie blew out through his teeth. 'I just don't know how I feel about it. Well, yes I do. I just can't really think of her as a mother. I had so little time and opportunity to learn.'

'Poor Charlie,' Jenna said. 'You always seemed outside of everything that was going on. You and your football.'

He managed a small laugh. 'My castaway friend.' Something in that sound gave her some hope that there was still some compassion beneath the hard exterior.

'So you don't feel anything for her at all?' she ventured.

'Oh God, Jenna, I don't know. Maybe I feel something but I'm not sure what.'

'There's a glimmer of hope then,' she said, turning quickly. She caught him off guard, the vulnerable look in his eyes providing an element of hope.

'Don't push it. I said maybe.'

Jenna watched London passing by: the bridges, the big old buildings and hotels, Big Ben, Westminster Bridge and the London Eye, but she hardly took it all in. There were more pressing things on her mind.

'I don't want our mother to die and me to have to live

the rest of my life regretting that I didn't make my peace with her,' she said at last, and looked at Charlie again. 'I can't waste the opportunity I've been given.'

She was surprised to see the bright look of emotion in his eyes; surprised and pleased. Perhaps she was getting somewhere after all.

11

OLIVIA

Olivia couldn't wait to escape the meeting room, the lawyer and, most of all, her brother. She was sure he was secretly laughing at her, that they all were. How could 'that woman' talk about something so personal to Olivia in front of everyone? It was deeply humiliating. She had guessed all along that her husband was having an affair, but she hardly wanted that fact aired in public! Yet she had offered Olivia a way out. Now she had proof without having to sneak around finding messages on his mobile when he was in the shower, or picking up the extension phone in the kitchen when he was talking quietly on the upper level. He'd been clever. They'd been clever, her Michael and this Heather. Olivia had never seen her husband leave his office with anyone other than his colleagues in a group, or by himself. But now she had the ammunition she needed to put an end to this once and for all.

She went back to the apartment and called him at work. She wanted to hear his voice, to trap something traitorous in the sound of it.

'Hello darling, how did it go?' he asked. His interest sounded genuine and caring. 'Are you okay?'

Olivia took a deep breath, forcing herself to react as calmly and normally as possible. 'Yes, I'm okay. It was so strange seeing her though. I'll tell you all about it later. What time are you home? Shall I make dinner?'

'Sorry darling, it's going to be another late one tonight.

I tried to get out of it to come home to you but I can't. Don't wait up.'

'Okay, see you later. Bye.' Olivia put the phone down and started to shake, with the tremors of an impending volcanic eruption rippling through her. She knew that she couldn't put the confrontation off for much longer, unless she was prepared to burst apart. She went to the kitchen and made coffee. Then she sat down with pen and paper and the contents of a file containing most of their legal documents. This side of things had to be sorted out first. She leafed through the papers and spent half an hour making notes; then she picked up the phone and dialled her solicitor's number.

CORNWALL

12

BRENDAN

Brendan Moon sat motionless in the kitchen of Beach Lane Cottage, as if the slightest movement could have catastrophic repercussions. An unopened letter from a law firm lay on the table. All the other clutter that usually covered every inch of the surface had been pushed back from the letter, like crowds away from a potential bombsite. In a way it was a bomb: a blast from the past. It was a letter he had always been expecting, a letter that he was certain would blow his world into a new set of pieces. How he wished that Jenna were at home to open it for him. His hands were shaking so much that he couldn't even pick it up.

He downed the glass of whisky he'd poured from a newly opened bottle. Why had Jenna gone to London to see her sister in such a hurry? It wasn't like her to rush off like that, to leave Cornwall for the city. She hated the city. And now this letter had arrived and he needed her. Perhaps he should wait for her to get back before he opened it. Would that make him a coward? Of course it would.

Brendan was torn between wanting to read the letter and wanting to hurl it into the wood burner and pretend it had never arrived. But he knew, with a gut instinct and certainty that whatever lay inside would not go away, that it could not be ignored.

He stared at it for a moment longer and then snatched it up, sliced the envelope open with a knife, shook out the contents and began to read.

The letter had been far worse than he could have imagined, and it had left Brendan reeling in despair. He'd poured himself another glass of whisky and then another and another and another until the bottle was two-thirds drained. The glass from which he'd been drinking he'd taken up and hurled at the clock, unable to stand any longer the sound of its incessant passing of time. The clock had broken with a satisfying crack and the glass had shattered as it hit the floor.

Now Brendan tried to stand up but he almost keeled over. He grabbed the table edge to steady himself and then staggered across to the sink to splash cold water on his face.

'Got to get to town,' he muttered. 'Got to see Mary-Ellen.' He fumbled in his pocket and pulled out his mobile. With shaking hands he managed to press the last number dialled. It was Jenna's. He'd tried to call her the night before but it had gone straight to voicemail. It did so again. 'Call me, sweetheart, as soon as you can. So much to tell you,' he said, but knew how drunk he must sound. 'Please!' he added emphatically.

God knows how but Brendan found himself behind the wheel of his car, reversing a little too quickly out of the drive and leaving deep tyre marks in the mud outside the gate. As he accelerated forward he scraped along the wall and swerved away. To hell with it, Brendan had thought. What did it matter? And in that erratic and dangerous mood, he'd driven off to the Blue Moon Café, bumping from bank to bank, veering and swerving out of control, with the whisky bottle rolling around on the passenger seat of the car,

Miraculously Brendan and the car arrived in one piece in Looe. He parked it haphazardly beside the river and tumbled out of the driver's seat into the road. Surprisingly, there were few people about to see this spectacle and, thankfully for everyone, he had not encountered anyone else on the country lane during his erratic drive from home.

The last remnants of whisky had been consumed during the drive; the bottle was now empty on the floor.

The Blue Moon Café overlooked the river, with East Looe on the opposite bank. As Brendan rolled up there were about half a dozen people eating lunch at tables by the window. One or two glanced at the man staggering around outside; it looked as though someone had been doing a spot of lunchtime drinking at the pub. Their smiles turned to dismay as Brendan pushed open the door and came in.

A young girl came over to greet her customer. She was new to the Blue Moon Café and hadn't yet met Brendan.

'Would you like a table for lunch, sir?' she asked pleasantly.

Brendan hiccupped and looked over his glasses at her. 'Do I know you?' he asked.

The girl looked at him. 'I don't think so, sir,' she replied.

'Where's the old bitch?' he asked loudly, drawing the attention of the diners. He liked that.

'Excuse me?' the girl said in surprise.

'I repeat,' said Brendan, 'where is the old bi…ah, there she is!'

Mary-Ellen, alerted by the raised voice, appeared from the kitchen.

'What's going on?' she said, wiping her hands on her apron. She was surprised to see Brendan standing there. 'Hello darling, what are you doing here?'

'Surprise, surprise!' he said. 'Or were you expecting someone else, a swarthy fisherman from Plymouth for instance?'

Mary-Ellen blanched. She looked at him in alarm and confusion, and then the smell of whisky hit her. She gathered herself enough to take charge of the situation.

'You don't look well, darling,' she said and took hold of Brendan's arm to steer him to the kitchen but he shook her off.

'What I have to say can be said right here, in front of all these good people.' Then he pointed a finger at her and shook his head.

'You, my girl, have been very naughty. Very naughty indeed,' he began and threw his arms wide, knocking a plate from the counter; it clattered to the floor, sending its contents flying.

'Whoops!' he said, wobbling as he tried to get his balance.

He certainly had the attention of the customers now.

'Brendan!' said Mary-Ellen angrily. 'For God's sake, what's got into you? You're making a spectacle of yourself.'

He laughed out loud at that remark and hiccupped again. 'Oh my dear, I've only just begun.'

Then he turned to the diners. 'Good people, let me ask you something. Do we like liars? Of course we don't but I must tell you, and I do so with a swelling pain in my heart, that this woman, the woman whom I loved and trusted, has been lying to me! I seem to attract this kind of woman.' He staggered towards a table and the customer seated there, an elderly man, leapt up in alarm to steady him.

'Thank you, kind sir, and now I shall continue. Where

was I?' He looked at Mary-Ellen. 'Ah yes, this woman has been cheating on me, after all that I've done for her. Cheating on me with a fisherman from Plymouth of all places!' He waited for their reaction but there was only an embarrassed silence.

'Lost for words, eh? But don't be shy. Tell me what you think. It's dishonest and it breaks the Lord's commandment to commit adultery, don't you agree?'

At this remark there was a disbelieving snigger from Mary-Ellen. 'What a hypocrite,' she added. 'I thought you didn't believe in 'the Lord'.'

Brendan swung back to her, furious that she should find anything remotely comical in his remark. 'It's unforgivable,' he said. 'Unforgivable I say!' he roared, and everyone seemed to visibly shrink. A couple near the door got up and left hastily, throwing cash onto the table.

Mary-Ellen was unnerved. She turned to her waitress, who was looking pale and anxious.

'Call the police please, Sarah, and tell them we have a drunk in the café. Tell them we'd like them to remove him because he is causing a disturbance and upsetting the customers.'

'Hah!' said Brendan. 'Wait until they hear what I have to say.'

'I don't suppose they'll be in the least bit interested,' she retorted. 'I on the other hand have broken goods, and fearful customers.'

Brendan stared at her, trying to focus as best he could. 'Do you deny this relationship?'

'What's the matter with you?' she hissed. 'Why are you doing this?'

136

'I repeat,' he said, 'do you deny this relationship?'

'I don't know what you're talking about,' was her reply.

Brendan laughed grimly. 'Mistress of Deceit and Lies,' he retorted, then steadied himself with some effort. 'Think I'll take a seat.'

He stepped backwards and sat down heavily into a chair that slid a foot back with the force, grating loudly on the slate floor.

'I've decided to get rid of you,' he said. 'I'm cutting you out of everything: the house, the café, my life. You and your fisherman won't see a penny.'

Mary-Ellen tried to remain composed, but he'd seen the look in her eye.

'Hah!' he said. 'Shocked you, haven't I, but I mean it. In fact, I want you to go right now. Get your bag and leave my café!'

'Don't be ridiculous, Brendan!' she began but was alarmed into silence when he yelled back at her.

'Now, I say. Go. Leave this café, my daughter's café. My wife's café!' he added for emphasis and remembering the contents of his letter.

'I'm having you ejected from the café when the police arrive. We'll talk later about this when you've sobered up,' she warned. 'Did you drive here?'

Brendan didn't reply. He suddenly felt tired and vulnerable. He wanted Jenna. He wanted Rowena. He was confused about everything. He wished he'd never read the damned letter, to never have discovered that Mary-Ellen, the only other woman he'd loved, was a liar and was plotting against him and his daughter.

'Oh for God's sake, pull yourself together,' Mary-Ellen

said in a tone of disgust.

He looked up at her. 'Why, Mary-Ellen? Why did you do it?'

'Alright,' she responded. 'Do you think you've been a good man to me or to your wife before me, a good father to your children? I don't think so. Most of the time you're drunk. The rest of the time you're painting, or not, depending on how hung over you are or how depressed you are. You expect everyone around you to be supportive and to pick up the pieces. What time have you ever given to those close to you? Where were you when Jenna, an eleven-year-old, was brimming with guilt about her mother's disappearance; where were you when Charlie cried himself to sleep every night? Drowning your own sorrows instead of helping your children deal with theirs. And it wasn't Rowena leaving that made them fall apart. It was you!'

Brendan slumped forward with his head in his hands. The people in the café had nearly all left.

At that point a police car pulled up outside and two officers got out and entered the café.

'Having a spot of trouble?' one of them asked.

'Yes,' Mary-Ellen said shortly. 'This man is drunk and he's been causing a disturbance. I'd like him removed.'

'He came in shouting and swearing and thoroughly upset our customers,' Sarah chipped in. 'And he drove here,' she added triumphantly.

'I see.' The policeman turned to Brendan. 'Is this true, sir?'

Brendan looked up at him dejectedly. 'I'm afraid it is,' he agreed. 'Are you going to arrest me?'

'Your name, sir.'

Brendan sighed. 'Brendan Moon, but you know full well who I am.' He recognised the young police officer as the grown-up son of one of his drinking pals. He'd known Steven Jago all his life. Why, Steven had gone to school with Brendan's own children. Now he was married with two young children of his own and was a community police officer.

'How's your family, Steven?' Brendan asked.

'They're well, thank you,' the policeman answered politely. 'I'm afraid I'm going to have to ask you to come with us to the police station to take a breathalyser test. We can't allow you to wander around the town in this state, and we certainly can't leave you in charge of your car.'

Brendan held out his arms with his wrists pushed together. 'Very well then, take me away,' he slurred and almost fell off the chair. 'Sorry, Steven, I had some rather disturbing news,' he added by way of an apology for his behaviour.

Mary-Ellen watched the two policemen help him up and lead him out of the café.

Just before they went through the door, Brendan turned back to Mary-Ellen.

'The deed is done,' he said. 'The deed is done.'

Then they were gone, leaving her ashen faced. The few remaining customers were looking at her. She turned quickly and disappeared into the kitchen.

Sarah went over to a table to clear some empty dishes. 'Well, that's got rid of that disturbance,' she said and smiled at her customers. 'Would you like dessert?'

And with that, the Blue Moon Café returned to its business.

13

MARY-ELLEN

At the end of the day Mary-Ellen sat alone in the kitchen of the Blue Moon Café. Sarah had gone and the closed sign was hanging up at the door. Now she had time to think about everything that Brendan had accused her of.

She was angry and alarmed. His allegations were true. But if he'd considered the reasons, instead of always thinking about himself, he might have understood a bit better. How did he know, she wondered? Had he followed her? Had someone seen her with her new lover, Daniel?

She'd long since tired of Brendan, of his drinking and his moods and his dark impenetrable bouts of depression. She was sick of hearing people say: 'Well he is an artist and creative people tend to be, by nature, a bit on the temperamental side.' A bit! It was more than a bit with Brendan. Years ago she had imagined that he might change for her but she soon discovered that it was in his nature to be the way he was; nothing was going to change that. He could be so damned morose, but she'd loved him in the beginning, despite it all.

Mary-Ellen cast her mind back to the years before Rowena disappeared. They were good times. Of course she had never stopped wondering what happened to her. Had she suspected her husband and best friend of having an affair? Had that been the reason? The guilt had hung heavily around Mary-Ellen and it was for that reason that she had put her heart and soul into helping the family. She was a young girl when she fell for Brendan. He was the most charismatic man she'd ever met, despite his moods. Brendan had needed something to distract him from the din and disorder in that house; well that's what she'd thought back then. Olivia, for instance; what a disruptive force she'd been. Lucky for them that the au pair had arrived when she did. After Rowena disappeared Mary-Ellen had assuaged her guilt by dedicating her life to the Moon family. She and Anya had helped the children through the worst period; and she continued to help after Anya had gone back to Norway. For some time she'd hoped and believed that Rowena would return, but the weeks and months went by and she didn't. She'd looked after those children like a mother, run the café and looked after Brendan. She had in fact taken over Rowena's role, rather than created a new one. God's sense of irony!

Jenna was the best thing about the Moon family. She had always been very fond of her. Much later they had run the Blue Moon Café and the gallery together: Mary-Ellen during the week and Jenna at the weekends and during the school holidays. Mary-Ellen had managed them alone when Jenna took her teaching job and then went off to Africa.

It had been Mary-Ellen's idea to take on the premises next door and turn them into an art gallery. Yet she had never been offered the chance of a partnership in the business, as a mark of appreciation. She'd never been sure who exactly owned the business, and sometimes she felt like such an outsider, as though Brendan and Jenna had put up a barrier to prevent her getting too close.

Yes, she was with Daniel. She was making the most of what was left of her life; she reckoned she'd wasted the best years on the Moon family, one way or another!

How dare he come here today, accusing her in front of her customers. And what exactly what had he meant by 'The deed is done'? What deed and how had it been done? More importantly, how did Brendan know about the new man in her life? As far as she was concerned, nobody – apart from her solicitor, whom she'd consulted about common law rights – knew anything about it. Even Daniel, her fisherman, didn't know about her true intentions: how she was planning to gain what was due to her.

Brendan had filled her with unease. How much did he know? What was he planning to do, or had already done? And why had Jenna gone to up London so suddenly? She felt sure that whatever it was, it had something to do with today's events.

It left her with a strong sense of foreboding, and an increasing sense of anger and injustice at Brendan's treatment of her.

14

BRENDAN

Brendan had been given a stern warning about his behaviour at the police station, but no charges were made. No one had actually seen him driving his car to Looe, and although he'd made a nuisance of himself in the Blue Moon Café, he was of course the owner. He thanked them profusely, and Constable Steven Jago had driven him home.

He was sleeping off the effects of the whisky when the phone began to ring. Groggy and disorientated, he slithered off the sofa and began to stumble around the living room looking for the phone.

He found it at last, on the floor under the table, banged his head as he came back up to answer it and swore loudly.

'Yes,' he said gruffly, when he finally managed to answer it, rubbing his temple with the other hand.

'Mr Brendan Moon?' an official voice asked.

'Who's asking?' he said, mindful of not giving himself away.

'The police.'

'Oh, the police. What have I done this time?' he asked sardonically.

'Are you the owner of the Blue Moon Café?'

'What? Well yes, of course I am.'

'I'm afraid I have to inform you that it's on fire. Can you come straight away, sir?'

Brendan took the phone from his ear and stared

horrified at it for a moment. A fire? Was he still drunk and dreaming all this?

'Did you say a fire?' he asked, putting the phone back to his ear.

'Yes I did, sir. Are you able to get to the café, or shall I ask the police to send a car?'

'If you know anything about today's events, I think it might be safer if you arrange for a car,' Brendan suggested, with a hint of irony.

'Very well then, sir, it will be with you shortly. Can you tell me if there was anyone in the flat on the top floor above the studio, or if anyone was likely to have been in the café?'

'What? Oh no, I'm sure not,' he answered but he felt confused and unclear about the conversation they were having. 'The café staff would have gone home earlier today,' he added, hoping he was right.

'Is the flat occupied at the moment?'

'No, it's empty,' he assured them, absolutely certain of that reply. 'Have you tried to contact the café staff?'

'Not yet, no. We were hoping to get their contact details from you.'

Mary-Ellen was probably in Plymouth with her fisherman anyway, Brendan thought sourly. 'Mary-Ellen Keane lives just along the lane from here, heading back towards Looe,' he said. 'But I don't know anything about the new girl.'

Brendan put the phone on the table and sat down heavily. He tried to think. A fire. How? There had never been so much as a candle spark in all the twenty-five years the café had been going. Why now? Unless...? He sighed. Maybe it was...? No, better to think it was just an accident, started by an electrical fault or something; nothing to do with the letter. Please God don't let it be that.

He stood up and looked at himself in the mirror over the fireplace. He looked dreadful. He climbed the stairs to the bedroom and raked a comb through his mop of unruly hair, washed his face and hands, and cleaned his teeth. Then he changed into a clean pair of trousers and a shirt, patted himself with some aftershave and went back downstairs to wait for the police car. There was nothing like bad news to sober you up.

Brendan decided not to call Jenna just yet, at least not until he'd seen the café and the extent of the damage for himself. He knew how upset she was going to be. Well that was an understatement; she was going to be devastated, knocked off her feet by the news.

He could see the glow in the sky as they approached the town. It looked bad. The fire was clearly still burning. If the fire brigade hadn't managed to put it out yet then Brendan was prepared for the worst.

The worst was worse than he had imagined. The fire had raged through the entire building. The shell of it was blackened by smoke and soot, but some flames were still shooting up into the sky at the back. The inside had been drowned from the water the firemen had used to put the fire out. There was nothing left.

Brendan had to choke back a sob. The Blue Moon Café, the last link with the past, was gone, reduced to blackened ruins.

Then he heard a small feline sound and looked down to see the kitchen cat, a little tabby called Libby, at his feet.

He picked her up and held her tightly to him. Libby

purred contentedly, snug against his warm jumper. 'At least you're safe,' he whispered. 'She wouldn't have forgiven me if you'd perished too.'

After Brendan had talked with the police and the fire brigade, he went and sat in the police car with Libby and called Jenna. It was such a difficult phone call to make and he was heartbroken when he heard the horror and dismay in her voice. Knowing nothing of the rest of the day's events, he couldn't begin to understand how broken and vulnerable she was.

'Darling, I'm so sorry,' was all he could manage and it sounded so inadequate.

'I'm coming home, dad,' she said and then the phone went dead.

Brendan leaned back in the seat. How could this have happened? Why had it happened? In a matter of hours his whole life seemed to be falling apart; first there was the letter, then the confrontation with Mary-Ellen, and now this.

A fire officer tapping on the window interrupted his thoughts. 'Excuse me, sir, have you got a moment?'

Brendan got out of the car to speak with him.

'It's too early to confirm for certain,' the fire officer said, 'but we've found evidence of kerosene on the ground floor. We could be looking at a case of arson.'

'Good God, you can't be serious!' said Brendan, staring at the fire officer in horror. His thoughts were racing. The situation was worse than ever.

'The police will want to ask you some questions of course. For instance, do you know of any reason why someone might do this?'

Brendan thought he was going to collapse. Any reason? Right now he could think of one word to sum it all up: revenge.

Instead he answered: 'I don't think I know of any reason.'

The fire officer nodded. 'We'll carry on with our investigations and make our conclusions known to the police, who will be in touch with you.'

'Thank you,' said Brendan.

When the fire officer had gone, Brendan breathed again. This was something he could never have contemplated happening. If it were true, then where would it end? Was the past – his wife's past, the woman who'd left so suddenly and had just as suddenly thrust herself back into his world – catching up with him?

LONDON

15

JENNA, OLIVIA AND CHARLIE

It was dark outside when the doorbell rang. Olivia had been writing and then talking on the phone to her solicitor for nearly two hours. She ended the conversation and got up to have a look at the video security camera. Her heart sank when she saw the faces of her brother and sister. Reluctantly she picked up the intercom receiver.

'I guess you'd better come on up,' she said and released the door lock.

The penthouse door was open when they got out of the lift, but Olivia wasn't waiting there for them. They wandered in and heard her in the kitchen, talking to someone on the phone.

'I'll just drop my bag in the bedroom,' Jenna said and left Charlie by himself.

He looked around him. Nice, he thought, and typically Olivia: modern clean cut, nothing messy. He chuckled when he remembered the chaos of their Cornish home and how much she'd hated it. He also remembered sneaking into her room to deliberately mess up her toys, and throw her clothes on the floor. Mean of him. But he'd had his reasons.

Olivia came through from the kitchen. 'Sorry,' she said, holding up the phone. 'Something came up.'

Charlie heard the coldness in her voice and knew how much she must hate him being there. 'How are you doing?'

he asked, to be polite.

She looked at him quizzically. 'Fine. Why are you asking?'

'Well, after what happened today I thought it might be polite to,' he replied equally sarcastically.

'Yes, well it's nothing I can't deal with and to be honest I'm not really bothered,' she lied. She hated the fact that he was here in her private space. Why on earth had Jenna brought him with her?

'Oh,' he said, not believing a word of it. 'Okay.'

They both turned to Jenna as she came back into the living room, glad of the distraction from their thoughts and feelings.

'Hi Olivia, sorry about running out on you this morning,' Jenna apologised.

Her sister shrugged. 'That's okay, you explained on the phone.'

She didn't mention anything about Rowena, but that was to be expected, Jenna thought. She was determined she was going to get them all talking about it sooner or later.

'Drink?' Olivia asked them both.

'Yes, a beer please, if you have it,' replied Charlie, and he wondered if Michael was a beer drinker. He couldn't quite picture him down at the pub with the boys and a pint in his hand.

'Just water for me,' said Jenna. She'd had a headache hanging around all day and it was now beginning to manifest itself with vengeance. It had probably been brought on by a combination of last night's alcohol and the day's stressful events.

'Still or sparkling?' Olivia asked, as if she were a waiter

in a restaurant.

'Oh tap's fine,' Jenna replied. Charlie rolled his eyes at her as Olivia disappeared into the kitchen. In return, she shook her head warningly at him.

'There,' said Olivia, returning with the drinks and placing them on the glass coffee table.

Silence fell as they drank and wondered what they were going to say, and how to say it.

Charlie spoke first. 'Jenna found out where mum is today. She's in a hospice in Primrose Hill. She spoke to Anya.'

'I know,' said Olivia and she looked across at Jenna. 'You didn't see her?'

Jenna shook her head. 'No. Apparently she was too tired after the meeting. I've told Charlie I'm going to try again. I won't give up until she sees me. Anya's going to try and arrange it.'

Olivia shook her head. 'I admire your perseverance, but you won't catch me trying to see her.'

'I've said the same,' said Charlie.

Jenna put her drink down and leaned towards them. 'Can't you forgive her? She's explained why she left. She did it for us!' Why couldn't they see or understand the sacrifice she had made for them. It didn't make sense that they were still being so unreasonably bitter.

'No,' said Olivia in a matter of a fact tone. 'She did it for her. Otherwise she would have taken us with her. They put whole families under Witness Protection Programmes.' Olivia had already checked the details on the Internet.

'Maybe it was more complicated than that. You were too young to know what was going on. I don't believe mum

151

would have left us because she wanted to. I could see it in her eyes today. I think it broke her heart,' Jenna protested.

'If you're talking about the affair with Mary-Ellen, I bet mum did know; and if she did, it would have been the perfect excuse to take us all away and leave dad.' Olivia sat back crossly in her chair with her arms crossed, reminding Jenna of her as a moody child. 'Why leave us with an alcoholic?'

'Olivia's right. She could have taken us all, and dad as well,' Charlie chipped in. 'Got him away from the problem. A new start and all that.'

'Do you think mum told him?' said Jenna, her head recalling those whispered moments beyond her bedroom wall, the fierce low voices discussing something important. 'About the drugs and the Witness Protection Programme?'

'Maybe,' said Charlie. 'It's possible he knew all along but kept it a secret.'

'Well if she did tell him and she wanted us all to go, he must have said no,' said Olivia. 'If that's the case then we are the victims and our parents the perpetrators of this whole damned story of our lives! I hate them both!'

'No,' said Jenna, 'it was the drug smugglers who were the perpetrators. If that hadn't happened to mum, then none of this would have either and our lives would have been very different.'

'Really?' said Olivia. 'Perhaps if she hadn't have been selfish enough to have a family in the first place, it would have been better for everyone! The way I see it is negative, whatever angle you come at it. Dad's drinking, Mary-Ellen, drugs, gangs, babies…'; but she broke off when she saw the stricken look on Jenna's face. 'Oh please!' she added.

'We need to get some answers, from both of them,'

said Charlie.

'I'm not having her bullied,' Jenna warned, 'if she does agree to see me or us.'

'Dad's a different story. I think it's time he was confronted and bullied,' stated Olivia plainly. 'And I'm the one to start that conversation.'

'Your phone's ringing, Jenna,' Charlie said, catching the sound of it coming from the bedroom.

She got up and went to answer it.

Olivia and Charlie fell silent.

Charlie twisted the beer bottle round and round in his hand until at last he spoke up with some uncovered feelings. 'I really resented you, Olivia, when I was a kid. Mum gave what little attention she had mostly to you. Dad gave what was left of his attention, when he wasn't drinking or off shagging Mary-Ellen, to Jenna. Apart from Anya, who tried her best, I was alone. Charlie the misfit, the boy who wanted to play football and a father who preferred paint, whisky and women to his son. Can you understand how I felt then?' He emphasised the 'I' because he felt that she was thinking only about herself as usual. 'And then I was packed off to boarding school,' he finished.

Olivia said nothing. Maybe he was right but she was dealing with her own feelings and too much time had passed to start caring about Charlie now.

He took her silence for the indifference that was intended. 'Well, why would you want to know all this now? It never hurt you, never will. You've got your own problems to sort out.'

Before Olivia could reply, Jenna appeared at the bedroom door, ashen-faced. 'What?' said Charlie.

She shook her head, unable to speak.

Olivia got up and went over to her, taking her by the arm, as she seemed to slump. 'Who called you?' Mum, she thought. She's died. She sat her sister down on the sofa and went to get her some water.

When she returned and Jenna had sipped at the water and appeared to have stopped shaking, they asked again what the phone call was about.

'It was Dad. There's been a fire…' her voice tailed off.

'Where?' Olivia and Charlie said in unison.

She sighed deeply before speaking. 'The Blue Moon. It's burned down. I have to go,' said Jenna, getting up from the sofa. 'Dad needs me and I've simply got to get home.' She was trembling from shock and disbelief. The Blue Moon, her beloved Blue Moon Café, gone. Her legs buckled and she sank back down on the sofa.

Olivia took hold of her hands. 'It's too late to go tonight, Jenna, there won't be any trains,' she said gently. 'Best to stay and leave first thing tomorrow.'

Jenna shook her head. 'I don't want to wait. I just want to go home,' she wailed.

'I'll drive you,' said Charlie suddenly. 'We'll have to go over to Vauxhall first to collect my car but that won't take long. We could be back in Cornwall by the early hours.'

Jenna looked up at him with such relief and gratefulness on her face that he felt a rush of brotherly tenderness towards her.

'Coming?' Charlie said casually, turning to Olivia.

She opened her mouth to say 'no' but something else seemed to take hold of her and it came out as 'yes'.

Charlie was as surprised as she was.

154

CORNWALL

16

BRENDAN

Brendan was stunned when Jenna called back to tell him that all three of his children were on their way down to Cornwall: Charlie coming back to a father he hadn't seen and a place he hadn't visited in years, and Olivia to a place she had always hated. He realised of course that they were coming because of Jenna and the fire, but it was a mystery why they were all together in the first place.

He hurried around the cottage, tidying up; he collected dirty towels from the bathroom and did the washing up; he even vacuumed the living room floor to clear up the mud he'd traipsed in earlier. The beds were made but they hadn't been used or aired for a long time. There was nothing he could do about it now. Tomorrow maybe.

He checked the fridge; there was some milk, but nothing much else. He'd go out first thing and get some bread and cereal and other provisions.

Finally he sat down with a mug of black coffee and laid his head back on the chair to think.

The letter lay on the arm of the chair. The letter. Somehow its arrival hadn't surprised him. He had been expecting such a letter for many years now. A lawyer's letter informing him that Rowena, who had remained the legal owner of the house and the business, was planning to sell up, to get rid of it all. He'd always meant to try and do something about shifting the ownership to himself and willing it on to Jenna, but he'd never got round to it and now it was too late. As to the rest of the contents of the letter, he was shocked beyond belief. To learn that Rowena was suffering from a terminal illness really saddened him. She had suffered so much and had made so many sacrifices; to end her life in this way was truly unfair. If only things had been different; so many things.

The revelation about Mary-Ellen was almost heart stopping. He couldn't imagine how Jenna was going to take the news. They had been friends since Jenna was a child and they had run the café and the gallery together.

It was not long ago, he thought, that he'd told Mary-Ellen that he was going to discuss with Jenna the legal possibilities of giving her part ownership of the business and the house. It was the least they could do after all she'd put into the business and their lives over the years. But somehow he had never got around to doing it. To discover now that she had been cheating on him was unthinkable, and he was glad he hadn't taken that step. Yet he knew it was probably his own fault; he was a difficult man to live with.

Jenna was his main concern now. But how was he ever going to break the news to her that not only had they lost the café but that also the house was going to be sold; and the mother who had vanished was alive and the owner of everything they had.

He awaited the arrival of his children with a mixture of eagerness and trepidation.

17

THE RETURN

For most of the journey they were silent. Olivia sat in the front with Charlie, and Jenna was curled up on the back seat. Olivia wasn't very communicative, mumbling a response when Charlie asked if she minded him putting the radio on, for instance. Yet there was a hint at the relenting of their animosity, a hint of a truce, albeit a slightly uncomfortable and unfamiliar one. It was as though some of the years were peeling back to reveal things they hadn't considered about each other. The catalyst, of course, was Jenna.

Olivia's phone rang twice on the journey; each time she took it out of her pocket, looked at it and promptly cut the caller off.

Charlie made a shrewd guess that it was Michael. He wondered what she had decided to do about the revelations about him in her mother's letter but now wasn't the time to ask. Why should she expect him to be interested? Perhaps they'd talk in Cornwall. So much had happened in this waning day that it was almost beyond belief.

He glanced at Olivia when her phone rang again. This time she switched it off. She didn't return his look or say anything; she just stared ahead into the darkness and the passing car lights, or turned her head to the passenger window, staring at her own reflection and the flash of lights. Once, he realised she'd fallen asleep for about fifteen minutes, with her head against the window.

When he glimpsed Jenna in the rear-view mirror, he saw that she had her eyes closed too but he didn't think she was asleep; and as soon as they drove over the border from Devon into Cornwall she opened them, as though instinct had told her she had crossed the border and was on home ground.

It was eleven-thirty when they crossed the Tamar Bridge and continued on to Liskeard. They were almost home.

Jenna was awake and watchful as they crossed the bridge between East and West Looe. She had her head pressed to the window, staring out at the darkness and the occasional passing light.

On the other side of the bridge she asked Charlie to stop. There was no mystery about why. Without being asked, he turned into the road that ran beside the river and drove along a few hundred yards. It was dark, without moonlight, and a little river mist was obscuring the landmarks, but the streetlights soon helped to pick out the Blue Moon Café, or what was left of it.

As they drew up, Charlie heard Jenna give a small strangled cry. He stopped the car and Jenna opened the door and got out. As she took a step forward she stumbled. Charlie, who was watching her, started to climb out to join her. Jenna stopped him with a short sharp shake of her head. It was something that she needed to do alone.

The area was cordoned off and deserted. Black-and-yellow tape marked out an area in front and either side of the burned-out building and there was a police car parked in front of it. On one side was a newsagent; on the other, the gallery. It looked as though the gallery had not been too badly affected, except perhaps for some smoke damage inside. She hoped it was the same for the newsagent, which had been run by the same family for longer than the café had. Thank goodness for old buildings and the thick walls between them.

But the Blue Moon Café was gone. The black holes where windows had been looked like the bruised eyes of someone who had been punched. Overwhelmed by this indescribably tragic sight, tears began to stream silently down Jenna's face. The Blue Moon Café had been the last link with the past and with their mother. It was a friend; no, it was more than that, it was a family member. And now it was gone, up in flames in a matter of moments.

What would happen now? What of her mother's revelation that it was going to be sold? Was there insurance and who was responsible? Her father had always insisted on dealing with those matters and she'd let him get on with it, even though she knew he was not always capable enough. Now, in hindsight, she wished she'd been more responsible herself.

Eventually she wiped her eyes, took some deep breaths and, with a heavy heart, got back into the car. 'I'm okay,' she said. 'Let's get going.'

They could see the lights of Beach Lane Cottage as they turned down the narrow lane that continued on towards the shore; and then the headlights swept across the lawn as Charlie swung into the shingle drive in front of the house.

Jenna jumped out almost the minute the car had stopped, but Olivia and Charlie remained in their seats, staring like mesmerised rabbits at the cottage in front of them, lit up by the headlights. The cottage they had once known so well now looked alien and forbidding to them, after all the years of absence and forgetting. A fleeting thought crossed Olivia's mind as she sat frozen with trepidation; she wished Anya were there.

'Come on, you two, it's freezing out here,' Jenna said, bending her head to look back into the car. Yet she understood their reluctance to move.

Her brother and sister opened their doors and slowly got out. Charlie went to the back of the car and opened the boot to get out the bags they'd brought. As he shut down the lid, he saw Brendan standing in the doorway to the cottage, illuminated by the bright headlights. It was a strange moment. He looked at the man standing there with that irritating swaggering stance, hand on hip, wearing the same old clothes by the looks of it: corduroy trousers, a fisherman's jumper; and the same unruly, but now heavily streaked with grey, mop of hair. His father.

Charlie said nothing and made no move toward him. He wasn't ready for hugs or any other such intimate gestures. He was here for Jenna and that was all. As far as Charlie was concerned, it was his father who had a mountain of ground to make up.

'Hello Charlie,' Brendan said but he knew already to keep his distance, to reveal nothing of the stomach churning anticipation and anxiety he was experiencing. If Charlie thought it was difficult, Brendan had no idea how he was going to cope with having all his children back under the same roof. He was sure the tension would bring him to breaking point, and he owed it to his children to deal with it without running away to the pub or tanking himself up with the contents of a whisky bottle. There was so much old ground to cover; there were old scores to settle and, he hoped, to banish one day. If only he could wave a magic wand and make everything bad from the past disappear.

Olivia hung back, not wanting to approach her father or have to pass by him to get into the cottage and risk being caught in an embrace. Now she was here the thought of actually having to stay in the cold, shabby place and relive her youth was both awful and terrifying. What had she been thinking when she agreed to come with them? Charlie handed his father a bag and she saw him pass through the living room with it to the back of the house. She grasped the opportunity to slip inside and ran straight up the stairs to her old room.

As she pushed open the bedroom door, Olivia couldn't help but gasp. Time here was at a standstill. Everything was as she had left it: the bed covered in the old patchwork quilt Rowena had made, the same green curtains, her books, a dolls house, everything was still there. She was taken aback. It had never occurred to her to ask Jenna what they had done with the cottage in the years since she and Charlie had left.

She heard someone coming up the stairs behind her and turned quickly; with relief she saw it was Jenna. She stared quizzically at her.

Jenna shrugged. 'We didn't need the rooms so we just left them.'

'I can't believe it,' said Olivia. 'It's the last thing I expected.'

'Go on then,' said Jenna.

With some hesitation, Olivia stepped over the threshold

and back inside her childhood.

If he were truthful, Charlie would admit that there was something quite exciting about coming back to the cottage. Like Jenna, he had always loved the location of their family home, with just a downhill run to the beach and the wildness of the Cornish coast. He was looking forward to exploring and discovering some of his old childhood haunts and secrets again; to wander along the sea's edge with Jenna; to skim a pebble into the waves; to throw a stick and kick a ball. But there were also a lot of demons lurking, that he'd need to watch out for.

'Tea?' Brendan called out as Jenna and Charlie put their bags in the hallway and followed him through the living room and into the kitchen.

'Okay,' said Charlie, but wished he'd been offered something stronger. He decided against asking though, in case it caused any controversy. For all he knew, his dad might be on the wagon, and he didn't want to upset Jenna.

'I'll do it, dad,' said Jenna, but Charlie caught hold of her jacket and gave her a warning look.

'Show me around, Jenna, I want to see what you've done to the old place.' The last thing he wanted was to be alone with Brendan. Not yet.

'Nothing to see,' she said. 'I'll go and help Olivia and see if she wants tea.' She wrinkled her nose at him, like she used to do, and left Charlie by himself. Get on with it she seemed to be telling him.

He looked around him. Jenna was right. Everything looked scarily the same, apart from a new chair in the corner, Mary-Ellen's maybe, some new paintings on the wall, and a couple of large pots and plates. Mary-Ellen's work, he guessed again. Then he realised that the walls had been painted a pale sand colour. He remembered they used to be white; and the one across the fireplace had been dark purple. Now the whole room was softer and warmer. A fire had been lit in the wood-burning stove that was tucked into the large chimney alcove at the far end of the room. He glanced at the old bread oven in the side of the chimney and idly wondered whether his football was still in there, or if it had been discovered and cleared away. He'd check later.

Charlie wandered over to a cupboard in the corner to look at the photos on top of it. He toyed with opening the cupboard door but wasn't sure if he should. To do so might reveal some of the answers about his father's drinking habits.

'Would you like a drink?' said Brendan, startling him.

Charlie turned quickly and shook his head. 'No thanks, tea's fine.' Did he detect a slight sign of amusement on his father's face? What was that about? God, what were they going to say to each other?

'I must say I was very surprised to hear you were all coming home, that in fact you were all together in the first place. Was it just the fire? Or has something else happened?'

Brendan's question took Charlie by surprise and he had to think quickly before he replied.

'I was just taking Jenna back to Olivia's. We sometimes meet up when Jenna comes up to London. I stayed for a drink, and then your call about the café came through. Neither of us wanted her to travel back alone in the state she was in.' He shrugged. 'A spur of the moment decision I suppose.'

'Ah,' said Brendan, not believing a word of it. Something else had happened, he was sure, and he wanted to get to the bottom of it. He was beginning to wonder if it was something to do with the letter he'd received from Rowena's lawyer. 'I hear you're up on a drugs trial,' he added bluntly.

Charlie felt uncomfortable. He didn't want to discuss it with his father. Why should he? When had Brendan ever bothered to contact him or ask him how his life was going? The last thing he wanted now was an argument and condemnation for the way he lived. As far as he was concerned, his father had absolutely no right to voice any opinion about his life.

'Yes, but I'd rather not talk about it,' he said dismissively.

Brendan stared at him for a moment and then nodded. 'Okay, Charlie,' he said and changed the subject. 'Do you know why Olivia asked Jenna up to London?' But he never got a reply because the girls came down from upstairs.

Olivia sat down on the old sofa and sipped at her tea with a pinched, uncomfortable expression.

'Bedroom okay?' said Brendan, amused by it.

Olivia nodded. 'It hasn't changed much.'

Brendan smiled. 'No it hasn't, has it; still full of all your old junk. Do feel free to take any of it if you want to. The same goes for you,' he added, turning to Charlie. Olivia and Charlie exchanged perfunctory glances.

Charlie was beginning to wish he hadn't been so hasty in offering to bring Jenna back. He had a feeling that he and his father were going to end up rowing again. But he wanted to keep the peace, for Jenna's sake. He hoped his father did too.

'Are you all right, darling?' Brendan asked Jenna. She went across to him and perched on the arm of his chair, her arm resting on his shoulder.

'Yes I'm fine,' she replied, but her tired and drawn face told him otherwise. 'We stopped on the way and had a look. I had to.'

'Oh poor you,' said Brendan. 'I just can't imagine how it started. We haven't had a fire or any incident there since the place opened twenty-five years ago.'

Olivia idly wondered if it wasn't the gang Rowena had mentioned, seeking their ultimate revenge.

'We'll get to the bottom of it with the police and the fire brigade, I'm sure,' said Jenna.

Brendan nodded and smiled grimly. 'Of course we will. Now why don't you all go and get a few hours rest before the morning. Then I thought we could all go into Looe.'

'Is there any hot water?' Olivia asked. 'I'd like a bath after that journey.'

Brendan chuckled. 'There might be a bit left in the tank, but the system doesn't fire up again until 6.30am. Can you wait until later?' He saw a hint of exasperation cross her face. Of course she'd be used to constant hot water in their apartment in London.

'Okay,' she said briefly. 'Well, I'm going to take your advice and rest up.' She left the room without another word and disappeared upstairs. They listened to her footsteps shuffling around above them.

'Me too,' said Charlie. 'You should try and sleep too, Jenna. You must be exhausted.'

She smiled at him. 'I will. Thanks for bringing me back, Charlie. I really appreciate it.'

'No problem,' he replied. Jenna gave him a hug and he briefly acknowledged his father before leaving the room.

Brendan and Jenna sat in silence for a moment, each with their thoughts about the last twenty-four hours and what it had thrown at them; each wondering how they were going to explain.

'Dad,' Jenna began at last. 'There's something I have to tell you. Something that will explain why we were all together today.'

'I have the oddest feeling that I know already,' he said.

She looked surprised. 'Really?'

'Yes. Is it something to do with your mother?'

Jenna stared at him open-mouthed and nodded. 'How do you know?'

Brendan reached into his pocket and pulled out the letter. He handed it to her and she began to read. When she'd finished, dumbfounded, she handed him her own letter. It was his turn to be surprised.

'We all saw her today,' she explained. 'This morning. That's why I went to London. A meeting was arranged with Olivia a few days ago. And then mum arrived in the wheelchair, and Albert Findlay, her lawyer, explained about the terminal brain tumour.' A sob caught in her throat.

'Oh you poor darlings. What a terrible double shock for you all and how brave of you all to agree to such a meeting.' He was shaken to the core by the news that they had actually seen Rowena that same day.

'It was hard, dad, and when I saw mum everything just came flooding back. Not only that but it's also the first time we've all been together for years. Olivia was hard as nails about it and Charlie pretended he didn't care, but I know he did. Her solicitor read us each a letter, with advice about our lives. You'd imagine our reaction to that would be "How dare she presume to give us advice!" but the strange thing is that we all seemed to agree with her. Olivia came off worse, I think. She learned some awful things about Michael. We must be kind to her and you've got to make an effort, however badly behaved she might be.' Jenna looked beseechingly at him, but then she remembered his own discovery about Mary-Ellen's infidelities. 'Oh dad, I'm forgetting about your problems and what you know now about Mary-Ellen.'

He smiled wanly. 'I'm afraid I've already started on that one. I got arrested earlier for turning up drunk at the café and confronting her. Had to sleep it off at the police station in Looe. Steven Jago was very kind to me.'

'Oh,' she said and chuckled a little. 'Well it was understandable I suppose. How did Mary-Ellen react?'

'Defensively. She denied everything but it was in front of customers and I didn't help my cause by being drunk.'

'Never mind, dad. As long as she's out of our lives. I can't believe she would do that to you after all you've given her.'

'Oh I don't know. She's had a lot to put up with me and my drinking and my moods. And what have I given her? I'd thought about a share in the business some time ago, but did nothing about it; I hadn't even considered that it wasn't my business to share out.'

Brendan felt even more useless and inadequate. The inheritance he'd imagined for Jenna simply didn't exist.

'Well, she won't get a penny of anything,' Jenna said with resolution.

Then they looked at one another, with the same

revelation dawning on each of them.

'Do you think she could have had anything to do with the fire?' Jenna said.

'I suppose anything is possible,' Brendan replied. 'But I have to say my first thought was that it was related to revenge by that gang.'

'Oh God, how awful. Do you really think it could be? I'd honestly rather it was Mary-Ellen than that. Can we find out from the police?'

Brendan shrugged. 'I don't know. I'll make some enquiries.'

'What shall we do if it is Mary-Ellen?'

'Let the police deal with it. I'm not going to interfere, Jenna. If it was Mary-Ellen then she'll have to deal with the consequences.'

Jenna yawned. 'I'm too weary to think anymore. I'm going to bed and you should too.' Then she remembered something. 'Did you know that Anya is mum's nurse?'

Brendan's mouth dropped open in astonishment and he shook his head. 'No idea,' he said. 'It wasn't mentioned in my letter. How on earth did they get together?'

Jenna told him everything Anya had told her.

'It's as though we've completed a circle,' said Brendan.

'Yes, that's what we all thought,' Jenna agreed. Then she stood up. 'I'm off to bed,' she said. 'Don't sit up all night worrying or drinking,' she warned.

'I won't,' Brendan promised. 'See you in the morning, my sweet.' After she'd gone, he got up and fussed about with the fireguard around the grate and poked the burning logs into a safe position. Then he glanced momentarily at the drinks cupboard. He was longing for a tot to help him sleep but he'd promised Jenna. And anyway, after the day's events, it really was a bad idea. He still felt rough. With a deep sigh he left the room, closed the door and started up the stairs.

But it was impossible to sleep. Now stone cold sober, he recalled, again, everything about the disappearance and what had happened afterwards. The pain he felt was as real now as it had been then, as was the guilt for the sham he had made of her disappearance, putting posters up all over the countryside and towns, deceiving his children. He'd known all along why she'd left. It was why he couldn't react normally with the children, why he drank to forget what he knew and the fact that he'd agreed to it in order to make his own life easier. How he'd paid for that terrible mistake. Two of his three children despised him and why shouldn't they. He knew that Olivia had always blamed him for Rowena's disappearance. When she discovered that he'd known all along what had happened to her, all hell would be let loose. He was scared about how they would all react. Even Jenna? Would she hate him too?

Olivia splashed cold water on her face from the sink in her room, brushed her teeth and changed quickly into her nightdress. Then she slipped into the hard cold bed and lay there shivering, just as she used to do when she was a child, still as a corpse until she stopped shaking, and her body heat had warmed up the bed a little.

The sidelight was on and she lay there, looking at the ceiling, holding her breath, waiting to relax. God, it was the strangest thing being back in her room. Slowly she began to remember things: the sound of the pipes clanking as water passed through them, and of the floorboards creaking on the stairs and hall. And she recalled the rhythm of the sea when her window was open, as it was now, despite the cold breeze; she'd pushed at it when she'd first walked in, hating the musty claustrophobic smell that came from releasing things closed up for so long.

When was the last time she'd been here? It must be at least eight years ago, if not more. It was weird to find everything almost as she'd left it. So far she'd been afraid to open any cupboards, to see her past life in old clothes hanging there, or old shoes that had trodden so many paths in and around the family home. Drawers holding goodness knows what; contents she'd long since forgotten about, or needed. Everywhere lay reminders, dredging up good and bad things from the past.

She heard Charlie in his room next door and wondered if the door adjoining their rooms was locked or unlocked. It was always unlocked when they were children. Below she could hear the muffled voices of Jenna and her father in the living room and then the sound of them climbing the stairs and going to their rooms. After a while there was a kind of silence within the house, apart from its own voice.

Olivia glanced at her mobile on the bedside table. It was still switched off. She had nothing to say to Michael and she didn't care that he might be worrying about where she was. It was more than likely that if there were any calls, they would only be messages with yet another excuse for being late. Well she didn't care. She wasn't there.

She reached up and turned the bedside light off, closed her eyes and, against all expectations, fell very quickly asleep.

Charlie was not so lucky. He lay awake until first light, with a million thoughts tearing around in his head. The trial, the past, his mother, his father, his sisters, home, London…and so on and so on.

The moment he heard seagulls heralding daybreak he was up, pulling on his jeans and a sweatshirt, creeping out of the bedroom, downstairs and into the kitchen. The key to the backdoor, he discovered, was still hanging in the same place.

It was a clear and bright but chilly dawn. He took a coat from the line of hooks in the porch between the kitchen and the back door and then he was out, into the clean fresh coastal air. By God, it smelled good and he breathed in deeply, filling his lungs and stifling the mugginess of London that hung around in there.

Laughing softly he ran down to the end of the garden, past Brendan's studio, and checked whether he could still vault the five-bar gate. He passed the test and hurried across the grass verge into the lane and then on down the steep path to the beach.

The first thing he did when he reached the shoreline was run the length of the curved west bay, where the tide was out, avoiding the rocks with their pools of trapped seawater hiding crabs and small fish. He ran until he found the old spot he was looking for, at the mouth of one of the caves; and he sat down to watch the sunrise.

He sat there for a long time, listening to the surf crashing and breaking, finding a rhythm again to match his heartbeat, tasting salt in the blustery wind. He felt like charging into the sea and he did, leaving his shoes behind and scampering across the rocks as sure-footed as a crab. Then, hopping across the sand, he wrestled out of his jeans and his sweatshirt and plunged into the waves.

The sharp cold ocean took his breath away but he swam on, through the frothing surf, farther and farther out, then he turned back, swimming until his feet touched the bottom and he could crawl back onto the sand. He lay on his back, exhausted, elated and very, very cold.

This was the memory he would take with him into prison when the time came, and Charlie was in no doubt that it would. There would be plenty of time to think about his future, too. He was glad he'd had the opportunity to come back home, to remind him that there had been good things about his childhood, despite the bad. He was older now, more able to look at aspects of his past life with a clearer mind. Yet he was still confused about the turbulent relationship he'd had with his father. Why had it been like that? Was it worth mending? Did either of them want to make the effort? Something was telling him yes, but he hadn't a clue how to begin.

'Hey,' said a voice. He opened his eyes to see Jenna standing over him. She was holding a towel and a bathrobe and she dropped them both on top of him. 'I saw you from my window.'

'I couldn't resist,' he said, rubbing his arms and legs, and then his hair, with the towel. He stood up and put the bathrobe on, pulling it around him and trying not to shiver. The warmth from the sun was not yet strong enough to banish the chill of that icy water.

'You're mad!' said Jenna. 'Even I don't swim in it when it's this cold. Come on, let's go back and get a hot drink inside you.'

They walked on the sand until the rocks got in the way and they had to clamber over them. Charlie pulled on his sweatshirt over the top of the bathrobe for extra warmth.

'I don't know why I ever left,' he said at last.

Jenna looked quickly at him. 'Yes you do. But those reasons don't have to stick forever.'

He inclined his head and said, as if he didn't quite believe it himself. 'True. And now I want to come back, I really do. To the simplicity of this,' he said sweeping his hand around the bay. 'I want to get back to the elements, nature, the better things in life; I want to go out with the fishermen for a day.'

She laughed. 'Wow, that's some revelation. But you'd soon start missing London and wishing you were back there, or slipping back into the old ways.' She was testing him, recalling his time in Newquay.

'No!' he said emphatically and stopped in his tracks, grasping her arm and pulling her to face him. 'No, I mean it. I think I could find myself here; perhaps not this very place, but somewhere along this coast, somewhere wild and deserted. Give myself a chance to find out what went wrong, and what went missing, besides mum, if that makes sense to you.'

'What would you do?'

'To earn a living, you mean? I don't know. Paint maybe.' He half laughed. 'Though it irks me to say it because of dad, and I never let him know it, I was actually quite good when I was at school. Had a couple exhibited locally.'

She looked at him incredulously. 'Why didn't you tell us? Have you still got any of the paintings you did?'

He shook his head. 'No. Not any that I could lay my hands on now. I sold them to pay the rent. And I didn't tell anyone because I didn't think anyone would be interested.' He remembered begging the art master, who'd been so keen to contact his father, not to.

'Oh Charlie. It's probably the one thing he would have been interested in. Well you'd better get started again; and if they're good enough, which I have no doubt they will be, you can put them in the gallery.'

But Charlie didn't hear. He was too wrapped up in his own thoughts and revelations. He linked his arm through hers. 'God, Jenna, I can't believe the change in me. But maybe it's too late, what with the trial and the possibility that I might have to do time.

She pulled him to her. 'Don't worry, Charlie, I'm sure it won't come to that. I'll come and support you at the trial if you like.'

'It's too much to ask, and it'll take up too much of your time. I told you yesterday, I have to deal with my problems myself, and you have to stop worrying about everyone else.'

'But would you like me to be there?' she persisted.

'Well of course I would, but it's not necessary.' He meant it. Jenna, he was beginning to realise, was really important to him.

'We'll see,' she said. 'I'm going to go back to London anyway, to be with mum.' Again it seemed he wasn't listening.

'Breakfast!' Charlie shouted, breaking into a run. 'I'm famished after that swim.' They raced each other back up the beach and halfway up the lane before dropping to a walk, their energy sapped, their breath coming in gasps.

'Beat you,' Jenna managed to say.

'I let you win,' he retorted, struggling to catch his own breath.

Brendan was up when they got back to the cottage, the two of them staggering through the door and collapsing into the chairs in the lean-to. He put his head through from the kitchen, peering over the top of the glasses resting on his nose, just as Charlie remembered him.

'Go and change out of those wet clothes,' he ordered. 'You'll catch a chill and make a mess.'

Charlie stood to attention and saluted, just as he used to do as a child, which caused Jenna to break into fits of the giggles.

'What's going on?' Brendan called from the kitchen, where he was making tea and whisking eggs.

'Nothing,' they said in unison, and then they put a hand up to their mouths to stifle the sound of their snorting laughter.

Jenna waved Charlie away upstairs, and went through to the living room to stoke the embers in the wood-burning stove. She managed to get a good blaze going. Then she went into the kitchen to stand by the range and warm her hands and body, which the wind had chilled.

'When shall we tell Charlie and Olivia about your letter, and that you know about our meeting with mum?' she asked her father. She wanted to add that she knew he'd known all along, but she hoped he would have the decency to finally own up about it. If he did, then she would be able to forgive the deception because now she understood why.

'Over breakfast,' he said quickly. 'I want it all out in the open as soon as possible. We all need to work together on this.' There was also the matter of the other revelation; it had kept him tossing and turning until morning, knowing how difficult it was going to be to admit it.

'I don't think Olivia is going to work together with anyone. In fact I think she'll be gone either today or tomorrow, back up to London to deal with her own problems,' Jenna warned. 'We mustn't stop her. It's an awful situation. I can't begin to imagine how she's feeling.'

'Or perhaps she'll stay for a while to clear her head. She needs to work out how to deal with Michael to ensure she comes off best.' He shook his head. 'I never did like him, or his pompous family. God, do you remember their wedding!'

'Oh dad, don't tell her that, it'll only make things worse.'

He grimaced. 'No, I won't. Poor girl. I've got some understanding of how it feels to be cheated on.'

Jenna put an arm around him. 'Of course you do, dad, and we'll deal with Mary-Ellen too.'

'What were you two talking about down there on the beach?'

She shrugged. 'Old times, mostly.' Jenna didn't feel it was her place to tell him about Charlie's plans. Hopefully he would do that himself in due course.

'Not about his trial then?'

'A little about it, yes. I'm going back to London with him to be there when it takes place. I need to go back to London anyway.'

'To see Rowena?'

She nodded. 'Yes. I want to give it a try anyway. She

177

may still refuse, but I don't want to give up. Do you mind very much?'

He shook his head emphatically. 'No, darling, I don't mind at all. I'm so touched that you would want to see her after all that's happened, but I know how much family means to you.'

'I know why she did it now, and that it wasn't her fault.'

Brendan sighed deeply, feeling the guilt rising up. 'What will become of all my little sea creatures?' he said. 'Charlie the crab always scuttling away; Olivia the seahorse, as beautiful as ever. And you, my little starfish, wait quietly, resting on the sand, the calm in the storm,' he added fondly, reaching out a hand to stroke her hair.

Jenna laughed. 'I remember that painting,' she said, 'and you won't believe where I've seen it recently.'

'In London? A gallery?'

'In London, yes, but not in a gallery. It's hanging in Olivia's apartment. She bid for it in an auction on eBay!'

It was Brendan's turn to laugh. 'Well I never. I knew she'd have to admit to my talent one day. But eBay of all places?'

'Olivia can show it off to her friends and they can envy her for its investment value, and perhaps for having a successful artist for a father. That's more like it I'm afraid,' said Jenna. Then she added quietly, 'I don't understand why you sold it.'

'Yes,' he chuckled, 'that's more like our Olivia. I agree, Jenna, I wish I hadn't sold it either, but I had my reasons at the time. Perhaps I should do another.'

'No you won't,' said Olivia, striding into the kitchen, and

they wondered how much she'd heard of the conversation. 'I'm not having my investment devalued with a copy.'

Brendan and Jenna exchanged glances. 'Morning, Olivia,' they said in unison.

'Good morning,' she replied. 'I came to check if the water is hot enough for a bath?' There was the usual touch of sarcasm in her voice.

'Yes, sweetheart, it should be fine,' Brendan replied, appraising his youngest daughter, and her rather haughty persona, with a hint of amusement.

Olivia turned on her heel and left them with a 'Thank you' thrown over her shoulder. A few moments later they heard Olivia stomping downstairs again. 'God, Charlie's in the bathroom,' she said crossly, as she burst back into the kitchen.

'He's warming himself up with a bath after a dip in the sea earlier,' Jenna explained.

'Must be bloody mad,' Olivia exclaimed and took the mug of tea Jenna held out to her.

Brendan almost made the mistake of piping up with 'Just like old times then' but he stopped himself, realising how futile those words would sound.

'How long are you planning to stay?' he said instead, but even that could be misconstrued.

She managed a wry smile. 'Sorry, I'm just not used to this kind of living. That's why I left, remember?'

Brendan nodded. 'Yes, we all remember, Olivia. So what made you come back?'

'Jenna I suppose,' she replied nonchalantly.

'That was good of you, but I must say I was surprised to hear the three of you were together in London.'

Olivia didn't reply. She glanced at Jenna, but her sister was looking out of the window.

Charlie was creaking the boards above them as he walked back to his bedroom; and Olivia, seeing her opportunity to escape, rushed upstairs to claim the bathroom.

A little later they were all together again at the kitchen table, eating breakfast. But apart from the sound of eating, and the purring of Libby, who had taken to her new quarters very well, there was silence.

The silence had to be broken and Charlie was the one to do it. 'Are we all going into Looe this morning?'

'Well Jenna and I have to go to visit the police and meet the insurance agent, but you and Olivia can do whatever you wish,' said Brendan, stirring his coffee and preparing to light up a cigarette. But he thought better of it when he saw the look Olivia gave him.

'I'll go,' she said. 'Might as well have a look round the old place now I'm here.'

'I was thinking the same,' said Charlie. 'I'll join you.' He was mildly amused to see that same old shadow of disdain cross her face. He still found a sense of fun and satisfaction in needling her.

'Before we go, there's something you all need to know,' Brendan announced. The tone of his voice drew their immediate attention.

'It's about your mother and a letter I received recently.' They all exchanged surprised glances. 'Yes, I got one too. Jenna told me all about your meeting in London yesterday and about the letters and what they contained. I think you were all very brave to agree to be there at all. It must have been such a shock.' He took a deep breath. 'I'm afraid I have some even more shocking news for you.'

They looked at him expectantly and he took a deep breath. 'What you really need to know is that I knew all along why she left us. I knew about the Witness Protection Programme.'

Olivia and Charlie stared at him in disbelief. Jenna breathed a sigh of relief. Brendan waited for their reaction with anxious trepidation.

'What?' Olivia said eventually. 'You let us think she abandoned us. You let us torment ourselves with a million reasons why and you knew why all along!' Her voice had risen. 'I can't believe you'd do that to us! To watch our family being destroyed when a few words could have explained everything!'

'Olivia!' said Jenna.

'No, don't try and stop me. I can't believe this. How could you be so selfish? How horrible...' her voice broke off and she put a hand to her mouth, overcome with emotion.

Brendan looked at her sadly. 'I'm so sorry but I had no choice. I was sworn to secrecy. I should never even have known about the Witness Protection Programme but in a heated moment before she left, Rowena told me everything. I couldn't tell you, not without endangering all of us. And you were too young to understand what it meant.'

Olivia was shaking her head. 'Unbelievable,' she said, 'and typical. You could have told us when you were older, but it was all about you, wasn't it? You and the...the thing you had going with Mary-Ellen. Oh I can imagine how convenient it was to let Rowena go out of your life and pretend it was the best decision for your children.'

There was so much venom in her voice that Brendan was visibly shaken.

'Stop it!' Jenna cried. 'Stop making assumptions.' But she thought again of the whispering and the arguing beyond her bedroom wall, sounds that still haunted her.

Olivia looked at her with ugly pity. 'You can think what you like and I shall do the same,' she said, turning away from them all, overwhelmed by her feelings.

'Okay, that's enough,' said Brendan. 'Olivia's right, I was being selfish. Your mother and I had fallen out of love, or so I thought, and yes, I could see a new life ahead of me with Mary-Ellen. But my main concern was the safety of all of you. I promise you that. We both thought it was better for you to remain in Cornwall, in the house and the environment you'd been brought up in, for the stability.'

There was a choking sound from Olivia, who didn't believe a word of it. 'Stability!' she exclaimed sarcastically. 'Was that what we had?'

Brendan put his head in his hands. He could hardly breathe for the pain from the knife that had been plunged into his heart by his daughter. But he knew he deserved it.

Olivia pushed it in a little deeper and twisted it. 'So you just let her go,' she said quietly and bitterly.

Then Charlie broke in, completely changing the subject. He hardly seemed to be aware of the fiery exchange going on around him. 'Has anyone considered the fact that Mary-Ellen might have had something to do with the fire?' Charlie didn't actually care one way or the other about Brendan's revelation. It was academic as far as he was concerned, although it was also beginning to make sense. What mattered was now.

They all turned to stare at him, even Olivia.

Well,' said Brendan, 'it had crossed my mind. She might be miffed that I've found her out, but arson? I can't quite believe she could be capable of that.'

Charlie shrugged. 'Just a thought,' he said.

'It's just not the sort of thing I could imagine her doing,' Brendan said doubtfully.

'Well, I wouldn't cross her off my list of suspects, that's all I'm saying,' said Charlie, and carried on eating the remains of his scrambled eggs.

Olivia suddenly got up and ran upstairs. They heard her stomping around and then she reappeared with her bag packed.

'Off already?' said Charlie goadingly.

She gave him a withering look. 'I take it no one else thinks the conversation we were having is important. I do and I can't stay here now because of it. I'll catch the train back to Exeter this morning.'

'Well, that was short and sweet. I don't know why you bothered to come at all,' said Charlie challengingly.

'Neither do I. I've got far more important things to do,' she said coldly. 'I can't imagine why I thought things would be different. Deception seems to be the "in" word.'

'Ha, well your husband would know all about that,' said Charlie.

'Oh shut up, Charlie!' Olivia reacted angrily. 'At least I'm going to do something about it.'

'Olivia, don't leave like this. We're all upset about everything that's happened but we should stick together and help each other,' Jenna broke in, trying to calm the situation.

Olivia shook her head. 'No, Jenna, it won't work. I'm too angry about it, and too remote from this place now to ever be able to try and understand.'

Jenna looked quickly at Brendan but he didn't react; he pretended to be reading the newspaper.

'Copping out, I'd call it,' Charlie muttered. 'When all's said and done, it's actually all about you, Olivia, even though you insist it's everybody else's fault. I'm pretty pissed off with the life I was dished up too, but I reckon most of it was subsequently my doing and my responsibility. You can't go on blaming the past and others forever.'

Olivia laughed out loud. 'Oh like you've done, you mean,' she said sarcastically. 'I think taking responsibility is exactly what I'm doing. In case you've forgotten, I've got to deal with a phoney husband and the possibility of losing my job!'

Brendan smacked his hand down on the table, and they all jumped. 'That's enough!' he ordered. 'If Olivia wants to go, then let her. She has got important matters to deal with. We all have. Now, I'd like to go into Looe to deal with mine and Jenna's.' He got up from the table and went to get his coat and car keys, hiding the tears of regret and despair that had suddenly overcome him.

Charlie grabbed his own jacket and car keys and he and Olivia followed them out. Jenna was waiting to lock the door behind them.

At the sight of the two cars, Olivia hovered uncertainly, wondering which was the better of two evils. She watched Jenna get in the front with Brendan. Charlie looked at her challengingly, and she quickly got into the back of her father's car. At least she wouldn't have to put up with yet another argument with her brother, and he was bound to provoke one.

18

LOOE

In the grey light of a sunless day, the burned-out ruins of the Blue Moon Café were a wretched sight. Standing in front of the once thriving business she had been part of for so many years, and the blackened shell that remained, Jenna was reduced to tears again. Her heart felt so empty, its dull and hollow thud beating against her chest. She felt the sickening rise of anxiety and panic and turned away, looking for someone or something to reach out to. Out of nowhere a friend appeared and took her arm to steady her. Others who were passing had also stopped to view the smouldering ruins. They offered comforting words, these friends and locals who thronged around her, each lamenting the tragedy of the Blue Moon Café, which had been such a central part of the community for so many years. It had been more than just a business; it had represented a part of her life that had been snatched away in a veil of mystery.

A car drew up, and the insurance agent got out; and so Jenna and her father had to turn their attention to practical matters. They were unable to go inside the remains of the building; it was still ringed by black-and-yellow police tape, as the fire brigade had declared it unsafe. Council workers were already boarding up the gaping holes where once there had been windows and a door.

While Jenna and Brendan talked to the insurance agent, Charlie went to stand by the railings overlooking the river, lost in thought and, to a certain degree, some nostalgia.

Olivia followed him to have a look at East Looe, on the far side of the bridge, the place where she had spent her teenage years in rebellion, sullen moods and plans of escape.

She remembered the day she almost ran away to London; the day she was humiliated by her father in front of her friends; the day she had all her hair cut off. Turning back to the Blue Moon Café, she unearthed some hazy memories of milkshakes and carrot cake with her mother and Anya.

Everyone kept telling her what a disagreeable child she'd been, but it was hard for her to remember how she had behaved at such a young age, how she'd really reacted when her mother vanished from her life. It was all so vague, but the pain and the empty space deep inside told her more than memories could.

At school she had been diligent and attentive, wanting to succeed. She remembered having friends in the classroom, and then the friends she'd hung around Looe with in her teens. Yet she couldn't remember feeling that anyone had really warmed to her. She couldn't remember her father warming to her either.

Had Michael warmed to her? She knew he admired her, but why was he planning to divorce her? She thought she had done everything he wanted. She'd been a good wife, a clever wife. She was a successful hostess who wined and dined people from the City when Michael needed to clinch a deal. He had told her he admired her for the way she looked, for her intelligent conversation when they were alone, and for her contemporary style and attitude. But could she ever say he'd 'warmed' to her? Now she suspected not. She was a cold fish; she was aloof. She found it difficult to be anything else; she could not easily let go of her feelings and open up. That wasn't her style at all. Olivia kept everything close to her chest because she was afraid of something: rejection or disappointment?

The question now was this: did she want to fight for Michael? Was he worth the effort? She had a lot of soul searching to do, which didn't come easily to her; and for that she needed to be alone. Olivia had briefly imagined that coming back to her roots in Cornwall might help, but she found her family too stifling; the house and the place were too crammed with memories she'd rather forget. It had been a stupid notion to expect it to be anything otherwise.

The past here gathered like the waterlogged clouds over the sea, heavy and oppressive; memories rushed in like waves breaking on the shore, some crashing down, some the frothy breakers swirling with discarded pieces of life, hiding a deep sadness and suppressed rage.

'You all right, Livvy?' she heard Charlie ask.

'Yes, I'm fine,' she replied but she didn't look at him. She was still angered by his careless remarks and was now irritated with his term of familiarity. She didn't want to make friends with him; and she didn't want his opinion.

'What about Michael?' he persisted, but with a kinder tone to his voice.

Olivia shook her head in exasperation. She didn't just turn and leave, though, which she could easily have done and put an end to the conversation 'What about him?' she responded eventually, then added reluctantly, 'Oh I don't know, that's why I need space to think. And I need time to make the best decision.'

Charlie turned around and crossed his arms, resting his

back on the railing, a look of amazement on his face. 'You're not thinking of trying to patch it up, are you?'

'What if I am?' she responded challengingly. Then she sighed. 'It seems such a waste to just let it all slip away.'

'I don't think I could forgive that easily,' was Charlie's response.

'I'd just like to know where I've gone wrong.' Now Olivia was voicing her feelings aloud.

'Why do you imagine it's your fault? He's the one having the affair!' Charlie reminded her.

'Yes, but why is he?' She thought of him then with another, doing the things they did together and a dark shadow passed over her. She shivered.

'Maybe he's just a randy old sod and can't help himself!' he retorted.

She shook her head, tutting at Charlie's coarseness. 'No, Michael's not like that. It's more to do with us, our lifestyle, how busy we are. Maybe I haven't been an attentive enough wife.'

'Oh please,' said Charlie, 'don't start turning the blame on yourself.'

Olivia was silent. He was right. Why should she take the blame for Michael's actions? It was all such a muddle in her mind; like fighting a tangled ball of wool to find the beginning and the end of it.

'Have you turned your phone back on yet?' Charlie asked.

'Not yet, no.'

'Well turn it on now and let's see how many messages he's left you,' her brother said.

She took it out of her bag and switched it on. More

then ten message alerts popped up on the screen.

Charlie whistled. 'Impressive and desperate.'

'I think I'd better call,' she said and wandered off to a bench a bit farther down for some privacy.

Left alone, with Olivia on the phone and Jenna and Brendan talking with the insurance agent, Charlie decided to walk down to the ferry to make the short crossing over the river to East Looe, and find somewhere for a coffee.

The ferry crossing took him back a bit. How often had he set foot on the boards of the old boat as it chugged back and forth across the river on its brief journey?

On board he searched the face of the ferryman but wasn't sure if he knew him or not. He remembered the ferry had been run by the father of one of his primary school friends, Tom, but he couldn't remember their surname. It would come to him.

As soon as he found himself in the heart of East Looe he was transported back even further. Some of the shops he remembered were still there but others had gone. He wondered if he might bump into old school friends and found himself searching for familiar faces. Yet he doubted anyone would remember him.

Down at the beach area he sat at one of the outdoor cafés and ordered a coffee. It was only May and so the beach was not crowded like it would be when the season began, filled with screaming children and flustered parents eating chips out of paper, buying ice-creams and hot-dogs from a van, and fighting off the gulls that were very adept at sneaking up on you and snatching away your lunch. He remembered Brendan giving strict instructions to his children about not leaving food lying around or throwing it to the gulls for fear of a mass invasion. It happened once and they didn't have to be told again! Those birds had sharp beaks.

When they were old enough, Brendan would drop them off at the beach to play in the sand and swim on their own while he went to visit a gallery where his paintings were being exhibited, or to catch up with his artist friends in the pub. Later he'd collect them for lunch, if he remembered, and cart them back home again.

Charlie began to wonder about what really happened between his parents. As Jenna kept pointing out, he and Olivia were much younger, and to make assumptions without ever having bothered to find out the real truth of it was perhaps not the right way to go about building bridges.

Charlie doubted that Olivia would ever build a bridge to take her back, but he was prepared to make some effort to return. He knew the bridge taking him might be a little rickety, and in danger of collapse at any time, but he had made up his mind to try.

For a long time Charlie had been unable to care about anyone, or to care a lot about himself for that matter. He had never had a long-term relationship. The thought of rejection was too terrifying and there was no way he was putting himself up for that. There were girls for one-night stands and he had friends in the loosest sense of the word, but they were mainly acquaintances or colleagues that he drank with after work. He always ducked out of invitations beyond anything but drinks or dinner at a restaurant. He was a careful, canny loner who made sure that few people knew much about him. If they wanted to know more, he invented stories. He was pretty good at that, of building up a series of false surroundings that acted like a barrier between the real person and the real world.

He wondered how much Olivia had revealed to Michael about her brother. Details such as being expelled from school or living a wild life in Newquay were not the problem. It was the inner sanctum of personal details, such as how vulnerable he had been as a child, how his father had neglected him, and the rows between them.

At home he and Olivia were often immersed in arguments, racing through the house while Jenna tried to break it up. Everyone had thought it would be better with Charlie away at school, but they hadn't considered the holidays, when Charlie would come home. In his absence, Olivia had ruled the roost and she above all resented the intrusion of his return. His old school friends in Looe had found new people to hang out with and so he was once again sullen, lonely Charlie. After a couple of summers of hell, Charlie began to persuade friends at Cunningham Manor to take him home with them, rather than having to return to Beach Lane Cottage. He missed Jenna, but that was all. The family of Matthew Grant, his closest friend, lived in London and that made a great contrast to Cornwall. Once or twice, Matt had joined him in Cornwall when his own family were absent from London, and Charlie was delighted to put Olivia's nose out of joint!

Charlie's thoughts returned to Michael, and he wondered how much he really did know and whether he had slipped the idea to the police that, in view of his past, it could have been Charlie who was supplying the drugs to the City boys. A group of them had been caught with the drug in one of their apartments one night, after a tip-off and a raid. He hadn't been there, of course; but shortly after that,

Charlie had been pulled up and taken in for questioning, and then, because he'd been stupid enough to carry the packs of cocaine loose, they'd found traces of it in his bag.

Things had gone downhill after that, and it was the end of that particular chapter in his life. And he was glad. It had needed something drastic to bring him to his senses.

The insurance agent noted all the details about the employees of the café and the caretakers, Brendan and Jenna. He asked questions about Mary-Ellen and Sarah, and whether there had been any falling out with any of the current or past employees. Brendan felt obliged to tell him about what had taken place the day before, and he gave basic details about their relationship.

The insurance agent informed them that the insurance company would need to pursue a thorough investigation, and he warned that there might be a delay in paying out the insurance for the Blue Moon Café because of the suspicion of arson. He said the police would be interviewing everyone as a matter of course. He regretted that it was all he could offer them at the moment.

'We understand,' said Brendan. 'It's not exactly a straightforward case.'

'Well, aspects of it are. I shall put the claim through for cleaning up the gallery and the flat, which you will then be able to get on with fairly soon. At least you can reopen that part of the business,' he assured them.

'Thank you,' said Brendan, 'we appreciate your understanding.'

The agent handed them some papers to read and sign and then he left.

'Do you think they suspect us of the arson?' said Jenna when he had gone.

Brendan shrugged. 'I expect they suspect everyone at the moment. I shall be in the clear, drunk and incapable either in the police station or at home. And so will you; you were in London at the time.'

'Yes, so that leaves our prime suspect, Mary-Ellen, but maybe also a revenge attack from the gang of the past?' It was a prospect that sent shivers running through her. Exactly what were these people capable of? Her mother had thought it bad enough to vanish in order to protect her family.

Brendan looked grim. 'I find myself hoping that it was Mary-Ellen. But we can speak to the police about that. You know if it was Mary-Ellen then I feel that I am to blame. Half of what she said was true. I have neglected her. I have been an awkward old bastard and a drunk. She deserved more for all that she's put into this family.'

Jenna rubbed his arm. 'Don't beat yourself up about it now, dad. We all make mistakes, and most of us don't learn by them either.'

'Not a good example of the human race or fatherhood really, am I?' he said ruefully.

Jenna thought suddenly of Rwanda. She imagined having a father who had committed genocide. 'Oh you're okay,' she said, 'and it's never too late to make up for it if you really want to.'

'Yes, but do they?' he said, inclining his head to where he had last seen Olivia and Charlie, but only Olivia was there now, sitting alone on the bench.

'Hi Olivia, where's Charlie?' they asked, wandering over to join her. She thumbed behind her. 'He got the ferry over. Gone for a trip down memory lane, I expect.'

'Shall we all do that?' said Brendan.

'I could do with a coffee,' said Olivia, and walked off ahead of them. Brendan looked at Jenna and rolled his eyes.

Jenna watched, with concern, her sister ambling ahead of them. She'd seen the look of desolation on her face and sensed the anxiety that lay under the cool exterior. Although Olivia had been dismissive of her family and the home she grew up in, she was still with them. She could have gone back at any time, but she hadn't. Did it mean that deep down there was still some connection? Olivia stood to lose everything that was vital to her: her husband, her lifestyle, her job. But was it the Michael with social status and family connections, or was it the intimate Michael, the husband, the person that she was afraid of losing? For some inexplicable reason, Jenna found herself recalling their wedding day.

They were married on 2nd July 2005. It was the perfect day for a perfect wedding: clear skies and beautiful sunshine; a marriage between Olivia Moon, daughter of the respected, if somewhat eccentric artist Brendan Moon, and Michael K. Hobbs, son of Kevin Hobbs, a successful financier and acclaimed City stockbroker.

Amanda Hobbs, mother of the groom, slipped easily into the position Rowena would have taken as mother of the bride; perhaps not in quite the same way, but she helped Olivia to choose the perfect dress, select the most stylish bouquet, and she insisted on Claridge's as the only possible place for her reception. Amanda found Olivia charming, respectable, and a fitting bride for her eldest son. Olivia was enamoured by the lifestyle Michael's parents lived; they had a beautiful spacious flat in Belgravia, a small estate in southern France and a yacht in Majorca. There was nothing kitsch or distasteful about Michael and his family. It reminded her of the days she'd spent with her grandfather in London, dreaming of such a day as this.

The wedding took place in London. Olivia had said that she certainly didn't want to get married in Cornwall, nor did she want to be married in Michael's family church in Somerset. Both of them had agreed that London was the best setting and the most convenient place for their guests nearly all of whom, lived in the capital.

Jenna and Brendan were invited for dinner to meet the Hobbs family a couple of days before the big day. Mary-Ellen had not been included on the wedding invitation. They had been put up in a smart London hotel, a place, Brendan said, that made his head scream because of its dreadful taste, the dull artwork on its walls and its soulless character.

'Dad, can you stop ranting for just a moment?' Jenna had pleaded as they walked to the Hobbs's house for supper. 'This is Olivia's dream, not yours, and I want you to behave!'

He had looked at her over the top of his glasses with a mischievous look. 'Yes, my sweet, I promise I shall be on my best behaviour. God, I hope they have some decent art on their walls. I wonder if they have anything of mine?'

'Don't say anything rude, and don't drink too much,' Jenna warned him.

'All right, you don't have to worry, although I shall hardly be able to help myself if Olivia starts with her airs and graces. God, I know she's my daughter but she's so full of her own piss and importance,' he declared.

Jenna had sighed and tucked her arm through his as they arrived at the residence of Amanda and Kevin Hobbs.

It was the first time they had been introduced to Olivia's in-laws. Jenna begged her father to be courteous, whatever may happen.

Olivia had greeted them politely but was somewhat cool towards her father. There was a dutiful peck on both cheeks and a smile of welcome, but no hugging, no natural show of warmth.

'How are you, my darling?' he gushed, and watched with amusement as she squirmed at the unwelcome familiarity.

'Happy, thanks dad,' she replied and gave him a warning look.

'Is Charlie joining us?' he asked nonchalantly, referring to dinner and the wedding day.

'No,' she replied curtly. 'He never replies to my messages.'

'Oh dear, I was so hoping to catch up with him,' her father replied, and only she and Jenna detected the sarcasm in his voice.

Kevin Hobbs was delighted to meet Brendan. 'My colleagues were positively drooling when I told them Brendan Moon was to be Michael's father-in-law. You seem to be a legend in your own lifetime as far as the art world is concerned. Do come and tell me what you think of my own modest collection.' And off they went, the men, with a last word hanging in the air. 'Drink?' said Kevin.

Jenna had watched them disappear with a sense of doom. Please, please let him have what my father regards as 'good art' in his collection, she had prayed inwardly, and please let him be polite if he hasn't, especially after a whisky or two.

'Now, Jenna, come along into the drawing room and tell me all about yourself. Olivia doesn't give away a thing and I'm dying to get to know you,' Amanda Hobbs had insisted. Jenna followed the petite and exquisitely dressed woman and glanced down at her own outfit, which was shabby in contrast. It was the best she could do: a black silk dress from a market stall in Fowey, now creased and crumpled from its journey inside a suitcase, and a shawl thrown across her shoulders.

Amanda, Jenna observed in amazement, picked up a small bell as they entered the drawing room and rang it. A moment later a uniformed maid appeared and curtsied.

'Yes ma'am.'

Amanda turned to Olivia. 'Drink, darling?'

Olivia spoke her order of a gin and tonic to the maid. Jenna hesitated, unsure of what to request, so Olivia ordered for her, a glass of champagne.

Amanda ordered the same as Olivia and then they settled back into the depths of the soft sofa.

'So, Jenna, tell me about yourself. What line of work are you in?' Amanda asked.

Jenna had glanced at Olivia, who had pretended not to notice. Clearly her sister had told Amanda nothing about her family, except that her father was an artist. No doubt she'd beefed that up to her advantage. Now she didn't know what to say.

'I run the family business,' she blurted out, startling even Olivia.

'Oh, Olivia didn't say there was a family business,'

Amanda replied in surprise. 'Are you an interior designer?'

'Oh no, nothing like that. It's a café in Looe. And there's an art gallery attached to it,' Jenna explained.

'I see,' said Amanda, with polite interest. 'I expect you're busy with the demand for your father's work.'

Jenna smiled inwardly. Her life had been dismissed in seconds, in favour of the more interesting work of her father. 'Yes, he's busy,' she agreed. 'Nowadays it tends to go straight to London and abroad. He does lots of commissions.'

'Jenna often has famous people in the café and the gallery because of dad,' Olivia intervened. 'Why only last month there was a certain member of the royal family with Cornish connections.'

Amanda was suitably impressed. 'Did you serve him tea?'

Jenna looked horrified. 'Oh no, he didn't come for that. He just wanted to have a look at some of dad's watercolours, being a painter himself of course. It's only a small café,' she tried to explain, inadequately of course, and couldn't help but notice a look of exasperation on her sister's face. Jenna was cross. What the hell did Olivia want from her? She certainly wasn't going to act a part just to please her.

'How lovely,' said Amanda, and then she looked around the room as if she was searching for some inspiration. 'Perhaps you know Sara Dubois-Smith, Olivia's bridesmaid, or the family?' Amanda asked.

Jenna shook her head. 'No, Olivia and I never shared our friends,' she explained, 'especially since she moved to London.'

'I expect you know some of the Cornish families,' Amanda pushed, almost as if she was trying to convince herself. 'Your father must get invited to lots of dinners and weekend shooting parties.'

Even Olivia had to suppress a giggle at that remark. It was the last thing their father would do. He hated blood sports, or having dinner with snooty families and the small talk that went with it.

Jenna couldn't bear the thought of the conversation continuing. She glared at her sister, mentally willing her to do something.

'Do you think dinner's ready yet?' Olivia asked Amanda, consenting to Jenna's mental will.

'I'll ring the bell, darling, and check with Mrs Coleby,' Amanda responded.

Thankfully it was.

Jenna would have to admit that the food at the Hobbs's house was exceptionally good. The chef had served a celeriac remoulade with a lamb's lettuce and pear salad, topped with Parmesan shavings and a delicious light dressing. The main course had been a perfectly cooked rare rump of lamb with an almond, apricot and rosemary stuffing, creamed minted peas and a potato velouté. For dessert they were indulged with a chocolate fondant served with a passion fruit and raspberry sorbet and a spoonful of Chantilly cream. Cheese and fruit were served with coffee, which the butler brought to the drawing room, to where they had all retired. Olivia, Jenna noted, hardly ate anything.

'Brandy, old chap?' Kevin offered Brendan, who agreed immediately.

Jenna gave him a warning look, but she guessed that he was only accepting to compensate himself for the evening and what he would refer to as tiresome conversation. It just wasn't his cup of tea. Brendan was used to drinking with the Cornish locals, who had tales to tell, pints to drink, women to bed, lives to save, songs to sing. He wouldn't want to hear about the latest points on the Hang Seng Index or about the Wall Street crash of 1989 and how Kevin's company had bailed out the firms that had bloody well caused the problem in the first place!

'God, Jenna, how did we keep a straight face when Amanda kept ringing that damned bell!' her father had said as they walked back to their hotel later that night.

'Oh, they seemed okay dad, for Olivia. But yes, I suppose it was quite amusing.'

'Bloody pretentious, I call it! Pompous bloody behaviour!' Brendan said loudly, turning the heads of a couple of passers by.

'Dad, stop shouting. You're drawing attention to us. I'd like to get back safely if you don't mind,' Jenna remonstrated with him. She realised that he was drunker than she'd imagined.

'Jenna,' said Brendan with a more serious sound to his voice, 'I don't think I've ever asked you this before but do you ever imagine bumping into your mother somewhere, like here in London, for instance? Do you ever find yourself searching a crowd for her?'

Jenna hated it when Brendan had had too much to drink and tried to indulge her in these conversations and 'what if' questions.

'I don't really think about her at all,' she replied, as she always did, but it wasn't the truth. 'And yes, you always mention it when you've been drinking.'

'I don't know what I'd do if I saw her,' he carried on regardless.

'It's so unlikely to happen I don't know why you bother to think about it,' she said briskly, trying to prevent her father from falling as he turned to look at her, swaying dangerously.

He smiled at her. 'Dear sweet Jenna, you're always the diplomat, always the pacifier, the sensible one. What would we all do without you?'

She shook her head, embarrassed and irritated by his words. Good old Jenna, always the one to keep the peace. No one knew the true feelings that hid beneath that façade.

In a child's mind, the disappearance of a parent, whether through death, divorce or simply vanishing into thin air, as hers had done, often threw up the feeling that they were somehow to blame. When her mother left, Jenna was of the age when her mind was able to coordinate such thoughts and she had tortured herself with them. She often chastised herself for not having been a better daughter, for the times she'd run off and exasperated her mother, for the times she'd stomped off in a mood, or argued about helping with something because she was itching to go to the beach. Of course as she got older she realised that none of those things was the reason her mother had left, but as a child the thoughts had tormented her and left her feeling depressed and guilty.

Whenever she could escape to the beach alone, she would pound the rocks with pebbles, or dig holes in the sand with her bare hands, sometimes hurting herself. It was, she now realised, all part of the process of understanding and coping.

She might sit for hours on a rock, staring out to sea, thinking. Anya would come looking for her, perhaps afraid that Jenna was going to wade into the sea and drown. She had been asked not to go to the beach on her own, but Jenna had no intention of taking her own life. Who would take care of Olivia and Charlie and her dad?

Jenna wasn't vulnerable; she was simply trying to find a quick way to expel her grief. So she spoke aloud all her negative thoughts when she was alone, sending them into the wind to be broken up and scattered far away, to the skies, into space and the universe, or submerged in the sea; anywhere but inside her mind. When she told Anya what she was doing, the au pair had climbed onto the rock beside her; she hugged Jenna and told her she was squeezing the last drops of unhappiness out of her.

As she got older and more able to cope with thinking about her mother again, not a day passed by without Jenna looking for her mother in crowded places, in restaurants, in theatres, or, more bizarrely, scanning TV credits for her name.

The Piskies could have taken her of course. Jenna had believed in those little Cornish folk, who played tricks on people and once in a while stole them away. Every night for a long time she'd prayed to the Piskies to release her mother. Once she dared herself to imagine that Rowena had been abducted by aliens and would one day be returned to earth with fantastic stories to tell the world.

Nobody in her family had spoken of the more awful possibility that Rowena might be dead; that she might have been murdered, or abducted, or attacked and left for dead, or even that she had taken her own life.

Now, of course, Jenna knew that it had been none of the things she had imagined.

She and her siblings had grieved separately rather than being brought together by their father, which is what should have happened. This was because of his inability to deal with the disappearance. He sought refuge in his work, which kept the family financially afloat. But, apart from Anya, there was no other emotional support.

The only grandparent still alive, Grandpa Patrick Moon, lived in London. Although he came to visit every summer, it was difficult for him to travel in his ailing state. Jenna had long ago realised that Olivia was his favourite grandchild. She had even stayed with him in London a few times and never stopped telling them how wonderful it was. Jenna didn't mind too much. She had never felt comfortable in London anyway and was happy not to be sent there to stay. She liked her grandfather but only when he came down to visit them. For Jenna, Cornwall was like a security blanket and, for a long time, to be sent away from it caused her extreme anxiety.

The bells were clanging out across London as the smart white Rolls-Royce Phantom had arrived outside St Peter's Church. Olivia had emerged like a graceful swan in her impossibly beautiful and elegant silver and white wedding gown. It complemented her slender figure perfectly, with its strapless neckline, and an exquisitely beaded bodice and a gently draping chiffon skirt. The back was fastened by a line of bobble buttons that led down to a swirling train with a hint of embroidery at the hem. Her blonde hair had been fastened up onto her head. She wore diamond earrings but nothing at her throat. A narrow diamond cuff adorned her wrist, a wedding gift from Michael. She'd carried a cascade of oriental lilies, white roses and tumbling Singapore orchids with green foliage.

Earlier that day, at around eleven fifteen, Brendan and Jenna had arrived at the house in a car that had been sent for them. As they were ushered into the drawing room, Kevin, who had apparently been driving everyone mad with his incessant questions and appearances in the wrong places, relaxed; at last he had some male company. Jenna had been relieved to discover before they left that her father hadn't emptied the contents of the mini-bar in their room. For once, it seemed, he had taken notice of her and made a supreme effort to behave. He did, however, down the glass of champagne handed to him by Kevin. Brendan raised an eyebrow in response to Jenna's fleeting look, but she'd allowed him that.

Then there had been a flurry of activity outside the drawing room, with a lot of twittering voices, Amanda's raised above them. The door opened and Olivia had glided in.

'Darling, you look absolutely stunning!' Kevin had greeted his soon to be daughter-in-law.

Jenna had glanced across at Brendan and had been surprised to see that his eyes had filled up. Then she saw his lips move. 'Rowena' they said. She looked quickly at Olivia, but thankfully she hadn't noticed.

Olivia had waited for her father to speak first.

Jenna had guessed that she wasn't going to make it easy for him. She never had done. Her anger with him had always got the better of her, and Jenna had wondered who had insisted that she engage her father in the first place, to give her away. She was certain it wouldn't have been Olivia's decision.

Finally he'd approached her with his arms outstretched and taken her hands in his.

'Olivia, sweet thing, how beautiful you look. I'm so proud of you. Be happy, darling.' Then he'd taken her hand and tucked it under his arm.

'Hear, hear!' said Kevin and he'd downed yet another glass of champagne.

Shortly afterwards the cars had arrived.

Later, Brendan relayed to Jenna the conversation in the car on the way to the church.

'Dad,' Olivia had said, and turned towards him with a really stern look on her face, 'please remember what I said about mentioning nothing about Rowena today in your speech. I mean it,' she'd warned as he went to speak. 'I know she was my mother, but I still don't want you to mention her. You'll get emotional, and I don't want that to spoil my wedding day. Understand?'

Brendan had promised, but it had saddened him. He'd turned his head to the window to think about what it would have been like if Rowena had been there. And there he was, sitting next to a daughter who looked exactly like his wife.

The rest of the day had gone beautifully. Later on, after the dancing and endless champagne, the newly wed Mr and Mrs Hobbs had retired to their suite in Claridge's.

Jenna and Brendan had gone back to their own hotel, and returned to Cornwall the next day. It was more than six months before Olivia contacted Jenna again.

Back in East Looe, they found Charlie down by the beach, at a table outside a café, his arms folded, his legs stretched out, looking out across the beach to the horizon.

'Any fishing boats out there?' Brendan asked casually, as they joined him.

'One or two,' Charlie replied. He was thinking about how he would like to go out with them one day, just to see what a fisherman's life was like compared with his own. He wanted to feel the power of the sea all around them, the haul of the fish; he wanted to witness the rough life these men lived, men who had never known anything different.

'Maybe we could pick up some fresh fish for supper tonight from the Quay,' he suggested. 'Unless you have other plans.'

'Sounds okay to me,' said Jenna. 'I had Cornish Turbot and crab in a restaurant Olivia took me to in London.'

'Really,' said Brendan. 'Fresh that day?'

Olivia tutted and shook her head. 'The restaurant is renowned for its fresh seafood. Of course it was a same-day catch. London's not that far from Cornwall.' Though it's a million miles in other ways, she thought. Thank goodness.

'They're pulling the wool over your eyes,' Charlie lobbed in to the conversation.

Olivia shook her head and turned her chair away from them. She knew they were teasing her.

Brendan smiled to himself. He remembered that gesture from way back.

'The insurance is in good hands,' Jenna said to change the subject. 'The investigation into possible arson may delay some of the insurance payment for the Blue Moon Café; in any case, that payment won't be coming to us.'

Olivia turned back to them. 'You don't own it then?'

Brendan and Jenna shook their heads. 'No, your mother does,' said Brendan.

'Well of course she does, she was going to sell it wasn't she, along with the house. Isn't that what it said in her letter to you, Jenna?'

Jenna nodded. 'Yes, that's what it said. Now I guess she'll get the insurance instead of the sale.'

'What's going to happen to you both, where will you go?' Olivia asked but she didn't sound overly concerned.

'I've no idea. An old codgers' home for me, I expect,' Brendan joked although the whole prospect of moving out of Beach Lane Cottage made him feel rather anxious.

'Oh don't be ridiculous,' said Jenna. 'They wouldn't want you anyway.'

He looked at her with mock seriousness. 'But you agree I'm an old codger.'

'Mum said she would see you were okay after the sale, so maybe there will be enough to find you somewhere else, a studio flat or something,' she reminded him.

He sighed. 'I think I'd rather stay where I am.'

'You must be joking!' said Olivia. 'The house is falling apart. If you stay in it much longer, it will probably disintegrate around you, like a biodegradable box.'

'It's not that bad,' he protested. 'Did you get that line from one of your writers?'

'Yes it is. And no I didn't. If you ask me, she's doing you a great favour and you should be grateful.'

'Well of course you would think that way, Olivia, because it has no meaning to you, as it has to

Jenna and me,' he answered back snappily, irritated by her arrogant attitude.

Jenna's mobile was ringing again, interrupting a conversation just as it had done the previous evening.

They all looked expectantly at her as she took it out of her bag and glanced at the number. It wasn't one she recognised but she answered it anyway.

'Hello,' she said.

'Good morning, is that Jenna Moon?'

'Yes it is.'

'This is Angela Smith from Findlay Associates. We're representing Rowena Moon?' Her efficient clipped voice seemed to Morse code itself over the airwaves.

'Yes?' said Jenna and her heart sank. Had something happened already?

'I'm calling in connection with the fire that recently took place at the premises owned by Mrs Moon.' The precise tones continued.

'Oh, yes of course. How can I help?' Jenna said quickly when she heard her mother's name mentioned. She got up from her chair and walked over to the railings overlooking the beach. Her family watched her.

'Mrs Moon would like to see you at the hospice if you are available.'

Jenna's face lit up. 'Yes of course. When?'

'Are you in London at the moment?' Clip, clip went the voice like a typewriter. A group of squabbling seagulls tore at a discarded sandwich on the beach below and Jenna turned and walked away from the cacophony.

'No, I'm in Cornwall. I came immediately after I heard about the fire. But I plan to come back to London. I could leave later today or tomorrow?'

'Please phone us as soon as you arrive back in London and we'll arrange a meeting.'

'Yes, I will, thank you. I'll come as soon as I can. Is my mother okay?'

'I'm afraid I don't have that information.' The person on the other end of the phone clearly didn't want to enter into a dialogue about the state of a client's health.

'Okay, well thank you for the call,' said Jenna. 'I'll be in touch the minute I get back to London.'

Jenna returned to her family, her face beaming with joy.

'Good news we presume?' said Charlie.

'Wonderful news! Mum has asked to see me. It's about the fire of course, but it's a meeting, nevertheless.'

Olivia raised her eyebrows. 'Lucky old you,' she said, her voice dripping with sarcasm.

Jenna ignored her. She was looking at her father to see what his reaction was.

'I'm so pleased for you, sweetheart, but we must talk about the situation with the insurance company and find out where the police are in their enquiries before you go.' Brendan was genuinely happy for his daughter. He even felt an odd sense of longing to go with her and see the woman who had once been his wife, the woman who had made such a sacrifice for her family. Of course she still was his wife legally, but in no other way than that. Whatever had passed between them, Brendan would never have wished such an ending for her life.

Jenna nodded. She was ecstatic and would have agreed to anything just to have the chance to see her mother again.

'When will you go?' said Charlie, who now felt torn between taking his sister back to London and lingering on in Cornwall, of losing himself in the beauty of its deserted beaches, its jagged cliffs and old smugglers' coves. Yet he knew that London had to be the choice because of his bail conditions, and he had no intention of remaining behind alone with his father. It was far too soon for that. The thought of it genuinely scared him. Perhaps he needed Jenna more than he was prepared to admit.

'Tomorrow, early. Would you drive me to Exeter?' she asked.

'I'll do better than that. I'll drive you all the way back. I need to sort some things out and I should check in for my bail conditions.' Charlie offered.

'Disappearing so soon, my brood,' said Brendan and looked expectantly at Olivia.

'I'll take a train from here this afternoon, and get the train back from Exeter,' she said.

'You can come back whenever you want to,' Brendan said but she didn't respond. Sadly he doubted he would see her again for a very long time.

'Will you all visit Rowena?' he asked.

Olivia and Charlie shook their heads and looked away. They were both determined on that matter.

Brendan said nothing. It was none of his business whether they wanted to or not. They were adults now and they could make up their own minds. But he hoped they might change their decision, for their own peace of mind in the future.

Jenna was also determined to make them change their

minds but she held her tongue.

'So, from a family reunion to a family farewell in less than twenty-four hours,' Brendan said with regret.

'Don't worry dad, I'll keep in touch and I'll be back as soon as I can,' Jenna assured him. 'I'll go and see the lawyers and find out what mum has arranged as far as the house is concerned.'

'I suppose I should start clearing the old place out,' he said resignedly.

Olivia snorted. 'Is she prepared to wait another lifetime to sell it?'

'I'm afraid you're right on that score,' Brendan responded. 'I shan't know where to begin.' It was going to be a daunting and painful task, clearing the remains of a lifetime that had been so thoroughly and methodically torn apart.

'Why don't you hire a skip?' Olivia suggested heavily.

'Oh no. I, we, couldn't do that, could we, Jenna?' He looked to his other daughter for support.

Jenna was looking darkly at Olivia. 'For someone who never took any interest in the place where she came from, you seem to have a lot to say about it.'

Olivia shrugged. 'It's just my opinion.'

Jenna turned to her father. 'Don't worry, dad, there'll be plenty of time to clear it out, but please don't start until I get back. I couldn't bear you to throw anything away without me being there. And anyway I want to hear what mum has to say first.'

Olivia looked exasperated. 'There must be stuff in those drawers and cupboards you haven't looked at for years. Why on earth would you want to keep it?'

'I don't expect you to understand, Olivia. So let's leave it at that, shall we? It's really not your problem.' Jenna was having one of her rare moments of rising anger and she could feel the heat of it under her skin.

Olivia made a face but resisted commenting any further. She seemed to sense she was taking Jenna to the edge.

'Come along then, let's buy this fish and take it home,' Brendan intervened. He felt a mixture of pride, amusement and irritation for his children, his three grown-up children, for their strength, their failings and their ability to slip back into their old sibling roles. Of course he realised, with the benefit of hindsight, how much he had missed out when they were growing up, how he had failed them as they struggled to come to terms with a bewildering event in their lives.

He wanted to talk to Charlie about his involvement in the drug world. It wasn't because he wanted to accuse and condemn, it was simply because he wanted to understand; or maybe it was to torture himself with his own failure. Above all, he wanted to help his son now but he didn't know how to approach him, how to offer that belated help.

Brendan wanted to put them above everything else in importance for the first time in many, many years; he wanted to try and shrink the gulf of resentment, mistrust and indifference that had fallen like impenetrable rubble between them.

LONDON

19

JENNA

Jenna and Charlie left early the following morning, and arrived on the outskirts of London around midday.

Charlie dropped Jenna off at an underground station, and they parted with promises to keep in touch and let each other know how they were getting on.

Jenna found her way to Waterloo Station where she tussled with the swarms of workers and tourists to get onto the Northern Line to Chalk Farm station. From there, she walked to Primrose Hill, where she had booked herself into a guesthouse. As soon as she had checked in, Jenna called the solicitor's office; an appointment was arranged for her to visit the hospice at three o'clock the following afternoon.

Then she called Anya.

'Jenna, I was expecting to hear from you. I'm sorry it was the lawyers who called, but they insisted on making the arrangements,' she explained.

'That's okay. Thank you for persuading mum to see me.'

'It didn't take much persuasion. She wants to see you very much, but at first she just thought it was better not to. She didn't want to hurt you again.'

'But it would be worse not to see her.'

'Of course it would. So, we'll see you tomorrow. Take care, Jenna.'

Jenna now had half a day and a night to get through before the purpose of her visit to London, and she decided

215

to go walking. She already knew where she would go; she walked south to Regent's Park and into London Zoo.

In Rwanda, when she was on her exchange visit from the school where she'd been teaching, she and her friends had been granted some free time to visit the Parc Nationale des Volcans, and to track a group of mountain gorillas. They were driven there by a local from the town where their school was, and they stayed overnight in a hostel in Musanze.

In the chilly damp of a mountain dawn they had walked from the hostel to the headquarters, where they were to be briefed and prepared for a trek that could take them as little as half an hour or as much as four hours, depending on where their assigned gorilla group had moved to during the night. The treks were not through easy terrain. With so much rain in the forests, the paths were steep, slippery and muddy, and dense with trees, undergrowth and thickets of bamboo. When it rained, it really rained in the Rwandan volcanoes. But no one was worrying too much about the weather. There was a buzz of excitement amongst them, each knowing that they were going to do something quite extraordinary and, to a certain extent, unique. They were going to get up close and personal with one of the seven gorilla groups that had been acclimated to tourists, but which were still large, unpredictable and potentially dangerous wild animals.

She vividly recalled the sound of the guides reassuring the gorillas using gorilla sounds; the steady penetrating eyes of the silverbacks, the crashing and smashing all around them as the gorillas swung through the forest trees, and the glorious sight of a mother and baby lying together in the nest, watching the visitors. Only an hour was allowed to observe their group but it was an hour of utter joy and entertainment and frantic camera snapping, as something new happened with each passing minute. At one point, an infant gorilla sat right in front of them and copied their movements. And she remembered the guide ordering them back into the undergrowth when the silverback decided to walk right past them, and how she could smell and sense his power and territorial authority. It was one of the most pleasurable hours she had ever spent in her life.

Now Jenna passed through the zoo gates and made her way to Gorilla Kingdom. London Zoo was home only to western lowland gorillas, not the mountain gorillas she had seen, but for Jenna they would be enough to remind her of an unforgettable experience.

She sat for an hour watching the gorillas, but because Chris had come to mind again, she was distracted by thoughts of what had followed when she arrived back from Rwanda.

Jenna had called Chris the minute she landed at Heathrow; it was early in the morning, and she was desperately excited at the thought of a reunion with him after so long apart. It had been difficult to make contact while she was away but they'd exchanged emails whenever she could get onto a computer; she had sent texts to him too, but sparingly because it wasn't easy to find somewhere with enough electricity to charge up her mobile.

He'd been so enthusiastic about her seizing the job opportunity and she'd loved him for that, even though they would miss each other like crazy.

He hadn't answered her call from Heathrow, but she guessed he was probably preparing for a lesson, so she sent him a text instead. When he hadn't replied to that one or the others she'd sent, by early evening, she began to feel slightly uneasy. He must have known when she was arriving back because she'd emailed him with all her flight details. Jenna had been half expecting to find him waiting at the airport for her, having made an excuse to the school.

Perhaps he was ill. She decided to pay him a surprise visit at home.

Chris was sharing a house with a few guys she'd met and liked so she felt no qualms about turning up on the doorstep. She'd banged at the door, but she could already see that Chris's car wasn't parked in the street and there wasn't the usual sound of music and activity coming from inside the house.

Jenna was beginning to feel something heavy and disagreeable in the pit of her stomach, a lump of anxiety. She drove to the pub Chris had taken her to on several occasions but she sat in the car, afraid of going inside. Several times she tried to reason with herself rationally. He was probably held up in meetings at the school, or so bogged down with paperwork that he hadn't had time to look at his mobile, let alone answer her messages. She knew the life of a teacher and the mountain of statistics and reports that had to be completed.

So Jenna had driven to the school. There was a parents' evening on. Ah, that was the reason, she'd thought, with a feeling of incredible relief. But when she got to the classroom there was another teacher, not Chris, speaking to the parents.

She'd gone in search of Chris's head of year. She'd greeted him with a smile. 'Hi Malcolm!' she said.

He'd looked at her oddly for a moment and then

appeared to recall who she was. 'Hello Jenna,' he'd said, with surprise in his voice.

'I was looking for Chris?' she'd ventured.

He looked even more puzzled. 'Chris? But you must know. Chris doesn't work here anymore. He was offered a job in London and he left about two weeks ago. I thought you'd know, but of course you've been away in Africa…' His voice had trailed off as he saw the stricken look on her face. 'I'm sorry,' he'd said inadequately and muttered an excuse about needing to hurry off. Jenna had nodded and stumbled back along the corridor. She'd sat in her car, shaking uncontrollably, and two hours had passed before she'd felt stable enough to drive home.

She was over the break-up now, of course, although it had taken a long time. Chris had eventually written her a letter. A letter! After a three-year relationship! It was as bad as being dumped by text. Her pupils had told her about that latest phenomenon. He'd rambled on about how they had grown apart and how they both had different paths to take. She'd found his explanation difficult and inadequate, and she was hurt and angry by his ability to let go so easily. She'd sent him a simple reply, scrawled on the back of his letter: 'Have a good life, Chris.' And that was it, her final lesson in the ways of men and women and relationships.

I am destined to be abandoned, she'd told herself, and to have a secular existence. She had been surprised by how long the hurt and pain had lasted.

A year later, she'd given up her teaching career to run the café full time with Mary-Ellen, as well as the gallery she and her father had bought next door.

The zoo closed at six and Jenna wandered back to Primrose Hill to find a restaurant where she could have an early supper.

On the way back her mobile buzzed and a text from Brendan appeared. *Hope you're okay my sweet, and all the Moon kids arrived safely at their London destinations. The house seems oddly empty today, even though it's not had an entire complement of Moons in it for such a long time. Let me know how you get on tomorrow. My love, dad x.*

Jenna sent a text back: *I'm fine dad, thanks. Will wait to hear news from Olivia and Charlie and let you know. Will send my news tomorrow. Went to the zoo today. Saw gorillas. Eat well. Love you. J x.* The 'eat well' was a code for 'don't drink', which she knew he would understand. She worried about him when he was on his own; and even more so now, after all the depressing events that had taken place.

She hardly slept a wink all night again, tossing and turning on an uncomfortable mattress, listening to the sounds of London that were not muted as they were in Olivia's double-glazed apartment. It seemed that cars whooshed by all night, sirens whined and doors banged; there were people sounds, and cats and a fox screamed in the streets. For about an hour just before dawn there was an eerie silence, but at first light it all started up again.

She awoke exhausted and thirsty and opened a bottle of water she'd bought from a little shop down the road.

There was still a long time to wait before she set off for the hospice. At breakfast, she ate only a slice of toast, her stomach too full of butterflies to find room for anything else. Then Jenna changed into the clothes she'd worn the night she went out with Olivia to the restaurant. This time she added a pair of silver and turquoise earrings from Africa. She sat around nervously, watching the clock, pacing the room and peering out of the window. She went out when they came to clean her room and found a small patch of grass with a bench to sit on. Later she went to a café for a coffee but she had no appetite for lunch. Twice she shook her watch to make sure it hadn't stopped but the second hand was still turning. Restless and unable to relax, she spent the time trying to calculate exactly how long the journey would take; and she eventually set off half-past two. At ten to three, Jenna arrived outside the hospice and knocked on the door.

'Hello Jenna,' Theresa greeted her. 'How lovely to see you again.' She led Jenna through to her office and gestured for her to sit down.

'Thank you,' Jenna replied and smiled nervously. 'I'm a bundle of nerves.'

'That's quite understandable,' Theresa said sympathetically. 'Just be prepared for the nurse to interpret most of what she says. Her speech has deteriorated and she tires easily from trying.' Theresa stood up. 'I'll let the nurse know you're here.'

Once alone, Jenna practised some breathing exercises. Gradually she became attuned to the sounds of the hospice. Low voices reached her from the hallway and a trolley clattered along a corridor, perhaps carrying pots of tea, or medical implements: a blood pressure pump, syringes, drugs. She pictured the patients in their rooms, some lying in their beds, breathing shallowly, struggling to speak, like her mother, but unable to. She thought about the last minutes ticking away, a nurse keeping a vigil at a bedside, stroking a brow or holding a limp, wasted hand. Jenna shivered as she imagined all of those things happening to her mother.

Theresa returned to the office and beckoned to Jenna. 'They're ready for you,' she said.

Jenna tried to get up but she was stuck like glue to her chair. Fear and apprehension grounded her, made her unable to function. She shook her head. 'I can't do it,' she said weakly.

Theresa closed the office door and took hold of Jenna's hand, which lay limply on the desk. 'I've seen this happen a hundred times before but for you there is an added fear. Not just an illness with an unknown factor, but the circumstances of your relationship too. The fact that you've come this far, Jenna, tells me that you are a brave and determined young lady. Am I right?'

Jenna nodded her head.

'Then let's take it all the way. Think about how brave your mother has to be, and what an incredible step this is for her. She has no idea why you've come here to see her. She might suppose you've come simply to reject her, to make her feel as you once did. Or to tell her how much you hate her. Oh I know you haven't,' she added, seeing the look on Jenna's face, 'but does she?'

Slowly Jenna began to understand and she rose up from her chair at the desk. It was now or never. If she backed out now, because of her fear, then there would never be another chance. That was the whole point, wasn't it?

Theresa took her arm and helped her through the door and along the corridor to the stairs. There were exactly eleven steps up to the turn and then another four; and then they were walking along the first-floor corridor, with a patterned floor and walls painted cream with paintings hanging on them. It suddenly reminded her of her first school.

Theresa came to a halt outside a door.

'Here we are then,' she said and smiled encouragingly at Jenna. 'Ready?' Jenna nodded and Theresa lifted her hand and tapped on the wood.

A moment later Jenna heard the sound of the doorknob turning and then the door opened and she was on the threshold of her mother's room. Anya reached out her arms to Jenna and embraced her in a warm and familiar hug. 'Come in, come in,' she said.

Jenna put one foot forward over the threshold but still she hesitated. She turned to Theresa, who was already walking back along the corridor. At the top of the stairs she turned back and smiled encouragingly.

20

OLIVIA

Praying that Michael would be at work, Olivia took a taxi from Paddington, where she had arrived back from Exeter, to their apartment in the late afternoon. Although she was sure he wouldn't be there, she pressed the buzzer before she got into the lift, and was relieved when there was no reply.

It was a strange sensation, returning to the apartment. She wondered if Heather had been there with Michael; and in the bedroom she could hardly bring herself to look at the bed. But Mrs Ashby had been in and seen to any untidiness anywhere. Nothing looked used or out of place.

Olivia went to the bathroom to take a shower. She felt as though she hadn't been properly clean for the past few days. The old family bathroom in Cornwall was as bad as she remembered, and the shower had not been the deluge she was used to in London.

She stripped off her clothes and stepped under the fall of hot water from a showerhead as big as a dinner plate in the en-suite bathroom. She let the water saturate her skin and the warmth of the droplets relax her tense body.

She didn't hear the key in the lock as someone came in, or the footsteps along the passage where this person stopped for a moment before hastily but quietly retreating. If Olivia had emerged from the bathroom a few minutes later, walked across the bedroom and glanced out of the window, she might have seen a young woman hurrying across the road towards the river.

Fifteen or twenty minutes later the apartment phone rang. Patting her hair with a towel and putting her bathroom wrap on, Olivia let it go to the answerphone.

'Hello. Olivia, are you there?' It was Michael. 'Please pick up if you're home.' She didn't respond and then the message time ran out.

It was then that she noticed a scent in the air, a perfume that was quite pungent and sweet, something like Chanel or Dior. It was not a perfume that she wore and she hadn't noticed it when she arrived. She looked around the apartment, half expecting to find someone there. She checked all the doors and windows but nothing was open or unlocked. Olivia felt uneasy but she sensed that the answer was very simple. She went into the kitchen to make some coffee.

The phone rang again but, as before, she left it.

'Come on, Olivia. For God's sake, answer the phone. I know you're there!' Michael raged from the answerphone.

She picked it up. 'How, Michael? How did you know I was here?' The reason for the smell of perfume had suddenly dawned on her.

'Olivia! Oh my God, where have you been? I've been worried sick.'

She grimaced. 'Not quite enough to prevent you giving someone a key to our apartment.'

There was silence. 'What?'

'Don't play games, Michael ...your 'someone' came into our apartment and must have been surprised to find me here too. She crept out without me knowing, and then let you know, which is why you're calling now. Am I right?'

'It must have been Mrs Ashby. Did she leave some laundry for me?' He spoke calmly, with an effort to sound convincing.

'Mrs Ashby doesn't wear Chanel, as far as I know.'

'Well I don't know who the hell it was!'

Olivia toyed with putting the phone down but she wanted to hold on. The long pause was as wide as the gulf she could feel growing between them. 'I think we need to talk,' she said simply.

'You're damn right we do,' he responded. 'Why on earth did you just disappear like that? Was it something to do with meeting your mother?'

'I think you have all the answers, Michael. I'll meet you at The White Swan in about an hour.'

'Why not at home?' he said.

'Because I want to meet you somewhere else,' was her simple answer.

Reluctantly he agreed and added weakly, 'Are you all right?'

'Fine,' she said and hung up. Her hands were shaking as she put the phone down.

It seemed Michael had given his girlfriend a key to their apartment. How bloody dare he! Of course it wasn't Mrs Ashby. She would have called out. Did he think she was that stupid?

She dialled the caretaker. 'Hello, this is Mrs Hobbs in Penthouse Apartment 4. There's a problem with our front door lock and I'd like it changed immediately. Can you arrange it for me?'

'That's fine, Mrs Hobbs. I'll have someone there as soon as I can.'

'Do I have to be here? I need to go out quite urgently.'

'No, that's not a problem. I've got a master key for the original lock. Just come to the office when you get back and I'll have a new set of keys waiting for you.'

'You're very kind. Thank you. And I'll take care of my husband's keys. He's away at the moment.'

She went to her bag and took out the papers she'd been working on for the solicitor, then she called an estate agent and arranged for someone to come round to see the apartment at ten o'clock the following morning. She had complete ownership and would not require her husband's signature to put it on the market. Olivia had bought the apartment from the proceeds of her grandfather's property in Kensington, after he died. She had never got around to adding Michael as a joint owner, even after their marriage; just like her mother, she thought wryly.

He was waiting for her outside The White Swan as she arrived in a taxi; he was pacing the pavement and looking, she thought with strange satisfaction, tired and drawn.

She paid the taxi driver and turned to Michael, who was hovering, seemingly uncertain about whether to approach her.

'I won't bite,' she said sardonically. She decided he looked rather sad and pathetic, which rather helped with the battle for her own feelings. She knew in her heart of hearts that she still loved him but, she reminded herself, this man, her husband, was cheating on her. This was no time to feel sentimental or forgiving.

She led the way through the door and found a quiet corner. Michael went to the bar and ordered a gin and tonic for himself and a slimline tonic for Olivia. There was no way Olivia was going to drink alcohol and allow it to cloud or soften her judgement.

They sat opposite each other at a round wooden table. Olivia leaned back in her chair and stared at her husband.

'What?' he said, shifting uncomfortably.

'I was wondering when and why you fell out of love with me. Or were you never in love with me in the first place?' Her gaze was hard and level.

He took a moment before answering her. 'You're being irrational and ridiculous. Of course I love you. What I would like to know is what on earth you thought you were playing at, disappearing without a word. Is it hereditary or something?'

Olivia didn't flinch even though it was an unnecessarily nasty thing to say. 'I had some rather interesting news,' she replied. 'I needed some time and space to think about it.'

'Something to do with that damn mother of yours no doubt!'

She didn't react but said levelly, 'Yes, it was something to do with our meeting. Tell me, Michael, what will you do when I sell the apartment? Will you move in with Heather?'

His face was a picture. 'What do you mean, sell the apartment?'

'I'm selling the apartment. I've had enough. I knew things weren't good between us but I hoped we might be able to get through it, and then I had confirmation of your adultery.'

He threw back his head and laughed. 'Confirmation of my adultery! Good God, Olivia, how ridiculously pious you sound!'

She continued. 'I repeat, 'confirmation of your adultery'. Then she looked at him faintly quizzically. 'Do you think if we'd spared each other half a moment from our busy lives to talk about our problems instead of pretending they weren't happening, maybe things would have turned out differently? As it is I don't think I can expect anything from you now. I don't think I want it either.' Suddenly she realised that there was no point in making the effort to try and put things back together again, because she simply didn't want to. Her brother was right. Michael was a cheat and a liar. She felt suddenly clear-headed.

'You'll hear from my solicitor. God, Michael, I wish it hadn't come to this, but both of us were to blame. We were just too wrapped up in our own lives to think about each other.' She put down her glass, stood up and walked away.

The minute she left, Michael knew he'd made a terrible mistake. He ran after her but she was already in the taxi she had paid to wait, and it was driving away.

He tried frantically to find another, but there was no sign of a black cab anywhere.

Olivia was inside and working on her computer by the time she heard him banging on the door and shouting her name, unable to use his key because the caretaker had been true to his word and the locks were already changed. She'd picked up both sets of keys and instructed the caretaker not to let anyone into the apartment unless he had her agreement. The caretaker had a date that evening.

She simply turned up her iPod and let the music wash over her.

21

JENNA

The room smelled of freesias and herbs. Then Jenna saw the flicker of flames from scented candles. The warm sight of the candles and the gentle perfume helped to calm her racing thoughts.

Rowena was propped up on pillows in bed. She lifted her hand slowly as Jenna approached and attempted a smile. Jenna was shocked at how thin her mother was in the last stages of her illness. Where was the beautiful girl from the photograph, with her long blonde hair, her pretty face and her wide open smile? She felt an overwhelming need to cry out but managed to hold it back. Instead Jenna went to her and planted a soft kiss on her forehead.

'Hi mum, how are you doing?' she asked, as if they'd never been apart, and sat down on the chair next to the bed. She reached out a hand, needing all her strength to stop it from shaking, and put it over Rowena's own, resting on the bed.

Rowena looked at her and mumbled something that sounded like 'I'm okay.'

'The pain is under control at the moment,' Anya told Jenna, 'but it's hard for her to talk. Can I read you another note that she and I wrote together over the past couple of days? When I say we both wrote, I mean that I've taken the gist of what she wants to say and filled in the gaps. I read it out and she has approved it.' She looked at Rowena, who nodded her agreement.

'Of course,' said Jenna, and her hand involuntarily squeezed her mother's.

Anya drew out a piece of paper from her pocket and unfolded it.

Dear Jenna, I can't describe how blessed I feel to have a daughter who seems so ready to forgive and forget all the hurt and pain my actions in the past have caused our family. To see you here is worth my life. I mean that. Life can be cruel and life can be generous. I've had both in mine. I'm sorry to be leaving you again, but I'm happy to have you here if just for a few precious moments. I realise that my passing on will give all the family the chance to move on and forget…

'…to grieve and forgive,' Jenna interrupted.

Rowena raised one finger towards her daughter, and Jenna realised that she was indicating that Jenna was the only person who would do that.

'I'm sure they all will eventually,' she said soothingly but Rowena shook her head.

'No,' she muttered.

Anya continued reading. *Have you decided what to do with your life?* the note asked. 'You can answer that,' she said to Jenna.

Jenna turned to her mother. 'Well I suppose dad and I will have to find somewhere else to live but, mum, I'm not sure I want to. I understand why you think it would be good for me, but I have some news. Charlie wants to come back to Cornwall and start painting. Apparently he was rather good at it at school but of course he never told anyone, least of all dad. They don't…they didn't…get on,' she explained, 'but maybe that could change for the better. I've made up my mind to keep the gallery going, now the Blue Moon's gone, and to do something else to bring in an income. I'm not sure what yet. Maybe it will be supply teaching, maybe something different. Charlie and I could share the running of the gallery, and we could also share the house until he finds his feet again.' She paused for breath and to give her mother a chance to take in everything she had told her.

Slowly Rowena nodded. 'Good news, Charlie,' she mumbled.

Jenna nodded vigorously. 'Oh yes, it is good news. Of course we don't know what will happen at the trial. If he goes to prison, he could fall into bad ways again.'

'Charlie needs to remember what Rowena asked him to do,' Anya intervened.

'You mean about helping other people who have been involved in drugs and are trying to get out of it?'

'Yes. She was very specific about that in the letter, weren't you, Rowena?'

Rowena nodded in response. 'Must try,' she mumbled.

Jenna looked thoughtful. 'Well his drug problem started down in Cornwall, so perhaps he can find a project there, as well as getting started with painting. We must get him away from London.' She turned to look at Rowena again. 'Mum. About the house? I love it there so much and I really wouldn't be happy anywhere else. It's part of me and it's part of you and that's what makes it so special and important for me. Olivia hates it of course, but Charlie might move back. He could use dad's studio to paint. Dad seems resigned to moving out, but I don't want to leave. Now the café's gone, it's all there is to remember you by and quite simply I love it there, its my home.' It was a second impassioned plea, and Jenna desperately wanted her mother to agree.

Rowena looked searchingly at Jenna for a few moments before she attempted to reply. Then she nodded her head and said, 'Think.'

'Thank you,' Jenna replied, assuming she meant she would think about it.

Rowena began to cough and Anya went to fetch her a drink and some medication. Jenna held her mother's hand until Anya returned. It broke her heart to see her mother in such a terrible state. How many times had she imagined a reunion? But it had never been one such as this. Yet not once did Jenna imagine feeling resentful towards her. That was hard for Olivia and Charlie to understand. Both of them were openly angry, hurt and resentful. Jenna wasn't quite sure why she didn't feel that way too, after the hurt she'd suffered as a child. Perhaps it was something to do with spending time in Rwanda and seeing what real depths of misery children could suffer and yet still survive. To see their families slaughtered in front of them, to be attacked and raped. After teaching such children in Rwanda, Jenna had returned with the feeling that nothing she had experienced came anywhere close to that. Unfortunately Chris had thrown her back onto the self-pity pile for a while, but eventually she got out of it again and memories of the dignity of the Rwandans she had met, who were trying to get their lives and their country back on its feet again, had served to put self-pity into perspective for her.

'I think that might have to be enough for today,' Anya told Jenna as Rowena's coughing subsided and she lay back on the pillows with her eyes closed. 'Where are you staying?'

'I'm in a guesthouse in Primrose Hill. It's not at all far

from here.'

'There's a room here at the hospice if you would like it. It's free at the moment.'

Jenna was thrown by the suggestion. Did it mean the end was imminent?

'I just thought it would save you time and expense,' Anya explained, noting Jenna's worried look.

Jenna turned back to Rowena and saw that her mother was staring at something with a shadow of a smile on her face. Jenna looked down and saw what it was: the silver fork bracelet.

Jenna touched it. 'I wear it every day,' she said. She was going to mention the shoe, but wondered if that might be too much sentimentality for her mother to handle.

Rowena started to cough again and Anya indicated that Jenna must go.

'I'll be back, mum,' Jenna said. 'There's so much I want to ask you about your life.' But Rowena's eyes had closed and she was already drifting into sleep from the morphine Anya had administered.

Anya saw Jenna to the door. 'Rowena has a diary for you when the end comes. It details all the events in her life that you might be interested in. Come back this time tomorrow, and if you decide you do want to use the room then just give the matron a call in the morning.'

'Thank you so much for everything, Anya,' said Jenna. 'It's such a comfort to know she has you around. I can't believe we've come full circle in our lives.'

Anya smiled. 'I was so fond of all of you back then and now the years have fallen away again.' She paused. 'How have Charlie and Olivia been since the meeting?'

Jenna shrugged. 'Okay, I suppose. They've got a lot to deal with. Poor Olivia, having to find out that her perfect life isn't quite so perfect. And as for Charlie, well we'll just have to wait and see.'

Anya nodded sympathetically and then asked, 'Do you think they'll come to see her?'

Jenna opened up her hands. 'I don't know is the answer. Frankly I doubt whether Olivia will. Charlie might, if I can persuade him, but Olivia's mind is Olivia's will and nothing I can say will change it. Both of them seem angry and confused.'

'Shall I talk to her?' Anya offered.

Jenna shrugged. 'You could try. After all, you have kept in touch and if anyone could persuade her it would be you.'

'What made you forgive your mother, Jenna?'

'I don't know exactly.' She decided against explaining about Rwanda. It probably wouldn't come out right anyway. 'Possibly because of the terminal illness, but it might also be because I never stopped loving her or hoping that we might find her again. Not to punish her, but to try and put my mind to rest. It was terrible to grow up and not know why she left us. Where she'd gone. Whether she was dead or alive. Whether we were to blame for her leaving. I've carried a feeling of guilt for so long that when I heard the real reason why she left us I almost collapsed with the relief of it. I don't want to spoil that feeling now with anger and resentment. There's been enough of that.' It was an impassioned declaration and Anya was visibly moved.

'We'll look forward to seeing you tomorrow,' she said, wiping a tear from her cheek. Jenna briefly hugged her, then picked up her bag and left.

She called Charlie on the way back to Primrose Hill, hardly noticing anything going on around her, or the beautiful day it had turned out to be. She desperately needed someone to talk to about her visit.

'Hi Jenna, are you okay?' he asked immediately, her name appearing on his phone screen.

The waver he detected in her voice, when she replied, was enough for him to know that she needed his support. He could hear through the cheery pretence at being okay.

'Yes, I'm fine. What about you? Have you seen your lawyer yet?'

'No,' said Charlie, 'but I have spoken to him. He's working on a trial date. What are you doing later?'

'Oh don't worry about me. I'll find somewhere to eat nearby and have an early night,' she said brightly.

'Would you like to meet up? I could come over to you,' he suggested. When he detected some hesitation, he added, 'I could do with someone to talk to.'

The slight deception worked. Jenna was happy to see someone who needed her rather than the other way around.

'All right, let's have an early supper. There's a nice Italian restaurant on Princess Road. I'll meet you at the wine bar next door at about six-thirty?'

'Great. See you then, Jenny Wren.' It was a little ditty he would use when they were younger. She was touched that he still remembered it.

As Jenna turned the corner to her accommodation, Brendan called. She wandered onto the grass of the green space nearby and sat on a bench to speak to him.

'Hi dad, how are you?'

'Hello sweetheart. I was wondering how you were and whether you've been to the hospice yet?'

'Just back,' she told him. 'It was good to see mum, and Anya had written down what mum wanted to say. She even managed to answer a few of my questions. I mentioned about the house but we'll talk about that when I get back. Is there any news your end?'

'Yes,' he said. 'The police have called to say that they questioned Mary-Ellen and have arrested her on suspicion of arson!'

'Oh no!' Jenna was horrified. She simply couldn't believe that Mary-Ellen, long-time partner of her father's and their family friend, could be responsible for such a crime.

'Grim news, isn't it?' her father agreed. 'I still can't imagine her being capable of such a thing. Although they did say that she had been drinking heavily when they arrested her.'

Privately, Jenna wondered what had gone on between Mary-Ellen and her father to provoke such an act of revenge. She had always thought of Mary-Ellen as a close friend, one who'd stood by them through thick and thin, and Jenna was pleased when she and her father had hooked up. He'd needed someone like Mary-Ellen, who was fun and lively, and able to draw him out of his moods.

But she could speculate forever. And it wouldn't change what had happened.

'God, what a damned mess,' Brendan said. 'I'm sorry you've been dragged into it.'

'It's not your fault, dad,' Jenna tried to reassure

him but even she wasn't convinced that her words were entirely true.

'How was my...how was Rowena?' he asked quietly.

'It won't be long now,' Jenna replied, equally as quietly.

'I'm so sorry, darling,' he said with such feeling that Jenna was taken aback. Jenna wondered what her father really thought about Rowena, and she might have been surprised at the compassion and the extent of the feelings he still had for his wife.

'Anya suggested I take up the offer of a room at the hospice, so that I can be sure to be there when it happens. I think I'll take it and stay on until the end,' she told him.

'Well, whatever you want,' he said. 'I can take care of things this end as long as I've got you on the end of a phone. Any news of your brother and sister?'

'I'm seeing Charlie later.'

'Good, good. How are things progressing with the trial?'

'I don't really know. His lawyer is waiting for confirmation of the date.'

'Well keep me posted about everything, darling, won't you?'

'Of course I will, dad.' She wished she could be in two places at once. She longed to be in Cornwall to give the support she knew that Brendan needed so badly, particularly to keep him from lapsing into temptation with drink. But in London her presence was needed twofold: to be with her mum and to help her brother.

'If it was up to me, Jenna, I wouldn't press charges you know,' he said before they hung up.

'I know, but we have to. The insurance won't be paid

unless we do.'

'Yes, that's what they said. So I don't have any choice.' He seemed to be convincing himself.

'Don't worry, dad. Speak tomorrow. Night, night.'

'Night, sweetheart. Take care and say hello to that brother of yours from me.'

Charlie had ordered two large glasses of cold white wine for them at the wine bar, and even Jenna was grateful for the effects of the alcohol; after the first few gulps the tension in her body started to melt.

'You okay?' Charlie asked, studying the tight look on her face.

Jenna managed a smile. 'Yeh. It's been quite a day, but not for any bad reasons.'

'Could she speak to you?' Charlie wanted to ask the right questions but, because of his own lack of enthusiasm, it was difficult.

'Sort of, but only a few words. She's very weak now…' her voice wavered and trailed off. She took a sip of wine to cover the emotion she was feeling.

Charlie rubbed her arm. 'Brave old Jenna,' he said.

Jenna gave a quick laugh. 'Not really. It's what I want. Unlike you.'

Charlie grimaced. 'Sorry Jenna. I just can't get my head around the fact that she's suddenly come back into our lives again.' He paused and then said with compelling honesty, 'It would be better if she were full of life so I could simply and more easily hate her.'

'Oh Charlie, poor you,' Jenna said. 'I understand. We're each just dealing with it in the only way we can. But now

239

we know why she left, that she did it for the best of reasons. Isn't that enough of a reason to forgive her?'

Charlie shrugged. 'I don't know. The trouble is, Jenna, I'm not sure if I care. I hardly remember her. Anya was more of an influence than mum was in my life.'

Jenna tried to picture it from Charlie's point of view. She must be the only child to remember the days when they were a happy family; before drink was Brendan's favourite friend, and when Rowena had seemed to be just an ordinary, but wonderful, wife and mother. Charlie and Olivia appeared only to remember the stormy days, with none of the sunshine she had experienced.

'It was lovely talking to Anya again,' she said.

Charlie smiled. 'Ah yes, the lovely Anya. How bizarre that she should enter our lives again when our mother is preparing to leave us for a second time. A double whammy for us grievers,' he said cynically.

'Don't, Charlie,' Jenna said, hanging her head and hurt by his flippancy.

'Sorry, but I'm just not handling it like you are. Look, let's talk about something else.'

She looked up at him. 'Like what? We don't exactly have anything in common, do we?'

'Yes we do. Cornwall. I've been thinking a lot and I really do want to come back, Jenna. I've been doing some Internet research and there's a drug rehabilitation centre near Plymouth. Maybe, when I get out, I'll see if I can do some volunteering there. I know I'm not a drug addict, but I can give advice about the sordid world of the dealer.'

'That sounds positive,' she said. 'If only we could get your trial on the road.'

Charlie's face darkened. 'I'll need all the help I can get, if they do decide to bang me up,' he said. He dared not imagine what a life behind bars would entail; the long days and nights; the prison routine; the company he would keep. The picture of his moment on the beach in Cornwall would be forever in his mind, helping him to get through it.

'Albert Findlay seemed to be very convinced that the sentence won't be as bad as you imagine. He's a good lawyer; he must know how those trials work. Unless there are invisible powers helping you.'

Charlie looked askance at his sister. 'Oh come on, Jenna, that's a bit far fetched. Things like that only happen in movies. I supplied a Class A drug. I'm hardly going to be up for the sympathy vote.'

'Don't underestimate the power of people,' she said solemnly. Or Piskies, she thought.

'Well I'll believe you when I'm facing the jury and their verdict,' he said, laughing despite the seriousness of it. 'Now let's go next door for that meal. I'm starving, and you look as though you could do with some fattening up.' He'd been shocked by Jenna's gaunt face and her baggy jeans. Surely she hadn't been that skinny a few days ago. It looked as though she wasn't taking care of herself and, despite the problems he had to deal with, he was still concerned for her.

'You can make me laugh and remind me again about the good old days,' he said with a wink.

'Oh Charlie, you're incorrigible,' she said sternly, but once again Jenna also had that warm comfortable feeling she had when she was in his company. She longed for them to be a real brother and sister, looking out for each other, sharing things in their lives. Maybe it was a pipe dream, but she would work on it. All she could do was have some faith.

22

OLIVIA

It hadn't taken Olivia long to get things moving with her lawyer. She had already filed for divorce, and received an offer on the apartment before it had even been officially advertised at the estate agents.

She searched her own publishing house for jobs in New York, as well as the Internet generally, and pulled up a few names in the business, people she hoped would be able to help. Suddenly Manhattan was appealing; it was far away from London, Michael and Heather, and her family,

Michael was still bothering her with phone calls and messages, and even Amanda had attempted to intervene and make peace between them. She left messages on the answerphone, which made Olivia's blood crawl: 'Darling, these things happen. It's the way men are, and I'm afraid we have to turn a blind eye. He'll tire of her eventually and be grateful to you for not making a fuss.' What? Was she living in the Victorian age?

And yet a year ago Olivia might have done just that in order to preserve her perfect marriage. Only it hadn't been quite so perfect, had it? What had changed her mind? Hearing it from her mother? Or her own intuition?

Olivia realised that there had been a shift within her, even before that recent revelation. Things had been gradually changing over the past year. She'd been restless for something more in her life. Michael had suggested that perhaps they should think about having a child, but Olivia had swiftly put an end to that idea, claiming work pressures and career moves as the problem. Privately her thoughts were different: children got in the way, and the responsibility of them was daunting. And how would having a child mend the rift in their shifting relationship?

Olivia came to the conclusion that perhaps she had been too hasty in marrying Michael, too wrapped up in the ideal of it rather than the practicality. Maybe that was because of her growing suspicion that he was having an affair, long before her mother had confirmed it. She sighed. It seemed her father had been right about Michael all along; but then, she thought cynically, it takes one to know one.

Idly, Olivia wondered how Jenna was getting on with her visit to the hospice. Olivia had not returned Anya's call. She felt confused about the fact that Anya had chosen to return to their lives in such a surprising way. She was also a little angry that Anya hadn't let her know, considering they had kept in contact. Now Anya was far too close to her mother for Olivia's liking.

Every time Olivia found herself beginning to wonder about her mother and the past, she would force herself to conjure up an irritating repetitive song in her mind until the thoughts were well and truly smothered up. It just wouldn't do to dwell on the past; besides, only Olivia knew what really lay dormant in the deepest recesses of her mind. She knew that if she allowed herself to dwell on any of it for a second, she'd be lost. The past days had confirmed that to her. Those locked-up thoughts were emotionally charged beyond imagination; they were like smouldering embers waiting to be stoked back up again into a fierce all-consuming fire. It was why she couldn't possibly meet with her mother and let the past into her life again. As far as Olivia was concerned, Rowena was a mother who had chosen to abandon her children. End of story. She refused to consider Jenna's reasoning about it.

It was for that reason that Olivia had chosen not to have children herself; you could lose them, leave them, hurt them. Olivia chose to believe that Rowena had left her family for selfish reasons; otherwise why hadn't she taken them all with her to a new life in Australia? Olivia had done some research into Witness Protection Programmes and she was certain it would have been possible. So why hadn't she? In Olivia's mind, the answer was that she simply hadn't wanted to.

In a few days Michael would receive the divorce papers. Although they would stay married until it all went through, Olivia would essentially be a single woman again: free and independent. It was an exhilarating thought.

Olivia had to return to work the following day and it was there she knew she would be vulnerable to Michael's persistence. He might even come over to the office. She would leave strict instructions at the reception desk and with the switchboard operators that under no circumstances did she wish to see her husband or receive calls from him. Let them gossip about it; she didn't care what they thought and, anyway, she had no doubt that they knew the story already. Olivia Hobbs, the cool, sharp, rather haughty woman in editorial, who had a good eye for acquiring a winning author but about whom they knew very little, versus Michael Hobbs, the successful, wealthy investment banker from a good background. Let battle commence!

Twice that morning Olivia had spoken to Joanna Mills, who was just finishing her twenty-third book. Joanna was very successful and she brought the publishing house a generous and steady income with each new novel, and with her back titles too. You couldn't rush Joanna into finishing, though, and the author was only too aware that her publishing contract was safe for the time being. But it was a fickle world. Authors could be worshipped and adored by publishers one minute but the door could be closed the next. Olivia didn't much fancy the idea of being an author in such a heavily competitive environment.

Joanna hung on to her winning formula, and she was popular with a large but particular international audience. Her books had been translated into many languages. She wrote British historical fiction in a fresh, bawdy kind of way that a modern audience could relate to. Two of her books were already in line for a television series.

Joanna liked the full attention of her editor and, with the book launch due in three months things were coming to a head. They may not agree to grant Olivia time to go skipping off to the New York office. She would just have to convince them otherwise.

Life was precarious and unpredictable but, nevertheless, she was finding out that it could also be exciting.

23

ANYA

A nya had always suspected that Brendan had known the truth about Rowena's disappearance, whatever it might have been. She'd heard whispers of it through the bedroom walls, when Brendan and Rowena had argued late at night.

She had stayed with the Moon family for nearly two years after Rowena's disappearance. As just an au pair, she had felt a strange responsibility for the three young children. Even when she finally left the family, she was reluctant to do so, but her parents were urging her back to Norway to train to be a nurse, as she had always wanted to do; and four years later she had her degree. She had to admit that the Moon family were just a distant memory by then, and it wasn't until later in her life that she started wondering about them again. It was around about that time that Olivia had contacted her out of the blue.

The other compelling reason to leave was the fact that she couldn't bear to observe the ever more public relationship between Mary-Ellen and Brendan. At first she was grateful for the help that Mary-Ellen offered, and her kindness towards the children, particularly Jenna. Olivia was still a handful and now a child without a mother, and Mary-Ellen often took Jenna and Charlie off her hands for a few hours so that she could devote her time to pacifying the child.

Less than a year after Rowena's disappearance, Mary-Ellen began to spend more and more time at Beach

Lane Cottage, arriving after the café had closed and staying for dinner; and as time moved on, she sometimes stayed overnight.

It wasn't Anya's place to say anything, but she was concerned about the effect this was having on the children. Charlie, a sweet funny little boy, was becoming more sullen and quiet. She and Jenna could raise a little joy in him when they went to the beach and kicked a football around with him, or flew the kite she'd asked Brendan to buy him as a distraction, but he cried too easily over silly things and he was a difficult child to communicate with.

Anya could see the distance growing between Charlie and his father. She despaired at Brendan's neglect of his son but on the one occasion when she tried to bring it up as a subject, she was knocked right back down by a defensive Brendan.

'With all due respect, Anya,' he had told her in that polite but cool tone he reserved for her and the children, 'it really is none of your business.'

'But can't you see how the children are reacting?' she'd protested, knowing she was crossing a line but determined to make him understand.

'They are my children and I think I know what is best for them,' he had coldly reminded her.

'You don't seem to realise how hurt they are. They need you to be there for them as a priority, not to show them that someone else is more important,' she persisted, purposely referring to his relationship with Mary-Ellen. 'And as long as you employ me to look after them, then it is my business.'

Brendan had looked at her menacingly and she'd almost given in her notice there and then, believing she was on the

248

verge of being sacked in any case.

'I appreciate your concern but I repeat, it is none of your business.' And then he'd gone, as he always did, to his studio, not to paint but to swallow down more whisky.

Not long after that, he'd sent Charlie to boarding school. She'd felt guilty about that, wondering if she'd tipped the balance of that decision.

Many, many times it was on the tip of her tongue to tell him that she suspected he knew why Rowena had disappeared, but she never did. She didn't dare to. She knew how much Rowena had loved her family. How could someone so caring walk away from a little girl like Olivia, who needed her mother so much, even though she was such a tiresome child? How could she turn her back on the vulnerability of the lovable Charlie, or the strangely mature but sweet nature of Jenna? What could have happened to make her do such a thing? None of it had made sense. There must have been more to it than a simple disappearance. For a while she had wondered if there were more sinister reasons involving Brendan and Mary-Ellen, but the police didn't seem to think so.

And now she knew the reason, and everything had fallen into place.

Anya hoped she'd done her best to help the children cope with their loss. Towards the end of her contract, she felt that Mary-Ellen would rather she wasn't there at all. Brendan, though, was reluctant to push her out. Despite their differences, he knew very well the important part she had played in creating calm in an otherwise volatile and miserable household.

Anya was shocked to the core when Rowena

contacted her again, particularly when she learned of the circumstances.

The funny thing was that Anya was looking for a new direction in her nursing career. When Rowena called to ask if she would take care of her until the end came, Anya couldn't help thinking that it was all meant to be.

24

CHARLIE

Safely back in Vauxhall, Charlie had spent his time watching television, logging on to his computer and searching the Internet for drug rehabilitation centres, past drug trials and other relevant information. He was frustrated with the wait for a trial date. It could be next month or he could have to wait a year. Simply not knowing didn't help his nerves, or his feelings of vulnerability.

Charlie had no doubt that he was a wanted man. Of course he'd always covered his tracks, and Vauxhall was his safe house. He called it his safe house because it was the one place, as far as he was aware, that nobody knew about. For the purpose of his City job, Charlie had rented a smart apartment in his own name but he never lived there. Any mail sent to that address was redirected to a P.O. Box number; from there it was sent in a large envelope every week to the Vauxhall address in the name of Mike Hewitt. His salary was paid into one bank account but immediately transferred to another.

Jack Solomon had made it quite plain that Charlie was no longer welcome at the bank. No point trying to take them to a tribunal, Charlie thought wryly. Maybe he'd write his memoirs and shatter that old City boy network. It was already the end of his career so what did he have to lose?

As for the drug world, Charlie had never got himself close to the inner workings of it. It was too dangerous and he had no aspirations in that direction. He bought off the streets, changing his supplier and location frequently; it was dropped by him and collected by someone else, and neither of them knew who the other was.

But after dabbling for so long in the drug market he guessed that someone knew who he was. Now that his own cover was blown they would want to make sure he didn't blab. They didn't know he had nothing to blab about. They wouldn't care about finding out either, only about shutting him up. He was really going to have to watch his back now.

For the first time in his life Charlie desperately wanted to take a path with a focus that was not driven by drug dealing and financial gain. He'd had enough of living on the edge. Yes he had money in the bank, from legal and illegal earnings, but when he saw what happened in the City and the massive bonuses that were handed out, he didn't feel so bad about it.

Charlie dreamed about finding a nice girl, someone he was going to meet in Cornwall when he went back; she would love him for what he was and not for what he did or the money he had.

All the girls he'd met in his City life had been looking for a glitzy and glamorous life; holidays on private yachts in the Caribbean; private chalets in exclusive ski resorts; private jets to Paris at the weekend. The girls who worked in the bank had terrified him with their ruthlessness in such a male dominated environment. He longed for a normal relationship with a normal girl, but constantly asked himself whether he was worthy of it?

His future was uncertain, and the trial was a dark cloud on the horizon. Charlie knew he was facing the toughest challenge of his life, but still he couldn't shrug off a feeling of liberation that was strongest when he was around his sister Jenna.

But in another of those most private moments, alone and vulnerable to his feelings, Charlie would let himself remember his mother. He saw a tall, slender and pretty blonde woman, with fine features. Olivia, he had come to realise, was the image of her.

Rowena was a bit of a hippy with her long skirts, and in the summer she often went barefoot. He remembered following in the footprints she left in the sand when they walked along the beach. She always had the same silver chain and cross around her neck, and a silver wedding band on her finger. That's what he saw when he thought about her. But there was something else he remembered, every time he tried to recall her face: a shadow fallen half across it so that he could never quite remember the whole of her. It seemed to have been part of her persona, because it had always there in whatever she was doing: working in the Blue Moon Café, bending over him in the evenings to kiss him goodnight, or driving him to Looe in her funny battered up old Fiat. He could best describe it as a smudge that blurred the whole image but he never forgot her eyes, which were cornflower blue. Not quite as startling as Anya's but still memorable. He and Olivia had those eyes, but Jenna's were dark brown, like her father's.

Despite that memory, Charlie couldn't let Rowena back into his life quite as easily as Jenna had done. It was better not to. God knows he had enough to deal with right now. He wanted to be there for Jenna, but by doing so he was inextricably caught up in her need to share the daily news about his mother.

Like Olivia, he was afraid of what might happen if he turned the key and let himself back into the past.

25

BRENDAN

It had taken every ounce of his strength and willpower not to turn to the whisky bottle after his three children went back to London. He wanted to make an effort for them all, but particularly for Jenna. Hearing her on the phone once or twice a day helped, even though the subject they mainly talked about led to the resurrection of some difficult and painful memories.

Brendan was as surprised as anyone would have been at the depth of his feelings about Rowena and her imminent death. All the years that had passed since she'd left seemed to melt away and he could picture so vividly in his mind her sunny smile, her gleaming hair and the neat white teeth he had always found so appealing. Of course all of this was in the early days, when they were happy; when they were a couple with their first-born, Jenna, and then when Charlie arrived. Had Olivia so upset their idyllic life? Perhaps it may have seemed so then, but now he realised it was not; some far more sinister factors had contributed to the breakdown of their marriage. Finding out about Rowena's secret past, when it began to catch up with them, had been a major one. He'd felt betrayed and unable to grasp what it really meant for his family. That's when his drinking had started. He'd tried to cover up what was going on by allowing the effects of drink to smooth the ragged edges and the harsh realities, but the dangers his wife had encountered and which were closing in around his young family were almost too much to bear. Drinking had enhanced his temper and his anger had driven him not only into the arms of the bottle but also into the arms of another woman.

He and Rowena had argued in secret, or so they'd thought, neither of them wanting the children to hear anything or to be upset. Rows in harsh whispers behind closed doors at night, or screaming and bellowing at each other out on the cliff tops, where they were not afraid of the cutting words being taken by the wind to other listeners; those words had damaged them beyond repair.

He had insisted that the children should be left with him and that she must leave and take her past and the present danger with her. He couldn't bear to leave his beloved Cornwall. What an arrogant, selfish bastard he'd been.

And when she finally did leave, without warning, it was as much a shock to him as it was to everyone else.

Now he'd come to a decision. He'd decided to book himself a ticket on a train to London. He wanted to be there for Jenna, and he was lonely without her in Cornwall. He also wanted to see if there was any chance that Charlie would let him back into his life; but, even more importantly, Brendan wanted to see Rowena.

When he'd first received the letter from the lawyers he'd had such mixed feelings about everything. With the revelations about Mary-Ellen, he'd found himself thinking about the past and the wonderful girl he'd married. Of course, with hindsight, he was ashamed of the way things had worked out. Now his poor wife was facing an early death, and he found himself needing to see her for the sake of putting things right. He felt utterly compelled to do it and wanted to get up to London before he changed his mind. If she didn't want to see him then so be it, but he knew he had to try.

At a quarter to three the next afternoon, Brendan's train pulled into Paddington station and he stepped off it into unfamiliar territory. After so long in Cornwall he was overwhelmed by the sheer number of people bustling and shoving and the noise they made.

Brendan took a taxi to the guesthouse that Jenna had been staying at, hoping to find her still there. He knew his arrival would be a shocking surprise to her, but he hoped that she would at least be glad to see him and pleased about why he had come. But Jenna had gone. It seemed she had decided to stay at the hospice after all.

He called her up. 'Hello Jenna, dad here,' he said when she answered.

'Hi dad, is everything okay?' she responded, sounding a little impatient and he guessed he'd interrupted a visit to Rowena.

'Yes, everything's fine. I was trying to remember where you said the hospice was. I wanted to look it up on the Internet to get an idea of where you are,' he lied.

'Oh, okay. It's in Primrose Hill, the only one.'

He almost said, 'Ah, not far then,' but stopped himself just in time. 'Thank you, sweetheart. It probably sounds silly, but I just thought I'd feel a bit closer if I could see it on the screen.'

'Oh dad!' she exclaimed. 'Are you sure you're okay?'

'Of course I am. I've been spending the time having a bit of a tidy up, but don't worry; I haven't thrown anything out or touched anything that belongs to you. It's my stuff mostly.' It was true.

'I'm just going in to see mum now, so I'll give you a call when the visit's over. I'm staying at the hospice now by the way.'

'Oh are you. I'm sure you feel easier being so close at hand, just in case,' he ventured.

'Yes, just in case, as you say. Speak later, bye.'

Jenna rang off and Brendan set off for Primrose Hill. He was pretty sure someone would know where the hospice was when he got there.

26

CHARLIE

Charlie had booked himself into a large hotel overlooking Vauxhall Park for a couple of nights. Something had spooked him and he wasn't sure if his safe house cover was still safe. He booked in as Mike Hewitt and paid in cash. From his hotel window he was able to keep an eye on the area and the building he'd vacated.

Everything he had, which was not a lot, he'd brought with him, effectively bank details, cards, passport and mobile, computer, binoculars and his clothes. If his suspicions were correct then he probably wouldn't be going back to his flat.

For twenty-four hours he stayed in the hotel room, ordering food from room service and keeping watch. Pretty soon he thought there was a pattern in the movements of two men; they hung around as though they were keeping watch. He watched them back through the binoculars, but didn't recognise them.

Later that evening, when it was dark, Charlie decided to venture out. He skirted around the park, keeping to the busier streets and turned up at the back end of the building; and then he hid in a shadowy area to keep watch. But no one showed up. Perhaps his mind was over-reacting; perhaps something had spooked them?

Making his way back to the hotel, Charlie took a wrong turn and found himself in a dark high-walled alleyway between two blocks of flats. He could hear televisions blaring and the voices of kids shouting nearby. He hurried to the far end of the alleyway but it only continued to bear right, with no visible exit. Was he heading for a dead end? Soon instinct told him he was not alone. Charlie felt the hairs on the back of his neck rising and adrenalin tingling through his body to the tips of his fingers. He felt really scared. Someone was following him. How stupid of him to take a wrong turn and put himself in such a vulnerable position. He broke into a run and heard a shout right behind him, through the darkness. Then he felt a heavy blow to the back of his head. He staggered forwards and then stumbled, careering into the right-hand wall; he bounced off that and hit the left-hand wall. His legs buckled and he crumpled to the ground. Footsteps shuffled around him and then he felt the blows coming and heard the muttered curses until he lost consciousness.

The last thing he remembered was the metallic taste of salty blood filling his mouth.

When Charlie finally regained consciousness he knew where he was, even though he couldn't see. His assailants had kicked his face so hard that his eyes were bruised and swollen. Charlie was in hospital. The sounds of monitor beeps and moans, and the smell, quickly gave it away. He heard someone moving by his bed and tensed up.

'Oh, you're awake. It's just the nurse,' she said briskly as he turned his head towards the sound of her. 'I need to check your vital signs.' He felt her take hold of his wrist and then set him up to take his blood pressure.

'How are you feeling?'

'Beaten,' he said, with a feeble attempt at making a joke.

'You'll live,' she replied. 'But someone had a go at you.'

'It was probably something I said,' he jibed. 'It's the Irish blarney in my Cornish blood. A rare old mix.'

'I know all about the blarney,' she said, and it was then that Charlie detected her soft southern Irish accent. 'The police were here, wanting to speak to you. I expect they'll be back.'

'Grand,' said Charlie. 'So how did I end up in hospital?'

'Oh, you've got some kids to thank for that. You were lucky. One of them had the decency to call 999 on their mobile. They're not normally so caring around here. But if they hadn't called, I doubt I'd be talking to you now.'

Charlie grimaced weakly. 'Thanks for the vote of confidence. What about my eyes? What's the damage there?' He was afraid to hear the answer.

'The doctor will be round later to talk to you about that. Stop talking now,' she ordered, 'and try to get some proper sleep. Is there anyone we can contact for you? Whoever beat you took your wallet, mobile and any identification, assuming you had something like that on you at the time. Unless it was the kids,' she mused.

'I guess I've been mugged of everything then, including my memory,' he said, But Charlie was just stalling and he knew better than to think he'd merely been mugged. He reckoned he'd suffered a brutal warning about the trial and keeping his mouth shut. They needn't have worried. Charlie made sure he never heard any names or used them when he was buying off the streets.

He had nothing to tell; and he would take the rap for the charges without implicating anyone else, even the guy in the bank. It was what he had always done since he was at school.

He'd give it a day or two, and then use the hospital phone to call Jenna. He hoped he'd be able to discharge himself by then.

27

BRENDAN

Brendan arrived at the hospice about half an hour after the phone call to Jenna. He knew she would still be sitting in with Rowena, but he couldn't wait to get there. He hovered around outside in a little garden square that was surrounded by railings and rhododendrons. His stomach was tied up in knots and his pulse was pounding with a combination of excitement and apprehension; you name it, he was feeling it.

Finally, just as Jenna had done, he plucked up the courage to go and knock on the door.

Theresa McCann opened it and smiled at him with an inquiring look.

He cleared his throat. 'Um, I've come to see my daughter and…and…also my…my… wife.'

Theresa nodded. 'What name is it?' she asked kindly.

'Moon. Brendan Moon.'

'Well,' she said, 'it's been quite a week for the Moon family turning up on the doorstep. I'm the matron here, Theresa McCann.' They shook hands and then she said, 'Come in please.'

'There are quite a few of us,' Brendan said apologetically.

'Well you're only the third one I've met. Now. Is your wife or your daughter expecting you?'

Brendan shook his head. 'Neither. I wanted to surprise Jenna. I don't know if Rowena will see me, but I wanted to be around to support my daughter.'

'I see,' said Theresa. 'I take it you and your wife are not together, although it's none of my business of course.' She'd gathered that much from her brief chats with the nurse, and her understanding that Mrs Moon had been living for some years on her own in Australia.

'No, we've been estranged for more than twenty years, but I still care about her,' Brendan replied, a little defensively.

'I'm afraid it's not possible for me to simply agree to a meeting. Would you like me to tell someone you're here?' Poor man, Theresa thought; he seems so nervous.

'Perhaps you could speak to Anya first. I don't want to upset anyone.'

'Ah yes, Nurse Claussen. I gather she worked for your family some years ago?'

'Yes, she helped us then, and now it seems she has come to the rescue again.'

Theresa smiled. 'Well isn't that nice,' she said warmly, and then she picked up the phone and called the room.

28

OLIVIA

Olivia's boss had been unbelievably kind to her, despite the time she had spontaneously taken off for her unplanned visit to Cornwall. She'd sent a brief email explaining that there was a family emergency and she needed a few days to sort things out. No one mentioned it; there was a reminder about a planning meeting and details of some new authors they wanted her to commission over the next eighteen months, but no reference to her absence. It was Olivia who threw in the spanner.

She looked at the expectant faces around the table and said, 'Well it all sounds so positive and exciting, but I was going to ask if there was any chance that I could transfer to the New York office?'

Ten stunned faces stared at her in amazement.

'But Olivia, there's such an opportunity here for you to move forward with your career!' said her immediate boss, Richard Clegg, the senior editor.

She looked at him in embarrassment and said, 'I know, Richard, but the timing is wrong. I'm so sorry to let you down, but I've got some…some…well to be perfectly honest, some crap things happening in my private life at the moment. I don't think I could concentrate and do the company justice if I remained in London. If you'd prefer that I leave, I'll just have to deal with it, but if there was a chance of a transfer, that would be fantastic.' She exhaled after that speech, glad to have the whole thing off her chest.

Now the ball was in their court.

Her boss looked at her thoughtfully. 'We'll have to discuss this, Olivia. We'll let you know what we decide. I appreciate your frankness.'

She smiled and thanked him and left the meeting, shutting the door and imagining it was the last time she'd ever set foot in that boardroom again.

The phone ringing in her office caught her off guard. Olivia was engrossed in her computer, checking out the New York office and the latest news in the publishing world over there. Olivia had always admired Marlene Soames, the senior editor for the JACOBI Imprint, which handled the historical fiction genre. She would love to have the opportunity to work with her. It would be such a great new challenge.

'Olivia Hobbs,' she replied, picking up the receiver absentmindedly, still looking hungrily at her screen.

'Olivia. Richard. Have you got a moment to come to my office?'

Olivia's head shot up but her heart sank. 'Yes of course,' she replied. That was a quick decision, she thought, and resigned herself to the worst.

Ten minutes later she was taking the lift up to the tenth floor, where her boss had his office. She liked Richard. He had always been fair to her and had even backed her up once or twice, when the going was getting a bit rough with a couple of clients. Richard's PA sent her straight through to his office. He greeted Olivia with a smile and waved her into a chair. He was on the phone so Olivia occupied herself with admiring the paintings on the walls. Her ears pricked up when he said, 'Yes, she's here with me now. Well thanks for your co-operation, that's very good of you. Yes, would love to meet up when I'm next over.'

Over? Olivia thought. She waited expectantly whilst Richard engaged in some small talk and then at last he put the receiver down.

'The New York office,' he said. 'I expect you gathered the gist of the conversation.'

Olivia shook her head with a puzzled frown and waited for him to tell her.

'It looks as though there might be a place for you after all in New York. They've agreed to an initial three months, which is all you can have without a green card of course. The application for that could take some time to process but, until then, you can at least go for an extended visit to try the job out. It turns out that your opposite number over there has been itching for an opportunity to come and work in London. What do you think?'

Olivia was astounded. She hadn't expected a transfer to be so easily won. 'It sounds a fantastic opportunity,' she said. 'Thank you, Richard.' Even though she was crowing inside, Olivia kept her cool as usual and didn't give away too much of her enthusiasm.

Richard nodded. Then he looked rather earnest and said, 'To be honest, Olivia, I know you're struggling with your workload at the moment and I hope the transfer will help you to settle down.'

Olivia looked at him strangely. 'Struggling?' she said.

'Nothing to worry about,' he reassured her, 'but I've noticed that some of the authors on your client list have put you through your paces over the last six months. This next book launch seems to be taking it out of you. I think a change of scenery is just what you need.'

Olivia had to bite back the words she wanted to growl at Richard. He seemed to be implying that she'd lost her touch. And yet they were going to add more authors to her list before she asked for the transfer. It didn't make sense. But she'd got what she wanted, the transfer. Then she wondered if Michael had anything to do with it. Had he had words with Richard and implied that she was emotionally unstable or suffering some sort of breakdown because of her workload? Well, if he had then he wouldn't be pleased to find out his plan had backfired when she told him she was off to New York. So she smiled sweetly at Richard and thanked him profusely; and she left before he could change his mind. Once she was in New York she would throw her heart and soul into the work and prove to everyone just how brilliant she was.

She returned to her own office, feeling the tremor of something new and vibrant in her soul. It was as though her heart and her mind had been set free. In fact she hadn't felt this good since the day she'd first left home in Cornwall.

The rest of the day was spent with her assistant, Judy, arranging flights to New York and finding somewhere to live for this temporary visit. Then they made appointments with her authors. Alexia, her replacement from New York, was due over in a week's time and they would have to spend at least another week handing everything over. Because of the book launch it seemed best that Alexia should come to London first. Olivia was impatient, wanting to take off before anything happened to change her mind, but she was going to have to wait just a little while longer.

29

THE HOSPICE

Anya answered the phone that rang whilst Jenna and Rowena were sitting quietly together, Jenna talking to her mother about things that had happened in her life. She told her about her teaching job in Looe and her visit to Rwanda, somewhere that Rowena had not been able to have her daughter followed. She told her that she had taught the children of the survivors of the genocide, as well as the children of the perpetrators; both groups often lived in the same villages and so they went to school together. It had seemed to her so harsh and difficult for the children to be put through such an ordeal, but the Government was determined that the scheme of reconciliation would help future generations to think of themselves as Rwandans first, rather than people of this tribe or that tribe. Jenna admitted that that it had been a humbling experience and it had helped put her own loss into perspective.

Occasionally Rowena lightly squeezed Jenna's hand, which lay inside her own, in response to a remark. She had not felt so peaceful for a long time. The pain even seemed to be easier. She imagined that it was because all the tension, sadness and fear had finally drained out of her and, as she crept towards her untimely death, she had at least one of her beloved children with her.

Jenna studied her mother's face, bathed in soft warm sunlight, her eyes closed. She knew her mother was listening as she rambled on about things happening in Cornwall, aside from their own family problems. It was just general chitchat interspersed with references to people that she thought her mother might remember. Jenna's other ear was tuned to Anya speaking softly to whoever was on the phone, and she heard her say, 'Okay, I'll have a word with Jenna and call you back.'

Jenna looked across expectantly and saw Anya beckon her over. 'I'm just going to have a word with Anya, mum. Someone called.'

Anya decided there was no easy way to say this, so she got straight to the point. 'Your father is downstairs,' she announced in a low voice.

Jenna gasped. 'Dad!' Then she glanced across at Rowena, who appeared to be sleeping. She lowered her voice. 'What on earth is he doing here?'

'He wants to see Rowena.'

Jenna couldn't believe her ears. Her father here, wanting to see her mother?'

'I told matron that it is entirely up to your mother and it depends on whether she is up to handling the emotion of seeing him. Did you know that he was planning to come to London?'

Jenna shook her head. 'I had no idea. No idea at all.' In fact Jenna was stunned to hear that her father had travelled up from Cornwall.

They were silent for a moment.

'I'd better go down to see him, hadn't I?' she said eventually.

Anya agreed. 'Wait there with him and I'll speak to Rowena. She'll need some preparation, mentally and medically, if she even agrees to this visit at all,' she warned.

'I know,' said Jenna. 'I'll just say goodbye first.'

Rowena seemed distant when she went across and Jenna guessed that the effects of the pain-killing drugs were beginning to wear off. Anya was already busy preparing the next dose. Jenna gently kissed her mother's brow and stroked her hand, then left to go downstairs to meet her father.

Brendan was apprehensive about the greeting he might receive from his daughter. He didn't usually do surprises, but something had compelled him to make the journey. Now he was here he found himself torn between wanting to see his estranged wife, and wanting to turn tail and rush back to Cornwall.

There was a gentle knock on the door and Theresa said 'Come in'; and then Jenna was standing in front of him. He held out his arms with an apologetic look on his face. Thankfully, Jenna came straight to embrace him.

'Whatever made you decide to come here?' she asked, searching his face.

'I suppose it was a bit of a whim. All my family were up in London and I just wanted to be here too. That's what comes of reunions,' he said ruefully. He couldn't deny that having all of them back under the family roof had roused a great deal of sentimentality in his bones. He knew full well and without doubt that he had blown the chance of ever being a proper father to his three children. It was too late for that. Of course Jenna had always been there, but what about poor Charlie and Olivia? Had he let them down so badly that they couldn't stand the thought of being anywhere near him anymore? Alcohol, mood swings and depression, his reclusive nature and of course the revelation that he had known all along why their mother had disappeared didn't help his case. But he couldn't just go on blaming himself forever. He wanted to do something positive about it, step by small step. Whatever it took to regain some ground with them, he was prepared to do.

'Oh dad,' said Jenna fondly. She looked at him so intently that he wondered if she could read the lines of pain etched on the inside of his head and sense the depths of sadness behind his own deep-brown eyes.

Jenna knew what he was capable of hiding in those eyes, too deep for many to get to the bottom of, or even to try. Wasn't it the same for her? Chris had once said that when they were together. 'What are you really thinking, Jenna?' he'd asked. 'How can I read anything in those deep dark pools?' Perhaps that had been the problem: her inability to communicate, her fear of letting people get too close.

'I don't quite understand why you want to see mum?' she said to her father, with a puzzled frown. 'After all that's happened.'

'Why not?' he shrugged. 'I know it's been a long time, but I don't think I ever stopped loving your mother, and it's not just the sentiments of a silly old man. Remember I knew why she left and even though I was involved with Mary-Ellen by then, I still had the fondest feelings for her. But things had gone so badly wrong between us, what with one thing or another, some that were my fault and some that were to do with her past life. I suppose I was angry about the position she'd put us all in. Now, with the thought of her dying I just…' something caught in his throat and he paused for a moment, swallowing hard. 'It's just that I have this urgent need to say goodbye. There, I've said it. That's why I'm here.'

Jenna hugged him. 'Well I hope you'll able to do that dad, but it's up to mum. She may not share your sentimentality and you'll just have to respect that.'

He nodded earnestly. 'Oh yes, I'm fully aware of that and I do utterly respect her wishes.'

Theresa stepped in at this point. 'Where are you staying, Mr Moon?'

Brendan looked at Jenna. 'In the guesthouse that Jenna was staying in, at Primrose Hill.'

Now Jenna realised why he had asked her about it.

'Well, Nurse Claussen will be some time with her patient, and I doubt it will be today that you are able, if you are able, to see your wife. I suggest you both pop out and have something to eat and then you can bring Jenna back here. Perhaps I'll have some news for you by then.'

Brendan and Jenna found a small café near the hospice but neither of them was hungry. They ordered coffee and chatted a bit about Rowena, and about what she and Jenna had said to each other so far. Jenna told him that she hadn't heard from Olivia or Charlie for a day or two. She was slightly worried about the lack of communication from Charlie. After their supper together she had not had a text or a return call in response to her messages. She had no idea where he was living and he'd warned her not to try and contact him at work, where he was no longer welcome. Charlie had never given out any contact details, apart from a mobile phone number, which he changed from time to time. She was worried something had happened to him. No, certain something had happened. Even though it was just a relatively short time that they had been close again, she knew that they could rely on each other. She toyed with calling the police but that might get him into trouble for absconding or breaking his bail terms. For the time being she would have to leave Charlie to his own devices, and hope that he was deliberately being elusive.

Right now she could focus on only one important event: her mother.

As she and her father sat with a coffee each in the café, Brendan told Jenna he'd made a decision. 'I'm going to move into the studio flat above the gallery. I don't like driving much these days and I'd prefer to be in Looe anyway. It's a lonely old place with no one at home in Beach Lane Cottage.'

'Well I'm there mostly,' Jenna protested. 'And if mum agrees, I'll be living there permanently.'

Brendan gave her a half smile. 'I suspect that Rowena will only let that happen if I move out. Those were the conditions I think. Don't forget that her purpose is to free you from looking after an old man who should have taken more responsibility for himself ages ago.'

Jenna sighed, but she knew he was right. 'Well if she does give me the deeds, I've got some ideas myself. I think I might turn Beach Lane Cottage into a guesthouse. It'd be some income for us both.'

Brendan held up his hand. 'No Jenna, it will be an income for you. I won't take anything from you in that respect. We've got the shared responsibility for the gallery and the income from it, and I shall continue contributing paintings for as long as I'm able to. And I have some ideas for the gallery, such as renting out studio space for local artists.

We could develop workshops for new and established artists and hold more exhibitions. What do you think?'

'It sounds like a great idea,' said Jenna and added enthusiastically, 'and I have another one! Charlie tells me that he was pretty good at art when he was at school. He had a small exhibition and sold some work. What about asking Charlie if he wants to help you? If he does do time, it'd give him something to focus on until he's released.'

Brendan looked at her in wonder and with a little bit of sadness too. 'Well, well, well. I never knew. That's how far apart we are. So he's the one who took the old man's creative genes. I bet that irks him,' he said with a chuckle. 'In view of that, your idea sounds like a good one, but after all the bad blood between us, do you think he would take the offer? I just hope that if he does go to prison he won't get caught up in anything bad there.'

'We'll have to be there for him as much as we can,' said Jenna stoutly. 'And I'm sure we'll be able to persuade him in the end.'

'God knows I owe him that much, Jenna. Why has it taken me so long to recognise it?'

Jenna was silent. They both now knew the answers to the past, but what mattered was the future. Unlocking the past had happened and, apart from her poor mother, they all had futures into which they must step with clearer minds and lighter hearts.

'You and I know it, Jenna, but I still fear for Charlie and Olivia. They need to face those demons from the past. They need to face Rowena, and finally close some doors. They have to do it for their own salvation. I could see that so clearly when you were all down in Cornwall. Despite their reticence, I sense that they know it too.'

They sat for a while pondering these words. It was a grand speech and it made Jenna all the more determined to change their minds.

Jenna asked her father if he'd had any more news about Mary-Ellen and her prosecution.

Brendan shook his head. 'No. Not yet. I think in all fairness I should see her, if I can.'

'Is she still in custody?' Jenna asked.

'I believe so,' he said sadly.

'Let it go, dad. It's water under the bridge now. I'm sorry for her getting mixed up with the Moon family in the first place, although that was your business I suppose. But surely whatever happened didn't warrant such drastic revenge. I doubt anything will change now, whether you try to see her or not.' Jenna looked a little wistful. 'I was always very fond of her, you know.'

'I know, Jenna, I know. But that doesn't, as you say, change what she did. We need that insurance to cover our costs and I know that neither of us must let sentimentality get in the way.'

It was true. There would be money needed to renovate the gallery, at least to repaint it, but thankfully none of the work stored or hanging in there had been too badly damaged. Jenna would need some money to set up Beach Lane Cottage as a guesthouse, an idea she was warming to more and more. She would put it to Rowena, who would probably like a business proposition, and see if that changed her mind about selling it. Jenna simply couldn't bear the thought of parting with the place.

'Do you think your mother has ever thought about

going back to Cornwall?' Brendan said out of the blue.

Jenna hadn't given it a thought. 'I've no idea,' she responded. 'But it's too late now, I suppose.'

Then she started to wonder whether Rowena ever thought about Cornwall and Beach Lane Cottage, or dreamed about it. After all, it was the land she'd been raised in, where she'd married her husband, and then borne and later abandoned her children. It was a place where she had known passion and happiness and, at one point, lived with the man of her dreams. It was also a place where she had suffered fear, pain and sadness.

'What made you think it?' she asked her father.

'Perhaps,' he said, a tad wryly, 'for the same reasons you were just thinking.'

She looked at him in surprise.

'Great minds think alike, sweetheart. It's all in the dark-brown eyes, remember?'

'Then,' she began tentatively, 'are you thinking about asking mum to go back to Cornwall now, at this stage of her illness?'

'Yes,' said Brendan. 'That's exactly what I'm thinking.'

'I don't know,' said Jenna doubtfully. 'There's a lot of past there that she could be too weak to cope with.'

'If you mean Mary-Ellen, she's well and truly out of my life now. I think we outgrew each other a long time ago. But that doesn't mean I don't value her support and the friendship and loyalty she showed to our family. That's what makes it so difficult to accept the current circumstances.'

'And perhaps we didn't treat her as well as we could have,' mused Jenna.

'Oh undoubtedly. She told me herself she thought we

had overlooked her after everything she'd given up for the Moon family.'

'This may sound awful, but mum's my priority now, and with Mary-Ellen gone, mum could go back to Beach Lane Cottage before…' she swallowed the words she was going to say.

'Before she dies.' Brendan finished the sentence for her and nodded slowly. 'It would complete the circle of her life I suppose,' he said sadly.

'Well it's something we could ask Anya about and then see what mum thinks, but not yet. It's enough for her to cope with knowing that you've turned up.'

'Yes,' Brendan agreed, 'quite enough. But let's not dismiss it entirely. We'll put it to Anya but, providing it's medically possible, the ultimate decision will be Rowena's.'

30

ROWENA

Rowena was well aware of the whispered conversation between Jenna and Anya. Being near death had honed her senses. She heard 'Brendan' in the sentence that also contained the word 'here'. But her brain, slowing with the returning waves of pain, struggled to make sense of it. Brendan here, she repeated over and over. Why? To see me? Had Jenna brought him here? But the darkness was creeping in and clouding her judgement; and the last thing she remembered was the soothing sound of Anya's voice as she administered a fresh dose of morphine.

She woke at around five-thirty the next morning. The sun was just rising over the rooftops and she could see it through the half-drawn curtains. It was what she wanted every day: to be woken by the first light of dawn. There was plenty of time to sleep during the day and the long nights, but to see the dawn was imperative; that way, she knew she had made it to another day. And dawn reminded her of Cornwall.

Some people might not want to continue in a condition such as she was in, but Rowena had loved life, despite its difficulties, and she wanted to eke the most out of every last day that she had left, especially now she had Jenna's visits to look forward to.

Not wanting to force Anya to rise early with her, day after day, she had a night nurse to look after her from nine o'clock in the evening until eight o'clock in the morning, when Anya took over again. Yet Anya had given strict instructions for her to be summoned at whatever time if Rowena showed signs of taking a turn for the worst.

Rowena would lie there for half an hour, watching the light spreading around her, seeking out the darkened corners of her room and snuffing the shadows.

Anya always came earlier than she needed to and sometimes took over from the night nurse if Rowena had found it difficult to settle. Rowena was so touched that Anya, a girl she had known for little more than a year or so all those years ago, should have such a strong affection for her, and her family, despite the fact that she had abandoned her children. Anya had responded so positively and warmly to the email she'd sent out of the blue. Rowena had briefly explained to her about why she'd disappeared. Without question, Anya had readily agreed to take care of her.

'It must have been lovely having Jenna here yesterday, listening to her talking about her life, especially that bit about teaching in Rwanda. Perhaps she'll tell you more about the rest of the family today or maybe about…' Anya paused and Rowena turned to her with her eyebrows raised.

She's not daft, thought Anya. I wouldn't be surprised if she hadn't already guessed about Brendan, or heard some of the whispered conversation between her and Jenna yesterday.

'Perhaps they'll all come to see you in the end. How would you feel about that?'

She was sure she saw a flicker of a smile on Rowena's face. 'Like who?' she rasped.

'Brendan,' said Anya, deciding not to beat about the bush any further.

Rowena gave a grunt and Anya leaned a bit closer to her. 'Why?' Rowena asked.

'I don't know, but I'll come straight to the point. He's here, in London, and he wants to see you.' Anya fiddled with the drip tube, read Rowena's blood pressure, then went to check her feet to make sure they weren't freezing cold as they often were. She would rub them, wrap them in a warm towel and place them on a hot water bottle. After that it was usually bed-bath time, and a clean nightdress and cardigan. Then Anya would sit with Rowena and feed her some liquidised energy food.

'You?' Rowena asked eventually, looking at Anya's eyes.

Anya knew she was asking her opinion. 'I'm only concerned about your health and strength and what the effect of such a visit might have on you.'

'Cop out,' breathed Rowena. 'I'll think about it.'

Rowena was perplexed. The last person she expected to want to see her, out of all the Moon family, was Brendan. Although a long time had passed, they had parted on difficult terms and such harsh words had been said. Had he forgiven her for what she had done, for breaking their family apart? Had she forgiven him?

On the other hand, what did it matter? What harm would come from seeing him now? She could handle it and she didn't have to be told how much it would probably mean to Jenna. Of course she and Brendan would be like strangers to one another. Or would they? And did it matter? Perhaps she owed it to him? After all she had been partly responsible for his demise: his descent into alcohol, the return of his manic depression. Hadn't she?

Sometimes Rowena longed so badly to see Beach Lane Cottage again; to hear the seagull cacophony and the surf breaking over the beach and rocks; to smell the wind; and to feel the warm spring sunshine on her skin. Not many moments had passed in all the time she'd been away without her thinking about it. But it must all remain in her imagination now. Should Brendan too? Or would the years roll back if she let him in again, back to when it was good? She recalled the days when Jenna was a toddler, when she allowed herself to forget all about the terrifying past; to enjoy the present and forget that one day that nightmare might be released and revived, free to terrorise her all over again, forcing her to leave the people who meant so much to her, and breaking her heart completely. She often wondered why, in those dark days after she'd left, she hadn't taken her own life. Perhaps she was determined that no matter how far away she was, she would never forget and never let go. But the years had rolled by and any hope for a reunion had faded. Her life had droned on and then it had suddenly delivered her prematurely to death's door.

She had returned to England, no longer afraid of the danger the return might put her in. What did it matter anymore? She was dying. What could scare her more than that?

Rowena had drifted off, as she often did when the morning sun had warmed her skin. Anya sat by and watched her quietly. It was heartbreaking to imagine what thoughts were tumbling through her mind: the best and the regrets of her life, and now the anguish of knowing she was close to leaving it all behind again, but this time it was absolutely for good.

'Anya,' said Rowena, suddenly opening her eyes. 'I want to see him.'

Anya took her hand and gently squeezed it. 'I'll let them know.'

31

BRENDAN AND ROWENA

Brendan slept fitfully, waking three or four times during the night. He lay in the dark, thinking about Rowena in the hospice and the pain she was enduring. It was his dearest wish now that she would agree to see him. He wished for it more than he wished for anything.

Jenna was also an insomniac. She drifted in and out of dreams of her mother returning home. It was now her dearest wish too and she prayed to the Piskies for their help. At dawn she woke with a jump and knew in her heart that everything was going to happen. Rowena would see Brendan and she would, within a short time, return with them to Cornwall. She had never felt so certain of anything before.

At eight o'clock, when she was ready to take some breakfast in the nurses' kitchen, her room phone rang.

'Good morning Jenna, it's Theresa. I have a bit of news for you.'

Jenna drew in her breath as the matron continued.

'Mrs Moon's nurse called me a little while ago to say that she, your mother, has agreed to see your father.'

'Oh!' Jenna exclaimed, letting her breath out. 'That's wonderful news!'

'Can I leave it to you to contact your father and also to prime him beforehand on your mother's condition?'

'Yes of course,' Jenna said. 'Do you know when he can see her?'

'Mrs Moon agreed to today. Well, apparently, her exact

words were: sooner rather than too late.'

What sad words, thought Jenna; such sad, sad words.

She called her father immediately, overwhelmed and excited by her mother's generosity of spirit.

'Hi dad, how are you this morning?'

Brendan felt himself relax as he always did when he heard Jenna's voice. Funny, it was how he used to feel in the early days when he was with Rowena.

'Hello darling, I was just thinking about you. Bit of a sleepless night for me. How about you?' He yawned.

'So, so,' said Jenna. 'Um, I've got some news'.

'Oh,' said Brendan. 'Good or bad?'

'Well mum's agreed to see you. What do you think?'

Brendan felt a huge lump in his throat and he couldn't reply. He sat down on the bed in his room and saw that his hands were trembling.

'Dad, are you okay?'

'Yes,' he managed to squeak out. 'Just a bit taken aback. I hadn't expected it to actually happen.'

'You still want to, don't you?' Jenna asked anxiously.

'My darling girl, it's all I want. But I'll admit to being terrified.'

'We need to talk first,' she said. 'I want you to be absolutely prepared. We'll meet at the café again about midday and take it from there.'

'Yes of course,' said Brendan, beginning to come to his senses. A spot of humour even crossed his mind. 'Of course she might want to see me just to tell me what a complete bastard I was.'

'Well there is always that rather compelling thought,' Jenna agreed. 'But it's worth the risk, isn't it?'

'You're damn right it is,' he agreed. 'See you later, darling.'

Anya spent almost an hour preparing Rowena for her meeting with her estranged husband. It helped to have something else for Rowena to think about. She washed her hair as best she could and dried it neatly. Despite the drugs and other chemicals that had been injected into her body over the past months, her hair still looked okay. It was paler and thinner of course, but it still had a little bit of lustre left. Rowena remembered how much Brendan had liked it.

Anya rubbed cream into Rowena's hands, put a touch of make-up on her face and applied a bit of lipstick. She found a pretty floral blouse in Rowena's drawer and some jade earrings in a purse. Rowena already had on her old silver wedding band, even though it was rather loose now. Lastly Anya brushed Rowena's teeth, plumped up the pillows and tidied up the bed.

She lit some scented candles, as she always did, and picked a small bouquet of flowers from the hospice garden to put on her bedside table. Then they settled down to wait.

At three o'clock on the dot, Theresa called the room to warn Anya that Jenna and Brendan had arrived.

Rowena's eyes betrayed her apprehension.

'Now, you must make the sign if you find its too much for you. Do you promise?' Anya warned.

Goodness, thought Rowena, as she watched them enter the room, he's aged! She eyed the still familiar figure. He was still wearing the same style of clothes that she remembered so well: belted cord trousers, a shirt and a proper jacket. His now salt-and-pepper hair flopped just over his collar and across his forehead; the last time she'd seen Brendan he'd still had his mop of shiny dark hair that he was forever tucking behind his ears, and the fringe that was always slightly too long over his eyes. It looked a little coarser these days! And he stills wears brown brogues, she thought with an inward chuckle, and bifocal glasses!

'Hi mum,' said Jenna, coming quickly to plant a kiss on her forehead. She looked down and smiled at her and asked, 'Ready?'

Rowena gave an imperceptible nod of her head and Jenna turned to her father, who was waiting by the door. She beckoned him over.

He looked terrified and so Jenna reached out and took his hand to pull him to the bedside, as if he were a child. Then she stepped aside and left them to it.

Brendan and Rowena stared at each other for a moment and then Brendan cleared his throat and said simply, 'Hello Rowena.' His voice revealed nothing of how shocked he was to see her condition. What had the world done to his beautiful wife?

'Changed,' Rowena responded and Brendan realised she meant that he had.

He laughed. 'Don't I know it,' he agreed. Then he added gently, 'You still look the same.' She tried to guffaw at that but he put a finger to his lips and looked sternly at her over the top of his glasses. 'May I?' he asked, indicating the chair by her bed.

Rowena muttered 'Yes'. Still the same old charming man, she thought wryly. Brendan wasn't sure what to say or do now. Here he was by the bedside of his dying wife, a woman he hadn't set eyes on or spoken to for more than twenty years, a woman who was changed beyond belief. It was an incongruous situation.

With her limited speech there was going to be time only for the most important things to be said, and the most pressing thing on his mind was how he should broach the subject of Rowena returning to Cornwall.

'I'm sorry it's come to this for you, Rowena,' he said simply and earnestly.

He saw her body respond as with a shrug and on impulse he lightly put is hand over hers where it lay on the coverlet in front of him. He felt no movement to indicate she wanted it moved.

'Aren't we lucky to have Jenna to keep communication going within the family?' he said.

'Just Jenna,' she muttered.

'Well, Olivia and Charlie have their own agendas to deal with right now,' he said generously.

'Mum had someone watch over us all and so she knows a lot about what we've been doing with our lives in general,' Jenna explained.

Brendan felt slightly uncomfortable, knowing what Rowena had discovered about his own eventful and somewhat illustrious life. Then he saw the silver wedding band on her left hand on the other side of the bed; and for a moment he thought he might break down. He saw her look puzzled at his expression and he raised his own left hand, which also bore a silver wedding ring.

'Silly old fools,' he ventured with a smile.

Rowena started coughing, as she always did when she was overwhelmed with emotion, and Anya came over and shooed Jenna and Brendan out of the way for a moment.

'We'll wait outside,' Jenna said, unable to bear looking at and hearing her mother in such discomfort.

Brendan sat down heavily on a chair in the hallway.

'Are you all right?' Jenna asked anxiously.

He looked up. 'Am I all right? Of course I am. But what about Rowena?' he said with anguish in his voice. 'I don't think I can bear it.'

Jenna rubbed his arm. 'We have to be strong,' she warned.

'Then let's ask Rowena right now if she wants to go back to Cornwall. There are only two answers she can give, yes or no. We have nothing to lose by asking, and everything to lose by not asking,' Brendan appealed.

'I agree, but how would she travel there?' Jenna said doubtfully.

'Supposing it's the one thing she would like to do but doesn't feel she can ask?' Brendan countered. 'I'm sure the hospice would approve, if its what she wants.'

'That's true but I think we should run it by Anya and see if it's feasible first? It would be wrong to ask her, have her agree, and then find out that it's impossible.'

'I know, I know. But I don't want her to die here, no matter how kind they are. It's not right. She should be home. I don't give a damn about the past. I want to take her home!'

Then the door opened and Anya slipped out. 'Sorry you two, she's sleeping now. She gets tired so easily; it's the pain. Why don't you get some tea downstairs and I'll come and fetch you when she wakes up.'

'Anya, what do you think about the possibility of mum coming back to Cornwall for…for the end?' Jenna said, gulping at the final words.

Their old friend looked thoughtful. 'In principle it's a great idea. She has already confided to me she has imagined herself going back. But it's a question of practicality and whether, physically, she is up to such a long journey.'

Jenna and Brendan nodded their understanding. 'But the fact she's mentioned it to you already makes you think she would like to go?'

'Of course,' said Anya. 'Let me think about the practicalities. We'd need a private ambulance, medical facilities at the house, a hospital bed and wheelchair access.'

'So it's not a complete impossibility?' Brendan said, hopefully.

'No. Not completely. Do you still have that old lean-to off the kitchen?' Anya asked, her mind racing ahead now with ideas.

Brendan nodded. 'Yes, and it's better than it was. I had it almost rebuilt to remove the draughts and leaks. And it's warm in there, especially with the sun on it, and there are no steps either.'

'Would a bed like the one she is in now fit inside, with room for me to move around either side of it?'

'Oh yes,' Jenna piped up. 'And there would be room for you, or whoever was watching out for her during the night, to sleep on the camp bed. We'd take it in turns, Anya.'

Brendan was so overwhelmed by the prospect of his wife returning to their family home that he suddenly lost the power of speech. He simply nodded in response to Anya's further questions, and inclined his head to Jenna to answer.

'Well, we must speak to the matron and let her be the final judge. If she and Rowena agree then I think it could be possible,' Anya said. 'You go off and have some tea or something in the day room, and I'll come and find you later.'

Jenna's phone buzzed in her pocket. She looked at it and was surprised to see Olivia's name on the screen. 'Excuse me,' she said and went outside into the garden.

'Hi Olivia, how are you?' she asked.

'I'm fine thanks. Look, I've got some news about Charlie. Someone left an anonymous message on my work answerphone.'

'Anonymous?' said Jenna, a little perplexed. 'Why?'

'It said that he's in hospital after being beaten up. I imagine that's why.'

'Oh my God!' Jenna cried. 'What hospital, and who beat him up?'

'I can only answer one of those questions. St Thomas' Hospital.'

'No wonder he hasn't been answering my calls. Do you know when this happened?'

'No, the message didn't go into any details,' Olivia confirmed. 'I was going to ignore it but something makes me think it's true.'

'Poor Charlie! Look, thanks for letting me know, Olivia, and I hope things are going okay for you.'

'Yes, things are good thanks. I've sold the flat, served Michael with divorce papers, and I'm almost certainly transferring to New York.'

That was more information than she had expected, and Jenna was suitably taken aback. 'Wow, that's a lot of decisions you've made.'

'Yes, and it's a great relief. So what about you, how

291

are things going with the hospice?' Olivia couldn't bring herself to say 'mum' Jenna noticed and she knew she was only being polite.

'Well I've got news too,' Jenna announced. 'Dad's here, and he and mum have seen each other, and we're hoping to take her back down to Cornwall.'

Olivia could hardly believe her ears. In fact it was almost sick making. Rowena and Brendan having a reconciliation and Rowena going back to Cornwall?

But she decided not to make any cutting comment. Instead she asked, 'How long has she got?'

'No one knows for sure. A week or so, maybe longer. She just seems to be hanging on.' Jenna didn't say what she secretly believed, that maybe Rowena was holding on in case Olivia and Charlie changed their minds about visiting her.

'Well let me know how it goes. Are you going to see if you can find Charlie?'

'Yes. I'll probably go along later. Thanks for passing on that message, Olivia. When do you leave for New York?'

'On Thursday, for a long weekend trip, and then for three months in about six weeks' time.' Olivia was unable to keep the edge of excitement from her voice.

'I hope it goes well Olivia. Keep in touch.' The line clicked and Olivia was gone. Jenna wondered if she would.

32

OLIVIA

Olivia put the phone down from her conversation with Jenna and, for no apparent reason, burst into tears. God, what was that all about? One minute she was so damn sure of her watertight decisions and the next a crack appeared, letting a small stream of insecurity puddle around her.

She was determined to stick by her decision not to see Rowena, but something was getting at her, making her question that decision. No matter how many old tricks she tried to exorcise the thoughts, nothing would dispel them.

It was exactly why she wanted to go to New York; to start a new life with fresh ideas and decisions that weren't clouded by the oppressive existence of her family. Let Jenna and Brendan and Charlie live their lives, and let her do the same.

So why did a few lingering doubts continue to hang around and clutter up her mind?

33

JENNA AND CHARLIE

Jenna made her way across London by bus and underground to St Thomas' Hospital, on the south bank of the Thames, in the early evening. She hadn't told anyone else about Charlie and had made some muttered excuse to her father about doing some late-night shopping before they went back to Cornwall.

Rowena had woken later on in the afternoon, refreshed and with a burst of energy. Anya wasted no time in putting the idea about Cornwall to her and, giving it just a moment's consideration, Rowena agreed.

After breaking the good news to Jenna and Brendan, Anya made a start on the plans. Brendan said he would stay until arrangements were confirmed and then go on ahead to Cornwall to get the house ready for Rowena's arrival.

Jenna's initial enquiries at St. Thomas' didn't show any record of a Charlie Moon having been seen in casualty, or admitted to the hospital, during the past week. But Jenna was certain it wasn't a hoax call and that her brother was there somewhere; and she wondered if he had used a false name. She decided to carry out her own investigations. She checked out the beds in the admitting ward but he wasn't there, and then she slipped into the general medical ward, tagging along with a group of visitors in order to get through the security door. She tried hard not to look conspicuous as she passed each room, scanning the beds for her brother's face. In the room at the far end of the ward, there was a corner cubicle with its curtains drawn. Visitors were settling down beside the bed of the only other patient in the room, and she slipped past to the curtained area. She pulled at one corner and peered into the slightly gloomy interior.

There was Charlie, his eyes closed, propped up on pillows, a drip tube attached to his arm.

'Charlie,' she whispered, not knowing if he was asleep or in a coma. Her heart went out to her brother. He looked terrible. His eyes were bruised and swollen, and his arm was in plaster. God knows what he'd got himself mixed up in this time.

'Charlie,' she said again and then, glancing behind to make sure no one had noticed her, she slipped inside the cubicle.

Her brother turned his head slightly and moaned.

'Charlie,' she said for the third time. 'It's me, Jenna.' 'Jenna,' he mumbled, 'what are you doing here?' He could have wept with relief to see her there if his eyes hadn't been so swollen and painful. 'How did you know?'

'Olivia. She got an anonymous tip-off and called me,' she replied.

'Olivia? Ah, so perhaps it was the bankers,' he said. 'How did you find me? I was admitted under another name.'

'I know, I had to sneak around wards and beds looking for you. Why didn't you have any identification on you?' she asked.

'Sorry. It's a long story. I used a different name for admission, and I had a feeling something might happen so I left everything in a safe place. I've been pretending I've lost my memory.'

'How bad are your injuries?' she asked, studying the bruising on his face and the plaster on his arm.

'It could have been worse. But hey, what about you? How's it going with the visits?' She could sense he didn't want to talk to her too much about what had happened but she was determined to get to the bottom of it.

'What did you mean, when you said it was the bankers?'

He grimaced. 'I don't think they liked the idea that one of their own was actually supplying them with the drugs they were taking. Funny huh? I was kind of warned that something like this might happen when I went to the Club the night before we first saw mum. I tried to keep a low profile. I've never told anyone where I live, bankers or drug dealers, but someone must have found out. Followed me I guess.'

'Even I don't know where you live. God, Charlie, you've really got yourself into a mess!'

'I think I have to agree with you on that one.'

Jenna smiled ruefully. 'Well that's the good news, and talking of news, I've got some too. Dad came up to London and mum agreed to see him. Now we're making arrangements to take mum home to Cornwall, for her last days.'

'Wow!' he reacted. 'That's spooky news. Beach Lane Cottage with mum in it again, and Anya too I suppose.'

'This may sound strange Charlie, but I think it's something that was just meant to be. I could sort of see it coming, from the minute we saw mum at the meeting again with Anya; a Moon family cycle of life. We seem to be homing in like bees on Beach Lane Cottage.'

Then Jenna told him the latest news about Olivia.

'Sounds good,' Charlie responded positively. 'She needs some fun in her life, don't you think?'

'Well she certainly sounded excited about it,' Jenna agreed. 'But I wish she'd come to her senses about mum, before she misses the chance completely.' She stared at her brother. 'You too.'

Charlie just shook his head. 'You just don't understand how I feel about it, or Olivia. It's different for us. Just accept that and do what you have to do without worrying about us.'

'That's easier said than done,' she responded, wondering how on earth she was going to get through to them both. One thing was for sure though; she wouldn't give up trying.

'Let's change the subject. I need a favour of you please,' he continued. 'Can you call my lawyer, this is the number.' He relayed it to Jenna, who punched it into her phone. 'Let him know what's happened and that I might not make my bail conditions this week.'

'Can I go to your flat and get a change of clothes for you?' she asked.

'No way,' said Charlie. 'It's too dangerous for anyone to go there. But you could buy me something to wear and get me a new pay-as-you-go phone. I'll pay you back as soon as I get out of here.'

Jenna said she would, and promised to return the next day.

NEW YORK

34

OLIVIA

New York never failed to please Olivia. It was like living on one giant movie set, and you were never sure who, or what, you were going to bump into on the streets; maybe a real-life Sex and the City girl or a scene played out from a cop movie. Stretch limousines cruised up and down the streets, with their passengers obscured by darkened windows. Once she'd been waiting in a taxi at a junction and Al Pacino had hurried across the road ahead of them, shuffling like he did in one of his movies; and she'd looked up and down the street, expecting to see cameramen. But he was just out shopping like everyone else.

'You see that, lady?' said the taxi driver. 'In New York the movies are the real thing.' She wholeheartedly agreed with him.

In the evenings she would wander into bars and restaurants and let the scenes there unfold around her. She delighted in the glamour of Manhattan, the heady artistic ambience of Greenwich Village, the edginess of the Bronx, and Harlem brushing the uptown part of Central Park.

Olivia had booked herself into a luxury hotel in Manhattan; it had a pool on the fifty-eighth floor, overlooking Central Park. Her junior suite was spacious and comfortable, and it had an adjoining business area where she could connect her laptop to receive her email and send replies back to London.

She arrived around two in the afternoon U.S. time on

Friday and went straight to the office to announce herself.

Alexia briefed her about her parallel role as editor in New York, and she was given some papers to read for Monday's formal meeting with the board of directors. She caught a glimpse of Marlene Soames, the publishing queen she was going to be working for. She had been pre-warned about this formidable woman, despite the fact that Marlene was only about five feet tall, and very petite. Apparently she had a bite worse than her bark! Olivia felt the adrenalin rising. What a challenge! She was doubly determined to prove her worth, and to get the respect and attention of Marlene Soames.

The weekend was hers to do with as she pleased, but Alexia invited her to join her for brunch at The Apple on Sunday, and for drinks at a cool Manhattan bar on Saturday evening. 'Don't worry, honey,' she said, 'someone is bound to take you on to dinner.' By someone, Alexia meant perhaps an author who had flown into town, or some high flyer in the sexy world of publishing, who was waiting to be entertained by a smart, good-looking woman in the publishing business. But the last thing Olivia wanted was to be out on her own with a man; a crowd was far safer. She would make sure she stayed in a group, rather than find herself on the edge talking one to one with a strange man.

In the early evening Olivia checked into her hotel. Then she booked a massage, a manicure, a pedicure and a hair appointment. She wanted to be sure of looking her best.

The masseur had to work for his money because her muscles were so strung up and knotted and tight. After that, Olivia felt too relaxed to venture out anywhere for dinner, so she ordered food from room service and then ran herself a deep bath with plenty of bubbles. She spent the evening snuggled up on the bed, wrapped in the soft hotel bathrobe and indulging in the spectacle of American TV.

Ten hours later she awoke to find herself still in her bathrobe with the television droning on in the background. It was morning in Manhattan.

She spent the morning at her hair appointment and manicure, and in the afternoon she took a walk through Central Park, loving the way the city skyscrapers leaned forward, crowding around the edges; yet there was a feeling of spaciousness within the park itself, with it fountains and waterfalls, trees and green space, which refocused the eye. Cyclists, runners, strollers, families and loners all took to the paths, the grass, the benches and the cafés to enjoy the sun and rejuvenate themselves from the hustle and bustle of their city.

Olivia's pedicure was booked for five o'clock. On the way there she made time to pop into a shop on Fifth Avenue to buy herself a pair of shoes to show off her soon to be pampered feet. She was looking forward to her first cocktail in the bar, and to surrounding herself with the people who moved in her world.

Happy with her day and confident to appear in public, with her great new hairstyle and strappy shoes, Olivia felt as though she'd arrived where she belonged.

LONDON

35

OLIVIA

Why then, after having the time of her life in New York, did she feel the need to call Jenna five days later? She was in a black cab, on her way from Heathrow airport to London.

Even her sister sounded surprised to hear from her.

'Hi Olivia, how was your trip?'

'Fantastic. I haven't felt so good for ages.' It was true, she hadn't. But had she called Jenna just to tell her that?

'Good for you, Olivia,' said Jenna. 'We're fine here too. Mum's with us now in Cornwall and it's all going well. You'd think that she and dad had never been apart.'

Well that was enough to bring a girl back down to earth. Oh God, Olivia thought, I don't believe it! How could they possibly be getting along after all that had happened in the past and all the years in between, when they hadn't seen or even heard from each other? Why am I listening to this?

'So it's all let's forgive and forget, is it?' she heard herself saying, and couldn't help the touch of sarcasm in her voice.

'Oh just be happy for them!' Jenna snapped, startling her. 'It's not all about you, Olivia. Charlie's here too and he seems to be okay about it.'

'Charlie?' said Olivia, taken aback at the thought of her brother there too. She'd actually thought of them as allies in their refusal to see their mother. 'How is he, after the attack I mean?'

'He's doing okay.' Jenna didn't elaborate. She was too

irritated with Olivia to have an in-depth conversation with her now, or to explain why Charlie finally decided to get close to his estranged mother. Even she wasn't sure exactly what had happened to change his mind, but she guessed it was probably something to do with the attack.

'I'm sorry, Jenna, it's too unreal for me, the Moons playing happy families,' Olivia apologised.

'I hope you won't regret the way you feel, Olivia, when mum dies. It's likely to be anytime now.' And Jenna put the phone down on her, again.

Olivia was quite put out. She sat back in the cab and thought about the scene being played out in Beach Lane Cottage. It just didn't bear thinking about.

She laid her head on the back of the seat and closed her eyes. Suddenly, with frightening vividness, a hot sunny day on the beach near the cottage popped into her mind. She was making a sandcastle with her mother, feeling their skin brush as they crouched together on the sand, chattering and giggling. Her eyes flew open again. That was close, she thought, I almost went back. And of course it was this going back that Olivia simply wouldn't allow herself to do because she knew her whole world would be in danger of falling apart if she did. It was for the same reason that she refused to have any contact with Michael. Distance was Olivia's way of remaining in control, of blanking the past and distancing herself from the people, the places, the memories.

Back at the apartment she found an official letter waiting for her. It was from Michael's solicitor, demanding access to the apartment to collect some of his belongings. Fair enough, she thought, and arranged for a lawyer to be there with her when he arrived. Then she emailed Michael's lawyer with a date and time, reminding them that although they had shared the apartment as a married couple, he had relinquished all ownership rights. In all fairness, though, she had offered him a 40/60 split, in her favour, from the proceeds of selling the property. She had also agreed that he could take whatever he liked from the apartment, except for her obviously personal possessions. But she had already put most of these possessions into store: paintings, sculptures, two silk Chinese rugs that had belonged to her grandfather, an antique cabinet and her music collection. She'd had all of these since way before she met and married Michael.

She didn't much care if he took all of the electrical items and the rest of the furniture. She wouldn't need any of it in New York.

Mrs Ashby had been given notice and had already left Olivia's employ, so there wasn't the usual welcome of supplies waiting for her in the kitchen, or the under-floor heating already switched on when she arrived home.

Olivia went to pour a gin and tonic but the fridge was out of tonic. Damn! She opened a bottle of white wine instead, cold from the refrigerator where she'd left it.

Something didn't feel quite right, which was disappointing, given the high she'd been on until she landed in England. Irritably, she realised it was Jenna. What had made her call her sister? She should have known a conversation with Jenna would put a damper on things. And now she couldn't get the thought of them all together in Cornwall out of her head.

Okay, fair enough, their mother was dying, poor woman, but why did Jenna feel the pressing need to get them together as a family again? The woman was a stranger to them all. She hadn't been a part of their lives for over twenty years. Why couldn't she just accept that Olivia couldn't go back?

That night she turned from one side of the bed to the other, drifting in and out of sleep and dreams, of the past, of the present, of Michael and inevitably of her family. During the day that followed she hid like a recluse in the apartment, glancing out of the window every now and then, expecting to see Michael standing down below. She felt unnerved and uneasy and confused.

Monday morning came at last and Olivia, who had spent most of the weekend trying to get over her jet lag, found that her sleep-deprived body had virtually given up on her.

She called the office and said she would be working from home. When she turned on her computer she found about fifty emails from Michael: some begging her to reconsider her decision because he realised how stupid he'd been; some complaining that his mother was constantly on his case; some attacking her for her selfishness. The last one announced that he now realised that they were made for each other.

'Wrong!' she said aloud, then emailed back a curt reply, saying she was sorry but nothing he said would change her mind and she sincerely hoped that he and Heather would be happy.

Back came an email saying that all he wanted, had ever wanted, was Olivia, not Heather.

Olivia diverted any further emails from Michael to junk.

That done, she emailed a report to Richard; then she spoke to Imogen to tell her who Alexia, her new editor, was. On a whim, and because they had been what could loosely be termed 'friends', she explained briefly the history behind her decision. Imogen insisted that they meet for dinner before her departure, and whenever she herself was in New York.

She also called Joanna, briefing her in less detail. A meeting was arranged to settle some outstanding matters. Joanna would probably try to persuade her to change her mind. The author didn't like change. She emailed the remaining, and less prominent, authors on her list about her move to New York, giving them contact details for Alexia and explaining the changes it would mean for them.

Then she made some lunch and spent the afternoon cleaning the apartment. She found it surprisingly therapeutic.

As she sat with a mug of tea, the last spot of vacuuming and dusting having been done, her phone started to buzz its way across the coffee table. Reluctantly she picked it up and checked who the caller was. Damn! It was Jenna. She put her finger on the red button to cancel the call, but something changed her mind and she answered it instead.

'It's mum,' Jenna announced. 'She's taken a turn for the worse.'

So why call me, thought Olivia crossly? I've already explained how I feel. 'Look, Jenna, I'm sorry, I really am, but what do you want me to do?'

'Nothing,' said her sister in a small voice. 'I just thought you should know.'

It was a last ditch attempt to get her down there, Olivia

thought. 'Well I do now, and thanks,' she said.

There was a pause and then the line went dead; Jenna had hung up again.

Why did Jenna keep doing this to her?

I'm going out, she thought, even if it has started to rain. Droplets had spattered the plate glass windows of the apartment.

She went into the room Jenna had occupied, to get her raincoat out of the wardrobe. As she was leaving the room something lying on the bedside table caught her eye. It was a small photograph. She picked it up but when she saw what it was she dropped it again like a hot coal. It was an old photograph of Olivia and her mother together in Cornwall. How had it got there? Jenna again? She must have deliberately left it there for Olivia to find. Were there no lengths and tricks that Jenna would not go to, to get Olivia to change her mind?

Olivia ran as fast as she could, through the crowds of people on the pavements, racing in front of traffic and across side streets, ignoring the angry horns and shouts, her bag bouncing on her back, her heart pounding in her chest. Come on, come on, she screamed inwardly at her legs, which were so heavy and tired threatening to give up on her.

She was almost there, printed-out ticket in her hand. She rushed through the doors onto the concourse, looking up at the numbers rowed in a line above her head. A last dash, through the barrier, then she was aboard, just as the whistle blew and the train began to pull out of Paddington Station.

Her last thought as she collapsed into her seat was

that you could never find a taxi in London when you really needed one.

CORNWALL

36

TOGETHER

'I tried,' said Jenna to Brendan in the kitchen of Beach Lane Cottage, 'but I don't think she's going to give in.'

'There's nothing more you can or should do, Jenna,' said Brendan. 'We have to respect Olivia's decision. She's a grown woman now and she knows what she's doing, or thinks she does.'

'At least mum's got two of her children here, and you of course,' she said. Jenna glanced through the window into the conservatory, where Charlie was sitting by Rowena's bedside. Despite the fact that he could remember less of his mother from his childhood than Jenna could, there were still some memories he'd buried and they were resurfacing. Now, after all the resistance he'd put up when they'd discussed her, Charlie was chattering away to the listening Rowena.

Libby the cat, who seemed to have taken an enormous liking to Rowena, was her constant companion; she lay at her side, purring contentedly, while Rowena's hand rested lightly across her back. Rowena seemed to find Libby's presence relaxing, and had indicated that she wanted the little cat to remain when they attempted to remove her. It was the rise and fall of her rhythmic purring that Rowena found particularly soothing, and the feel of her soft fur.

Charlie told his mother that he had been knocked off his bike in London, to explain the bruises and the plaster cast on his arm. Rowena was not so sure. She was too shrewd and streetwise herself for Charlie to be able to pull the wool over her eyes. Poor Charlie, getting mixed up in that dangerous world that she had been in. She prayed the judge would deal leniently with him.

She knew that Charlie was thinking of moving back to Cornwall and she had considered Jenna's pleas to keep the house for them. At least he wouldn't be running any more, and Jenna had mentioned that Charlie had a hidden talent for painting. Well that would put the cat amongst the pigeons, she'd thought with a hint of amusement.

It had surprised them all when Charlie appeared in Cornwall, having discharged himself from hospital, healing but still tender. His lawyer had called him to say that a court date had been set for just over a fortnight's time. Preliminary talks with the judge had indicated that although Charlie would undoubtedly serve a sentence, there was a chance it might be reduced.

Anya found Jenna and Brendan in the kitchen.

'Rowena wants to get into her wheelchair and be taken down to the beach this afternoon,' she told them.

'Is she strong enough for that?' Jenna asked, glancing at the frail figure of her mother curled up on the day bed.

'Not really, but does it matter? She's very close to the end now, Jenna, and I think that whatever she requests we should go with. Do you agree, both of you?' Anya asked.

They looked at each other and then nodded. 'Yes, you're absolutely right. Whatever Rowena wants to do, we'll do it,' Brendan agreed.

If his wife wanted to go to the beach again then he would make it happen for her.

Wrapped up in an old shawl and a blanket, with thick

woollen socks on her feet, Rowena felt the afternoon breeze on her face and the taste of salt in the air, as they wheeled her down the lane to the beach. It was moments like this that made her fight to hold on to the fragile life that was ebbing away, more quickly now, like the turning tide. Yet she could perversely say that she felt she was the luckiest woman alive, spending her last moments in a place she loved and with all the people she loved around her, well nearly all of them.

Not much in her life had been done through her own choices, apart from marrying Brendan and having their children. Yes, she had chosen to go to India and befriend those deceiving locals, but that was followed by choices that others, the drugs gang and the police, had made for her. Yes, she had made up her mind to leave her family and she had made mistakes there, costly mistakes. No matter how much news she had received through the sources she had employed, Rowena could never have known the inner feelings of her family and the way her mistakes had affected them. She'd often wondered what would have happened if they had all gone, as a family, on the Witness Protection Programme. How would it have worked out? At least they would have been together but she knew that she would have been looking over her shoulder every second of every day, fearing for all their lives.

Being here again in Cornwall was something she had imagined so clearly, but she had hardly dared dream about a reunion with them all. As for a reconciliation with her husband, no! And then he had arrived in London, wanting to see her, and she was surprised by the emotion it churned up inside her. Or was it just the unchecked emotions of a dying woman? He wasn't the same of course and neither was she. The last time she'd seen him he'd been a liar, a cheat, a drunk and a generally disagreeable man to live with. A lot of the blame for that lay with her. The poor man had known full well that his whole world, and his children's, was about to fall apart. It had gone against all the rules, to tell Brendan about her past and the Witness Protection Programme,

She was well aware that she was leaving her children for a second time, but at least this time they had the full knowledge of why, and they also knew why she had left the first time. Had she made her peace with them? She felt she had with Jenna and almost with Charlie; but not Olivia, her sweet little Olivia, who had probably suffered more than any of her children. She respected her daughter's wishes and reasons, but hoped that it wouldn't affect her life and her future.

There were so many things still to think about and worry about, but perhaps it was those things that got her through her final days. The pain was becoming more difficult to control, though God knows Anya tried her hardest to manage the doses and the time between them. Sometimes Rowena found it so hard to bear that she wished she could take up a knife and plunge it into her heart.

When the train reached Exeter, Olivia was in such a state of agitation that she could hardly think. Terror and apprehension consumed her. She wanted to turn tail and return to London, but she battled with that thought and forced herself to carry on. Four hours after she'd left Paddington, Olivia arrived in Liskeard, took her rucksack and a large package down from the rack, and joined the jostling travellers waiting to get off.

It was not the usual Olivia who alighted from the train onto the platform. This Olivia was wearing jeans, although they were Armani, a t-shirt and a fleece, and Michael's Berghaus waterproof jacket. She looked like a smart version of the regular visitor to Cornwall, ready for a cliff-top hike and dressed for the weather. She'd even found a pair of barely used walking boots in her shoe cupboard.

Her journey wasn't over yet. She had to catch the connection to Looe on the local line and then she still had to make her way to Beach Lane Cottage. It was half-past two and she still had at least an hour to go.

The last leg of the journey seemed interminably long. It was late afternoon when she got out of a taxi at the top of Beach Lane. She paid the driver who had brought her from Looe, hoisted her rucksack onto her back, tucked the large flat square package under her arm, and set off towards the cottage. The winding lane was flanked either side by cliff top meadows and irregular hedgerows, and as she walked she caught glimpses of the beach and the sea beyond. She could see a small group of people on the beach, and a couple of cars parked up in Beach Lane Cottage. It was now or never, and never seemed the better option, but Olivia forced one foot in front of the other, determined to see through the decision she had finally made.

Jenna had been right. She needed to do this, if only for herself and no one else. To be able to say that she had closed that door and had no regrets was a better option than to wonder 'what if'? for the rest of her life and to carry on wallowing in the negativity of resentment. The last thing she wanted was to have those thoughts hanging over her in her new life.

Jenna spotted a lone walker on the lane as she turned to watch a peregrine zipping across the sky behind her. She shaded her eyes and stared – a hiker probably.

Rowena's wheelchair was safely parked on the corner of the small concrete causeway at the bottom of the lane, where small boats were dropped off. Charlie had perched himself on a rock next to his mother, and he was idly popping pebbles over the rocks into the small pools left by the ebbing tide. Brendan had stepped onto the beach and wandered across to the sea's edge, carrying two buckets, which the children used to play with when they were small. The yellow one was filled with gritty sand. He filled the red bucket with seawater and returned to Rowena. He put the yellow bucket upside down on the causeway in front of her and, with a flourish, drew away the bucket, expecting to produce the perfect sandcastle; instead it collapsed into a heap.

'Not enough water with it,' Charlie commented; and then he stood up, took the yellow bucket and went off to show his father how it was done.

Brendan placed the red bucket of seawater close to Rowena's nose. He dipped his fingers in it and lightly brushed her lips.

'Same old salty sea,' he said, 'and I'm still no good at making sand pies.'

Rowena smiled. He'd always got it wrong: too much sand or too much water. But Rowena always got the consistency right, just like when she made pastry.

Here I am, she thought, back again in the place I love most in the world, surrounded by the people I love most in the world, although not quite all of them, with the sea breeze tickling my skin and the taste of seawater on my tongue. It couldn't get any better.

Jenna turned to check out the walker again, although she wasn't sure why. There were always walkers around, especially down their lane. She saw that whoever it was had stopped just before the cottage and was resting against the stone wall. She noticed that the figure had a large square package with them; it was a bit odd for a walker to be carrying such a big item.

Jenna felt the nip of the sea breeze as the afternoon sun dropped lower. She turned back to her mother, suddenly concerned. 'Are you warm enough, mum?' she asked, and pulled the blanket over her legs and further up around her body.

'Go back soon,' Rowena said.

Anya noticed the laboured breathing and wrinkled brow of her patient. She was in more pain than she was letting on, she thought. 'I think we've had enough for today,' she said and got behind the wheelchair to release the brake.

'Nostalgia,' Rowena breathed, 'not pain.' She guessed what Anya was thinking.

'I know,' said Anya, gently. 'But we'll start back now.'

'Who's that?' said Charlie. 'Someone we know?' He pointed to Jenna's walker as he and Brendan shared the pushing of the wheelchair up the incline.

'Looks like a walker taking a rest to me,' said Brendan.

Charlie wasn't so sure. He thought there was something familiar about this person. Then whomever it was stood up and started walking towards them, leaving the package propped against the wall by the gate to the cottage.

'Jenna,' said Charlie, but she didn't hear him; she was engrossed in conversation with Anya.

'Jenna!' he said again, louder this time. It was now clear to Charlie exactly who the walker was.

'What's up?' she said, breaking off her talk with Anya. Charlie was pointing up the lane.

'Oh my!' she heard Anya gasp, and Jenna followed her gaze to the walker, who was only yards away from them now, her face clearly visible.

'It can't be!' she exclaimed. 'Mum, it's…' but she saw by the expression on her mother's face that she knew exactly who it was.

No one spoke but then Brendan heard Rowena mutter 'Push'. So he started up the hill again towards Olivia, who had stopped where she was, waiting for them to reach her.

Rowena was struggling with her breath but she held out her trembling hands towards Olivia, who hesitated for a moment before she went forward and took hold of them. 'Hello mum,' she said and was taken aback by the tears filling her mother's eyes.

'Let's go indoors,' said Brendan, 'to make Rowena more comfortable.' He gave Olivia a kind look and pushed the wheelchair through the cottage gate and round to the back of the house, where Anya took charge.

Olivia picked up the large square package and followed her father into the cottage; when he was free, she handed it to him. Jenna and Charlie looked on.

'What's this?' he asked with a puzzled look.

Something that needed to come home,' she said, squirming at the sentimentality of her words but meaning them nevertheless.

Brendan tore off the brown paper packaging and held up a canvas board in front of him. A small sound emanated from his throat as he realised what it was.

It was the painting that had been hanging in Olivia's apartment, the painting he had done of his children, the painting he had called Sea Creatures. When times were hard, not least because he hadn't made a good enough effort to produce any work, he'd sold the painting to a gallery. He'd regretted that sale ever since. But somehow, in the great scheme of God and the world, here it was, and here were they, all home again.

Rowena Moon died a few days later at Beach Lane Cottage. She was surrounded by her family, who had all, eventually and so graciously, taken a dying stranger back into their lives as the wife and mother she had once been to them.

LONDON

37

IN THE END

Charlie wasn't present for the reading of Rowena Moon's Will in the offices of Findlay and Associates in London, six weeks after her death. He had already been tried and found guilty in a court in London of possessing a controlled substance with intent to supply it. Shortly after that he had begun his three-year sentence in a Category C prison in Devon. In view of the seriousness of his offence and the relative leniency of the sentencing, the judge had also imposed a fine of £50,000. Charlie knew he was damned lucky in every respect.

As promised, Jenna had been present for the trial, and just to see her face in the public gallery had helped him through the ordeal.

Another absentee from the Findlay offices was Olivia.

She had finally recognised and accepted that reconciliation with her mother had been the essential piece her life had required to settle the turmoil within her. She promised herself never to run away from facing difficulties again, and as soon as she returned from Cornwall to London, she contacted Michael and arranged to meet him.

That day they talked about everything: the grievances that they both had, their personal hopes and hang-ups, and all the problems they had thought about but never voiced to one another.

Michael told her that he and Heather's affair was over for good. He made no excuses for it happening, but he begged her to believe that the end of their marriage had never been what he wanted. On reflection, he wondered if it had been a subconscious shock tactic to shake both of them out of the habitual rut they had become stuck in. Olivia suspected Amanda might have had something to do with this revelation, rather than it being Michael's original idea. She was too cynical to believe that Michael had been duped into the affair. Whatever the case, she stuck by her decision to go to New York. Her feelings about Michael were still unclear and she certainly wasn't ready to resume their relationship now, if ever. But at least she was going without the nagging sense that she had left behind unfinished business anywhere in her life. Facing things head on was easier than she had imagined it would be.

Michael said he was prepared to wait for her, but she promised him nothing. She would see what transpired during her three months away. She was well aware that they might both discover a better life for themselves apart or they might discover that, despite everything, they were meant to be together.

As she stepped aboard her flight to New York, a few weeks after her mother's death, Olivia could hardly believe the feeling of liberation and elation she was experiencing. The hard steely edge around her thoughts and emotions had softened, and it was no longer uncomfortable or terrifying to let herself think about the past. Ahead of her lay three months of new challenges, new horizons, new acquaintances and a new life to discover. Three months might stretch to a lifetime. Who knew? Why, she might even phone her family while she was away and let them know how she was getting on.

Tucked away in her case, in the event that she might be brave enough to read it, was a copy of her mother's diary. Anya had passed the original to Jenna but had made a copy each for Charlie and Olivia, at Rowena's request.

CORNWALL

38

MARY-ELLEN

A few months later, at another court in Truro, Mary-Ellen Keane of Restarick Cottage, near Looe, pleaded not guilty to deliberately setting fire to the Blue Moon Café in Looe. Although the jury found her guilty of the crime, the judge was prepared to take into account her lawyer's plea of diminished responsibility. She was sentenced to three years' imprisonment. Arson, the QC reminded her, was a serious offence and the sentencing reflected this. However, having heard all the evidence, including her lawyer's plea that she was emotionally disturbed at the time of the offence, thus acting out of character, and that had never been in trouble before, the judge granted her a suspended sentence of eighteen months, and she was ordered to complete a hundred hours of community service.

Summing up, the judge said, 'On reflection, you must realise how, in a moment of revenge, you put in danger the emergency services who had to attend the fire, and innocent civilians, even if you had not intended to. For that reason, this court imposes immediate custody.'

The Moon family never heard from her again.

39

MID-SUMMER'S DAY

The right day came quite by chance.

When Jenna woke on this particular morning she glanced out of her window and down towards the shore as she always did, her eyes sweeping the familiar landscape. It was early; the sun seemed to be rising in a hurry, she thought, as the sky filled quickly with a faintly yellow luminous light, as though someone had pushed open a door into a brightly lit room.

She opened her window and the cool morning breeze refreshed her bed-warm face. She heard the surf sweep in and turn on the beach like a melody, regular and rhythmic. The whole thing never ceased to amaze and delight her, even though she saw it day after day. It was not always the same of course; sometimes the sky and the sea were so dark there was no visible divide, and the thudding waves that turned on the beach massed and charged like an advancing army. Not today though. Today was beautiful. Just right. Soft and gentle, as the sun rose higher; a hint of soft white clouds gathering on the horizon; the settled sea a shimmer of diamonds where the breeze teased the wave tips.

Midsummer's Day. It might have been a strange anniversary to acknowledge, the day that Rowena had first vanished from their lives. Yet somehow it seemed the right day to mark her final departure.

They waited until late afternoon, when the light was clear and translucent, and even the air seemed to quiver in anticipation. Patches of big soft white clouds had sailed in, and sunlight pooled amongst the moving shadows they cast on the beach.

Brendan and Jenna left Beach Lane Cottage together and walked slowly down to the shore. At the edge of the sea, Brendan unscrewed the urn that held the precious remains. He held it up against the clouds that nuzzled the deep blue sky, and set free into the breath of Cornwall, the spirit and ashes of Rowena Moon.

The End

valharris

This is the third novel by the author Val Harris.
Sea Creatures is published by CAVA BOOKS an
imprint of Gingercat Books Independent Publishers.
Val lives near Farnham in Surrey with her family.
For more information about Val Harris why not visit her website:
www.valharris.co.uk.
Ask her a question or leave her a message in her e-guestbook

Acknowledgements

I would like to thank the following organisations for their help
and information: The Society of Authors; Cancer Research; The Misuse
of Drugs Act; The Verger of St. Giles; Polperro Harbour Heritage Museum;
Plymouth Magistrates Court; South East Cornwall Visitor Information;
Hospice Care UK; the publishing industry; Cornish folklore; artists in
Cornwall; my visit to Rwanda and 'A Thousand Hills' by Stephen Kinzer

My special thanks to Angie Baxter; Nick Ovenden of NOMO;
and to everyone who has contributed to the making of this book.

Please note that although the book refers to some specific places, events,
and communities in London, New York, Rwanda and South East Cornwall,
all characters, cats, names, places and buildings are the work of the author's
imagination and are therefore entirely fictitious.